Wild Dreams

Maureen D. Mack

Orange Hat Publishing
www.orangehatpublishing.com - Waukesha, WI

Wild Dreams
Copyrighted © 2019 Maureen D. Mack

Wild Dreams by Maureen D. Mack
ISBN 978-1-64538-061-0

For information, please contact:

Orange Hat Publishing
www.orangehatpublishing.com
Waukesha, WI

Cover design by Kaeley Dunteman
iStock Silhouette Credit: Matrosovv

www.orangehatpublishing.com

For Rebecca Baumgartner and Bradley Baumgartner.
You have been my wildest dreams come true.

Chicago, 1969

"Sweltering hot in Chicago land," warns a voice from the radio that sits on my dressing table. I brush my auburn, sling cut hair bending first to the left and then to the right as I lather all traces of my natural curl with a thick glaze of hair gel. The look that dominates fashion magazines and television this summer is waist-long, blond, perm-straightened hair. But I've never been for following what is in, so I ignore the trend. I pile on blue eyeshadow in thick layers, line my eyes Cleopatra-style with black liquid eyeliner, and coat my lashes with layers of black mascara.

I pull a skinny hot-pink bikini on my hips and, on the matching bra top, clasp the eye of the hook to its fastener. I found the bikini at Wieboldt's, my favorite downtown Chicago department store. Barely-there swimwear is in vogue and the department store salesgirl dared me to be the first to flash a bikini on the Lake Michigan beaches. I use the bikini as an underwear layer on most summer days as I like to hit Morris Avenue beach on days when the temperature climbs over eighty. I step into a bright-turquoise, silken, calf-length skirt and throw over my head a sleeveless black top with turquoise, red, and black beads on the bodice. I crave the feel of lush fabric on my skin. My taste verges on the extreme. After all, if you can't be extreme at twenty-two, when can you?

Standing in front of a full-length mirror, I scrutinize the image that stares back at me. An inch shy of six feet, my body is too curvaceous to attract an agent in the modeling business, although Wieboldt's has expressed interest in me modeling their bikinis. With an hourglass proportion of 38-24-36, I simply don't have a skinny, flat-chested model figure. Mind you, I am not fat; I would have fit in well with the Marilyn Monroes of her time but not with the Twiggys of today.

The way that a just-graduated college girl spends her summer in Chicago, where I live, is light years from the way she would spend it in Cork, Ireland, where I was born. I shuttle between Cork and Chicago as if I am on Chicago's El racing toward downtown and back. Four or five times a year, regardless of the weather, I jet from Chicago's international airport to the new airport in Cork. Granted, most girls my age would think it is exciting. I have had to squeeze my friends to cover missed classes at Northwestern, and I had to charm my college professors with descriptions of my gallant but demanding father, who insists that he needs to see me more often than during the customary college student holiday breaks. For the few that waivered in accommodating such a class attendance arrangement, I would coyly mention that my father has been unusually attached to me ever since my mother's death when I was five years old.

Gallant, maybe, I tell myself. And yet I still harbor emotions of anger, betrayal, and abandonment when it comes to my father. While my memory of the events that brought me to the States at eight years old is fuzzy, I do know a summer-long visit turned into a permanent relocation to Evanston, Illinois. Since then, I have spent my life with my Aunt Catherine Lane, my mother's widowed sister. I am grateful for the way Catherine has negotiated a life for me that feeds my interests and my social needs. But it does not erase the fact that my father dismissed and severed me from Ireland. Even when I am at home, he is more interested in touring me around his hotels in Dublin and Cork and insisting that *my fancy Northwestern degree in business and marketing* be put to work behind the scenes at his hotels in Cork and Dublin. My father rarely talks with me face to face.

I slip turquoise thongs on my feet and insert large hoops into my ears. I have lived this bi-country lifestyle for fourteen years. My elementary and high school days in Evanston were a torturous experiment in adaptation. I hung on to my father's assurance that the arrangement was temporary; I would certainly return to Cork by high school. But one year piled on top of another. With each visit home, a gulf wider than the Irish Sea grew between my father and me.

"Aunt Catherine," I call out, striding from my bedroom to the hallway where I grab my bag, car keys, and jacket from a vintage tree stand. "I'm driving into the city to meet Sissy. Need anything?"

"No, I don't think so, Deidre." Catherine returns the call from another part of the house. This question-and-answer routine is a habit we have been practicing since I got a car of my own.

"Thanks anyway for letting me know where you are going. I will see you at dinner at the usual time this evening unless I hear otherwise from you."

I leave the compact, one-story brick house which sits among flat fields one block from the shores of Lake Michigan. I point my car toward the city to meet Sissy Evans. Sissy was my first friend when I arrived in Evanston as an eight-year-old and we remained close through high school and college, which is quite extraordinary.

Sissy is auditioning for a cancan dance position which she has never danced. With a little fast study, she feels she can show enough raw talent to capture a position in the dance line. Like many girls, we both began studying traditional ballet during childhood and Sissy definitely has the classic body type and raw talent to continue with it for at least seven more years. I nurture my ballet, as I love the structure and discipline of the lessons. But my tall and busty body proportions are all wrong to seriously pursue classical ballet, or so I think.

Sissy and I enter the dark Chicago dance studio from the alley door and Sissy heads backstage. Taking time to adjust my eyesight to the closet-like setting, I am slow to see the girl on the stage practicing high kicks in four-inch heels. As my eyes adjust, I lean forward to get a better view of the dancer. I am used to seeing a few tall ballet dancers, but not big-breasted women wearing fishnet stockings, French chamois bustiers, and bikini tap pants. Surprising even myself, I find that I am curious rather than shocked. Twenty more women join the lone dancer and form a cancan line while the dance choreographers, sitting in front row seats, make notes, chat with one another, and eliminate one at a time until there remain but eight on the stage.

I recognize one of the women as being a classmate at Northwestern as well as a ballet student in my weekly classes. I am surprised that she did not mention the cancan tryout or her apparent interest in this spirited and less restrained form of dance.

"Any more back there?" the director calls from the blackness of the auditorium. Sissy joins the eight dancers on stage. The audition music pounds again and I watch Sissy with admiration and awe as she steps and kicks her way through the bawdy dance number, not missing a kick and keeping a flashy smile on her face through the entire sequence.

"Okay, sweetie, that was good, real good, you're in, at least until we find someone who may be better," he grumps at her. To the remainder of dancers on stage, the director barks, "If any of you know of any girls who can dance, learn fast, and take direction, send them down tomorrow and we will try again."

"Wow, Sissy," I say as we cross the street, headed toward our favorite café. "Why didn't you tell me you were interested in cancan dancing?"

"Well, you know," replies Sissy. "It's not something you pass around unless you are pretty sure about the person you are sharing it with. This is a far stretch from the kind of dance we did at Northwestern, isn't it?"

"I was taken back a bit at first, I have to admit. But the more I watch, the more mesmerized I am with it," I confess. "I like the large moves and the fact that the women carry the strength of the dance as well as the grace and beauty. But it does seem a bit seedy."

Sissy leans across the café table and says in a whisper, "I know, but as a dancer, I have to start somewhere. I am not going to go straight from being a Northwestern dance major to landing a position in a Chicago dance revue. And with the competition in this city? Won't you just try out tomorrow?" Sissy begs. "If nothing else, just to have my back until I see what happens?"

I look into my friend's face and see the urgency there. "Not a word about this to my Aunt Catherine. I don't want this to get to my father when she intercedes on my part to stay in the States for a year longer."

"You aren't a little girl anymore, Deidre. You are twenty-two. You don't have to do what your father tells you to do."

"That's how it works here, Sissy. But in Ireland, unless I was married and living under my husband's roof, I would be still living at home and under my father's very big thumb. It is really backward in Ireland when it comes to women. I still need him on my side more often than not."

"Well, I am on my own in this windy city. And I need a job to keep me going. A job in dance! It'll be fun," Sissy says. Then she reminds me, "And since you don't have a job right now..." I have to agree with her about that.

County Cork, Ireland, 1955

Deidre placed one foot on the second story window sill, and then lifted the other. She gazed into the thick umbrella of the Glengarriff Woods nestled beneath the Caha Mountains. She positioned her hands on either side of the screenless window frame to steady herself. She leaned forward. She would fly over Bantry Bay and watch the sun's rising rays dance on the water. She would soar over the horses that pastured next to the large stone stables where the herd lived better than most of the villagers and where her mother's horse, now lonely and abandoned, stood. Deidre raised her eyes to the stars, stepped from the ledge, and plummeted into the twilight air.

The house echoed with Deidre's screams. Within minutes, her bedroom door flew open and a woman in nightclothes rushed to her bed. She gathered the girl in her arms and shook her lightly. Deidre pushed her eyes open; eyes that would rather remain shut and in flight. Colleen put both arms around Deidre and assured her that it was yet another nightmare.

Patrick Moran stood before the wall-sized picture window in his first-floor study, which framed his view of the rolling hills and fields, and watched his daughter. Deidre gained speed and made a sharp last-minute turn from the direction of the stables to the bay below the estate's sloping lawn. He shook his head disapprovingly at seeing his daughter outrun a boy, the son of his estate manager, two years older than she.

God, she is wild and free, he confessed to himself. When his daughter was younger, Patrick hadn't seen such fire for independence as she now displayed. Deidre had captured her father's heart in much the same manner as her mother had. But once Suzanne passed, six-year-old Deidre's response to being motherless had stunned Patrick. After a short period of self-imposed seclusion in her bedroom, she had emerged hell-bent on keeping in motion and throwing off his sister Colleen's efforts at shaping a gentle, obedient Catholic girl.

Deidre had been a constant weight on Colleen's mind. Colleen had been raised in the Irish Catholic tradition of putting the needs of the family's men far above her own. But lately, she found that she was quick-tempered with Deidre and, perhaps, even resentful. She had spent her youth being a surrogate mother to her brother Patrick after their own mother's early death, a common occurrence in Ireland. Just as she had begun to center her life on herself, Patrick's American wife, Suzanne, became ill within a few years of moving into Moran Manor as a bride. Deidre was born the following year, and Suzanne continued a long malaise until she succumbed to the wasting effects of tuberculosis. As she walked down the corridor that led to her brother's study, Colleen was deep in thought considering all that she and Patrick had been through together.

Patrick Moran's reminiscing was interrupted by a quiet knock. Patrick walked to the door, took a deep breath, adjusted his demeanor, and swung the door open. He said, "Good morning, Colleen."

"Thank you, and good morning." Colleen avoided her brother's eyes, and her face was fixed in thought. She placed the tea tray on Patrick's desk. She knew Patrick expected her to retreat and allow him a quiet morning but she decided to say what was on her mind. She stood in front of her brother and held his eyes with hers.

"It's Deidre again," Patrick stated.

Colleen nodded.

"She is just a child, Colleen. I rather adore her free spirit and boundless energy," Patrick said, attempting to soften her concerns regarding his daughter's noisy morning behavior.

"Free spirit, you say?" Colleen questioned in a quiet voice. "She is perfectly undisciplined." She drew attention to the word "undisciplined" by pronouncing each syllable separately.

Colleen continued. "What is to become of her? She has one friend, and that is the son of your business agent. We can't simply go on as if Deidre's behavior or isolation from girls her own age simply does not matter!" Allowing her words to settle, she took a seat. "Patrick," she proceeded carefully. "I know you think it is best to keep Deidre here at Moran, but I beg you to reconsider." Colleen continued to weigh her words very carefully. "Deidre has needs that neither you nor I am equipped to handle. Her nightmares are increasing and recently she has taken to sleepwalking and talking about being able to fly. Her behaviors are not normal and have become dangerous. If I had not walked into her bedroom when I did last night, Patrick, she would have fallen out of the window fifty feet to her death. Deidre would be safer and better off if she was at a girls' boarding school in Dublin. She would have companionship, supervision—"

"Absolutely not!" Patrick yelled as he rose and paced around the office. "What kind of a father sends his only daughter off to a boarding school at eight years old after her mother's death? Girls in the Moran family are not sent away; they remain at home where their fathers can look after them."

Colleen looked down at her tea. Then she raised her head and looked at her brother while he continued to pace in a circle on what was already a worn rug.

"Patrick. I am tired. I raised you and took care of Suzanne as best as I could during all of the years she was practically housebound. Now, I find myself looking after Deidre full time and running the house with only half of the staff that this kind of house needs. It isn't that I am not willing."

Colleen paused to reflect on her last words. "Then again, maybe that is not the whole truth in it. I am not willing to go on in the same way, Patrick. I am forty-five years old. I have never been married, but I would have liked to have had my own family. But mother, then you, Suzanne, and now Deidre—they all came first."

Patrick stopped in his tracks and walked over to where his sister sat. He pulled up an upholstered chair to face her. She looked older than her forty-five years with dark circles under her eyes and hair pulled back in a bun, a style more fitting to women much older than she. Addressing her in a quieter tone that he just had, he asked, "Do you regret tending to our family first, Colleen? Is that what I hear you saying?"

"No, Patrick. Don't put words into the air that I did not say. But time goes on and I don't have the energy, nor do I know how to direct Deidre toward a life that will make her happy. When I grew up in this house, it was a different time. Most girls that I knew, along with myself, had a basic education and then spent their time learning to ride horses, paint, and play piano. Once mother died, I became your substitute mother, and that's what other girls did when they were put in the same situation. But times are changing, and particularly for girls, Patrick. They go through high school and some beyond that—particularly girls from families of substance, like ours. I shouldn't think you would want

Deidre to be raised in isolation like I was, and so far removed from how most Irish girls of her social status are being raised today."

Patrick's shoulders stretched toward his neck and a reflexive scowl rose in response to Colleen's words. "Things aren't changing that much in Ireland. A girl's proper place is at her father's side, especially so when she has lost her mother. If things are too much for you, Colleen, then it is time for us to look for a live-in teacher for Deidre. That's how you can be most helpful. No more of this talk about sending Deidre to a boarding school in Dublin, or anywhere else for that matter."

Patrick dismissed his sister by returning to his desk and shifting his eyes down to the stack of papers before him. Colleen picked up on her brother's all-too-routine dismissal. She left her chair and was halfway out of the door when she stepped back into the office threshold while pulling a small envelope from her dress pocket.

"This came yesterday. It's from Catherine Lane. It was addressed to both of us so I opened it. She wants to come for a month-long visit. If there is a problem, she asks to be contacted at once. Otherwise, she will be here for the full month of July and maybe longer," Colleen pushed back.

Patrick rose to retrieve the letter. He looked down at the letter, which was now in his hand. "It seems as if Catherine was just here for Suzanne's funeral, but I guess it has been two years. Of course, we will do our usual best to show her the courtesy and welcome that Suzanne would want. But I hope her stay will be the shorter part of a month. Can't imagine what an American woman in the prime of her life would find to do at Moran for more than a week, even if she has come primarily to visit Deidre. Eight-year-old girls aren't that amusing."

~ ~ ~ ~ ~

Deidre watched the car from her perch at the window seat on the second-floor landing. A woman dressed in a long brown coat with a wide-brimmed scarlet hat and scarlet leather gloves emerged from the stopped vehicle. Deidre watched as her Aunt Colleen and her American Aunt Catherine exchanged hugs and pleasantries. Deidre scrutinized the American aunt's feet. She did not wear boots of any kind. Deidre figured that her aunt would spend little time riding horses or hiking the Moran countryside dressed like she was. The family butler, who had been at Moran longer than Deidre's father, walked behind the women and carried a large suitcase and a small cosmetic case. Deidre slipped off the window seat and made her way down to the first floor's main drawing rooms.

"Deidre, there you are. Come in and welcome your Aunt Catherine, who has come all the way from America to visit us," instructed Colleen once she caught sight of her niece.

Catherine lifted her head to see the small girl glide across the carpet and into the largest of the three drawing rooms that caught the afternoon sun. The bright coral of Deidre's sleeveless A-line cotton dress contrasted dramatically with the heavy, dark tapestries that covered the ceilings and walls of the rooms.

"Oh my! Deidre! How much I have looked forward to seeing you again! With all of the people that were here the last time I was at Moran—" Catherine stopped short when she realized her mistake, and then continued on in an attempt to cover her indiscretion. "Well, anyway, come take my hand so I can really get a good look at my beautiful niece. Your Aunt Colleen tells me you are twice as smart as she was at your same age." Catherine smiled, teasing them both.

Deidre slipped her hand into her aunt's outstretched hand. Catherine lowered herself and wrapped her arms around the girl, holding her tight.

"Tea is this way and ready for you, Catherine. Deidre, we will see you later," Colleen said, dismissing her niece.

"We aren't going to hold to those old-fashioned routines of separating children from adults, are we Colleen? Is it okay if Deidre sits next to me and has tea with us?" Catherine asked very politely, expecting her request to be granted.

Deidre quickly nestled next to her American aunt before Colleen had a chance to respond.

~ ~ ~ ~ ~

Catherine rose to another Moran morning frozen in time. If she were home in Evanston, she would throw a robe over her nightgown and dress for the day after her breakfast. Nightgowns are not acceptable dress outside of bedrooms at Moran. She stood in front of the closet and reached for a pair of lime-green pedal pushers but chose a long skirt with woolen tights. She slipped a hip-length, long sleeve cardigan sweater over the ensemble. She now understood how easy it would be to fall into the habit of dressing like Irish grandmothers if only for the warmth. Moran lacked central heating, and though it was halfway through an unusually warm Irish summer, mornings were as damp inside the house as they had been since it was built in the 1600s.

She made her way down the expansive hallway and the terraced second-floor staircase. Closed drapes kept the early morning sun out, and Catherine thought the house seemed more like a closed tomb than a home. Once she arrived on the ground floor, light flowed through the uncovered windows.

The cook was hard at work baking brown bread and boiling oats. She raised her head and nodded a silent greeting to Catherine, who made her way across the kitchen to find a mug. She helped herself to the pot of coffee on the gas stove's open flame.

"Good morning, Catherine." Colleen intercepted her just as she finished reviewing the day's menus with the cook. She was not surprised to find Catherine in the kitchen. Colleen had noted that Catherine was quick to dismiss most of the Irish traditions when it was within her power to do so. "Let's take advantage of this quiet time and settle upstairs in the morning breakfast room," Colleen said. The cook loaded warm bread, butter, and oats onto a tray and headed up the stairs with the two women following behind. They settled into the sole room with curtains pulled open and were greeted by the morning sun.

"So how are things, really, Colleen?" Catherine asked after they finished with the polite exchange of sleep inquiries and weather patterns.

Colleen deflected her question. "You have been here for some weeks now. How do you see Deidre?" Colleen asked.

"I see an eight-year-old girl who is without any kind of connection to girls her own age. She is anxious to please and socially outgoing. She obviously loves the outdoors as I have not taken so many walks or ridden a horse so much in my life. She is willing to do whatever I suggest for a day's activity. But aside from all of that, she is aloof when I ask her about friends her own age, or, more to the point, when I ask her how she is doing without the company of her mother."

Colleen nodded in recognition. "I can't disagree with anything you have said, Catherine. I can't help but think that your sister would want better for her. But Patrick has always been headstrong and dogmatic when it comes to honoring Irish traditions. And he is Deidre's father. What do you think I could do to persuade him to send Deidre to school in Dublin?"

"Have you asked Deidre what she would like to do?"

"Ask Deidre?" answered Colleen. "That is really not how things are done in Ireland, Catherine. At least, not in Patrick Moran's Ireland. Children are told what to do, especially girls. So are women. They aren't inventoried about their preferences."

"Yes, of course. Suzanne used to talk about how backward Ireland was when it came to children and women. But I may be just the one who can get away with breaking the rules, being an American woman who doesn't know any better," Catherine responded with a smile.

~ ~ ~ ~ ~

Deidre crept on bare feet down the hall to her Aunt Catherine's bedroom. She nudged the door open, expecting to find a dark room and her aunt still asleep in her bed. Instead, her aunt stood at her window fully dressed and taking in the view of the Moran estate.

"Auntie Catherine, you are up!" Deidre whispered. Catherine turned to face her small niece and smiled. "No one is up as early as we are," Deidre added with a broad smile. "And breakfast won't be put out in the breakfast room so early."

"No matter," Catherine replied. "I have a better idea."

In no time, Deidre and her aunt were carrying their makeshift breakfast out the kitchen's back door. They headed down the hill toward the water. "I feel like a naughty child again! Your mother and I used to plan secret breakfasts under the backyard tree before our mother was out of her bed," Catherine confessed. Once settled on the grass, Catherine pulled slices of brown bread, strawberry jam, and bananas from a barley sack that they had found in the Moran kitchen. They ate their stolen breakfasts as they watched the sun climb in the sky over the bay and an eagle soar overhead.

"Your mother and I would go on small little expeditions through the grassy fields that lead down to the beach at Lake Michigan. We would bring bathroom towels with us and lay on them in the sand while we watched the white clouds turn into all kinds of people. We spent hours just watching those clouds hang really low over us or drift across the lake on an adventure of their own."

Deidre listened intently but made no response.

"We were a few years apart in age. She was my only sister. I miss her very much," Catherine said quietly. After a moment, she continued. "We didn't have horses at our house like you do here, Deidre. But we did take riding lessons at a riding stable. And we went to classes at a dance studio in Evanston. I wasn't very good at dance, but your mother sure was. She loved to slide across the wood floors and watch herself in the wall-size mirrors as she twirled across the room."

Catherine waited for a response from Deidre or perhaps a question. But Deidre stared off into the bay.

They finished their bread and rose to walk back to the house. "Deidre," Catherine said, "I will be leaving Moran in a few weeks or so to go back to America, to my house in Evanston." They were approaching the drive to the house when Deidre stopped and turned to face her aunt.

"Could I go with you?" she asked. "I was just thinking when you were telling me about you and my mother that I would like to see where my mother grew up."

"It's a completely different world there, Deidre. I live in a much smaller house than this." She pointed up at the imposing estate. "Just about everybody lives in a much smaller house than here. Do you know that?" Catherine looked at Deidre to catch her reaction but saw none. "And, it is a long way away. Too far to come for a short visit. But, yes, you could visit at my house for a month, or even for a full summer. But your father would be the one to give you permission, Deidre."

Catherine smiled and took Deidre firmly by the hand as they walked up the stairs to the house. She had set the stage. She had assured her sister that she would do whatever Deidre needed in her mother's absence. She was also well aware that she was up against a formidable barrier, in the form of Patrick Moran, when it came to interceding on Deidre's behalf.

~ ~ ~ ~ ~

Catherine's body ached all over. She thought she would be accustomed to riding since she had been riding with Deidre for three solid weeks. She eased back into the overstuffed chair she had plopped herself into and put her feet up on a large square footrest. Expecting either Colleen or a housemaid, Catherine was surprised when Patrick walked onto the garden terrace and sat down. During her lengthy visit, he had never materialized much earlier than late afternoon. He either kept himself hidden in his study or left for Dublin or Cork before she was out of her bed. She could only infer that he had something on his mind. He sat down across from her on the matching overstuffed chair.

"How did the ride go this morning with Deidre? You have become quite the horsewoman since you arrived," Patrick said. His voice was absent of any inflection.

Surprised that Patrick knew about her activities that day, Catherine responded, "Deidre insisted that I ride her mother's horse, Spirit. It seemed to give her real enjoyment to see the horse with a woman rider on it."

Patrick chose not to respond to the riding statement but pushed ahead, adopting a more serious tone.

"I suppose Colleen has shared with you that I do not approve of Deidre leaving Moran for a boarding school in Dublin," Patrick stated.

"Yes, she did," Catherine quietly acknowledged. "And in some ways, I can see where you are coming from. You want her to stay close to home."

Patrick knew she was not going to let him off so easily. He had sized up Catherine during her visits to Ireland when Suzanne was still alive. And her presence at Moran these past weeks had proven to him that she was as headstrong as ever.

"Patrick, Deidre has asked if she can come and visit me in Evanston. She would like to see where her mother grew up—visit the stables where she learned to ride and go to the dance studio where her mother and I took dance lessons as children. I told her she would have to get permission from you as it is a long trip and she would be away for a month or more."

Patrick's eyes did not reveal any response as he took in Catherine's news. His sister, who stood at the patio door entrance, overheard the conversation. At Colleen's appearance, Catherine dismissed herself saying she needed to change from her riding clothes.

"That American woman is out of her mind if she thinks that I will ever allow Deidre to go the States and be under her influence. It would be the ruin of Deidre. You tell her so. She stays right here where she belongs."

"I think you need to be the one to tell Catherine since she asked you and you are Deidre's father. You have made it clear that I am not to interfere when it comes to Deidre in any way," Colleen reminded Patrick.

Patrick jumped to his feet and launched himself across the small space separating Colleen's chair from his own. His eyes squinted and his face reddened with heat from a temper out of control. Colleen leaned back to create as much distance as possible between herself and Patrick.

"Well, you got one thing right. You are not to interfere with anything that goes on in my house. My house! You will do exactly as I tell you, and if you don't like it, then go live in a walk-up flat in Bantry for all I care."

Patrick kicked the large footstool, sending cups and saucers flying. He stomped across the series of reception rooms, their walls lined with furniture, providing him with nothing to kick or throw as he made his way. Colleen watched him leave and quietly composed herself before climbing the terrace staircase to her second-floor bedroom.

~ ~ ~ ~ ~

On the last full day before she was to return to Evanston, Catherine accepted the housemaid's offer to pack up her suitcases. Thinking she would help, as she still was not acclimated to others doing things for her, Catherine soon saw that she was just in the way. Instead, she met Colleen on the second-floor terrace and asked where Deidre could be found. Catherine learned that her niece had last been seen walking toward the beach, another Irish ritual Catherine was not used to: children's freedom to come and go as they please without adult supervision.

Catherine descended the terraced steps that sloped down the hill, slowly taking in a last view of the bay and forest that surrounded the estate, an estate she had come to know from her daily excursions with Deidre. She expected to find her niece skipping rocks across the waves or roaming the beaches. She came to the bottom of the hill and saw Deidre crouched upon the sand, slightly hidden behind a short pile of driftwood. The child she had come to know over the past month possessed boundless energy and would never be found motionless on a beach—or anywhere, for that matter. Catherine quietly approached Deidre and, in a soft voice, called her name.

Deidre raised her head. Tears had left tracks on her cheeks, and her face was coated in sand.

"Deidre, whatever is the matter?" Catherine asked.

"I asked my father if someone should help me pack to go with you to America like we talked about. He just said no, I wasn't going anywhere. I can't go with you, Aunt Catherine." And with that, the child sobbed so hard her chest heaved as she struggled to breathe.

Catherine stooped to reach her niece. She scooped her up and pulled her into her lap. She sat on the beach of Bantry Bay in picture-perfect Ireland and rocked her distraught niece to the rhythm of the waves.

~ ~ ~ ~ ~

Catherine's departure date had arrived. She was dressed in the same brown coat, brown shoes, red hat, and matching gloves that she had arrived in. Her suitcase and cosmetic bag were stacked at the front door. Patrick had delayed his morning routine to see her leave in an attempt to put bad feelings to rest and to restore a good image of himself in his sister-in-law's eyes.

Catherine was standing at the bottom of the staircase when the butler deposited more suitcases next to Catherine's luggage. Colleen, dressed in traveling clothes, exited her bedroom and walked across the second-floor landing to meet Catherine at the bottom of the staircase. Patrick caught sight of Colleen and raised his eyebrows.

"What's this about, Colleen?" he asked in an authoritarian tone.

"Well, Patrick, soiléir agus simplí, it is," she replied using the Gaelic expression for "plain and simple." She then announced, "If Deidre is not going to Evanston, then I am." She showed not an ounce of emotion. "Furthermore, you should know that if I go, so does the cook. If I'm not here, she isn't staying. She doesn't want to stay in a house where there is no lady in charge. And, you will have to hire two more housemaids because they aren't staying either. But our family butler will remain. After a lifetime of service to this family, he has nowhere to go and nothing else to do."

"So, if I don't let Deidre go, you and the few women who keep this place going are leaving too? Who's to take care of Deidre? And, for that matter, me? Blackmail! That's what this is. You can't be serious!" Patrick looked at Colleen, then Catherine, then back at Colleen.

"Call it what you will, Patrick. I am done talking. I would love to spend the rest of the summer, or even a year, living with Catherine in America and seeing how American women live. And that's what I have, Patrick. A year's invitation from Catherine."

Patrick glared at Catherine as he realized his sister and sister-in-law had set him up. He could see no way he could get by at Moran without Colleen, not to mention the cook and housemaids that had worked there since he was a small boy.

Attempting to save face, Patrick softened his tone and replied. "Even if I were to change my mind about Deidre going, there isn't time to change the plan. Deidre is hardly ready to go."

Colleen corrected him. "I had her things packed up the day after our talk on the patio. I made up my mind right then and there that one of us was going to America. Deidre can go dressed as is. Catherine can help her into traveling clothes when they arrive at the Dublin airport. She'll have time. The only thing left to decide is who is going with Catherine—Deidre or me."

Blood surged to Patrick's face and coated his cheeks, nose, and forehead with waves of heat. He clenched his teeth and fists and struggled to keep them at his side. He had never experienced the feeling of being trapped and forced to make a quick decision with no agreeable options available.

"Then go. Deidre stays here."

Colleen picked up her bags and followed Catherine to the waiting taxi.

From the second story window seat, Deidre watched with tears streaming down her face. The taxi carrying the only two women in her life became smaller and smaller and eventually disappeared from her view.

Chicago, 1969

The wind blows in a westerly direction off of Lake Michigan, lifting anything that is not securely attached as I hold my hand to my hat and hurry down Michigan Avenue. I am late again for the rehearsal and expect a tongue-lashing from the show's production manager. The Chicago heat has been relentless all summer long, but I can smell crispness in the morning air, signaling the inevitable appearance of autumn.

With Catherine's help, my father eventually agreed to an extended stay in Chicago. Without providing a lot of detail, I convinced him that I needed a year to transition from college. I did not reveal that I would be working as a dancer in a ballet company. After I outlined my argument that a year or so in Chicago would prepare me to enter the family business in Ireland, my father silently nodded in agreement, adding that he did expect me to continue living with Aunt Catherine in Evanston. I would much prefer to live downtown with Sissy and some of the other dancers, but I know better than to push my father.

"Late again, Deidre?" yells Tony, making sure the others know I have failed to sneak in without notice. "No question, if you weren't so quick at learning new material, your ass would be out of here," he shouts in my direction. He turns his back to the dance floor and the others follow. Tony continues to shout over his shoulder to the dancers, knowing they will be close behind him. "We have exactly one month before this show opens, and we still have one hell of a lot of work to do!"

"Sissy!" I call out when the day's session ends and the troupe members head out of the building to Michigan Avenue's coffee shops and Chinese cafés, the favorite eating places of financially pinched dancers. I run to catch up.

"Wait up," I appeal to her, catching her by the arm. "Do you have time to catch an early supper around the corner?" Sissy's body language gives away her reluctance to hang with me, but her Midwestern nice manners get the best of her.

We finish off our shared bucket of rice once our entrees are gone. Sissy chooses her words carefully to explain why she has been avoiding me. "I don't have the leeway you do, Deidre. I need this job right now. I don't have a clue as to what I would do or how I would make next month's rent if I get fired from this show." Sissy bends over the table in my direction.

"Tony is not going to fire you! He does not like you, but sure as shit, he will never fire you. He knows which side his bread is buttered on." Sissy whispers so other dancers in the café do not hear our conversation. She says, "This is my full-time job. This is what I do, Deidre—the only thing I do, other than waiting tables."

"Buttered on?" I ask. I still don't translate some of the American euphemisms that well; even after all of the years I have lived in the States.

"Translation: money," replies Sissy, her eyebrows arched. I do not need to ask Sissy to explain.

I climb the platform steps to catch the last train to Evanston after a late Friday night rehearsal. Tony has invited the dancers from the troupe to go with him for a drink at his favorite off-Michigan Avenue bar. I know his invitation is an expectation. The others never miss a chance to cozy up to Tony. Getting in his good graces outside of studio time means a friendlier demeanor from Tony at rehearsals and better dance roles down the road. I never accept because I do not trust Tony. From the first day he learned that I am Irish, he has looked past me. He gives me little corrective feedback that every dancer expects in order to improve. Instead, he jeeringly asks, "Is that how they dance in Ireland?"

I slump into a seat on the train, thinking that after all of these years, I still do not fit in with the women. Conversations center on families, especially mothers and how much they either love them or resent them, or both. Once I answer the inevitable question about my mother's death, or how I live between Cork and Chicago as I do, most have little more to say. They either do not know how to ask about losing a mother so young or they feel that the extra work of walking on eggshells around the subject of mothers and death is just too much. I could go out of my way to describe my exciting arrangement of flying to and from Ireland for the past fourteen years, but I've never been a good liar. It hasn't been exciting; it was just what I adjusted to and learned to accept. While it is true that I do not have mother-daughter stories to share, I have, on occasion, shared stories of my father's hotel businesses in Ireland and how I envision women will one day move out of their homes and into the business world in substantial numbers. Until recently, I never realized that it isn't just my lifestyle that places an ocean between me and American women; it is also the way I view the world that sets me apart.

I climb down the platform at the Evanston station and slide into my sedan. In the privacy of my dark vehicle, I allow myself to give way to my emotions. The truth is I am lonely—very lonely. At the age of twenty-two, I should be at the top of the world. But tonight, I cannot see a world where I belong.

Chicago, 1971

The March wind gathers energy from Lake Michigan and, coupled with sleeting rain, makes navigation miserable. I hug the high buildings, looking for shelter under the overhangs as I edge my way from the basement apartment I share with Sissy and bolt toward the theater on Michigan Avenue. I am just minutes behind Sissy who refuses to wait for what she calls my dilly-dally morning ritual. With hot tea in hand, as I never did acquire the American habit of drinking coffee, I question my decision to become a dancer with the Michigan Repertoire Dance Company rather than pursuing a more serious-minded career in business or returning home to work in one of the Moran hotels.

I do not expect that I will become a principal dancer or, for that matter, even a secondary one. My body structure is still all wrong. I am lean and firm enough, given the rigorous rehearsal schedules, but there is no fix other than surgery to reduce my breasts—and even then, my hip bones are widely spaced and substantial in size. Coupled with my height, I am simply too much for a male dancer to lift. But the Michigan Repertoire Dance Company offered me a full-time position in the dance corps and a role as an understudy for the secondary dancers. I jumped at the chance. Sissy has blossomed in her dance development. Recently, she nabbed the understudy role for the principal female dancer in our company.

I pull open the dance company door, grateful to be out of the cold rain. My hair is soaked where the umbrella failed to keep me dry. My face is bare with just a hint of lip gloss. I wear heavy, shapeless jeans and urban street dweller boots to my calf. I am hardly a model of Chicago high fashion. But then, most dancers aren't when they are not on stage during a performance. Each day, six days a week, is the same: I arrive at the dance studio for the first of three dance lessons followed by a show rehearsal in the afternoon. It leaves little time to shop for food, do laundry, or sleep; much less have any kind of social life.

"Deidre," Sissy says, nudging me with her arm as we layer street clothes over our sleeveless tops and leotards. "Let's grab a tuna sandwich before heading back to the apartment." I nod and we head down Michigan Avenue towards Ziggy's that looks as if it has been there for a hundred years. Once we place our orders, we head toward the back corner where a pinball machine has stood ever since the bar opened decades ago. We are partial to the ancient machine with its old flippers, bells, chimes, and balls. Unlike the men who play it, we don't place bets on who will rack up the most points; we play to hear the machine drop balls and chime. We pile our bags, along with our food order, on a table close to the machine. It is late Friday afternoon but early enough in Chicago that there are few others in the bar.

The bartender keeps busy polishing glasses, readying the popcorn machine, and filling ice chests. He notices a male customer sitting at the far end of the bar. While he completes his various tasks, the bartender keeps one eye on the man, who is now off of his seat and leaning on the bar. The guy wears a casual pair of jeans with a white dress shirt hanging loose. He is average in height and not particularly muscular. "Maybe in insurance," the bartender says to himself. He moves closer when the man nods in the bartender's direction to refill his whiskey shot glass.

"Work nearby?" the bartender asks as he has not seen him in the bar before. The two men exchange polite conversation and the customer's attention turns to the women at the pinball machine. He casually asks if they are regulars. The bartender nods. The customer comments that they are real lookers, and based on their size, they don't look like either of them could hold much booze. The bartender shares that, based on the bits and pieces of conversation he has picked up, he thinks they are dancers with one of the local dance or theater companies. The customer looks at his watch, pulls a bill from his wallet, and lays it on the bar. He nods to the bartender and exits. Within seconds, he melts into the crowd of walkers on the street.

Sissy grows tired of the game, which is unusual as the customary pattern is for her to talk me into playing long after I become bored. As we pile on jackets and sling our purses over our shoulders, the bartender walks to the back of the room in anticipation of our departure, openly displaying a tab slip in his hand.

"Do you know that guy that was sitting at the bar a few minutes ago?" the bartender asks.

We both look in the direction of the bar and respond that we had not paid any attention. The bartender nods and lets us know that the man has paid our tab. We do not give much thought to the matter as it is hardly the first time a man has picked up our bar bill or sent drinks to our table. We figure it is his way of opening the door to conversation the next time he sees us at this bar or some other one.

Once we are out of the bar, I change the conversation to our plan of hopping on the El and heading up to Evanston for a quick girls' overnight at Sissy's parents' home. "I hope you don't mind, Sissy, but

I have changed my mind about staying with you at 'the homestead,' as you call it. Low on energy. Another time?"

"Sure enough. If you change your mind, just come on up. No need to call," Sissy advises. She heads for the train and I cross the street and head toward our apartment. After a hot shower, I turn on the television and grab a blanket before collapsing on the couch. I prop a cup of hot tea on a TV tray—every dancer's favorite beverage because it's calorie-free but soothing to the body. I make a mental note that Sissy would have arrived in Evanston by now and is probably being smothered by her much younger siblings.

I do not want to complain to Sissy that I am growing increasingly unhappy with my low-level dance position, nor do I want to tell her that I am thinking about moving on to something better suited to my interests and college preparation. I do not want to dampen Sissy's exuberance given her increasing success at the dance company. My mood will rebound with a good night's sleep.

Hours later, still under the sedation effects of a sleeping pill, I wake to a disturbance coming from the street. Lying still until I become more alert, I realize that the noise is a pounding at the apartment door. Has Sissy returned early and forgotten her key? I quickly consider the possibility and decide it is not likely. The pounding goes away. I fall back to sleep, but the pounding soon startles me awake again.

I check the clock. It is early Sunday morning. I reconsider and think it could very well be Sissy returning early, or maybe it is another dancer friend needing a safe house after a long night of partying. I unlatch the chain from the bolt lock and open the door a few inches to peer outside. The man from Ziggys pushes it open and says he paid the bill at Ziggy's and wants to get to know me better. He shoves his way past me. He closes the door behind him, blocking it with his frame.

Groggy from the sleeping pills, I desperately will my body to a full alarm state. What flashes across my brain is the horrific murder of eight Chicago nurses by deranged killer Richard Speck just five years earlier; an event that terrorized me and Sissy when we were seniors in high school. I know I have to divert this man to give me time to think more clearly. I ask if he brought any alcohol in an attempt to act as if I expected him to be here. I slowly back away—the wall phone is across the room—but he anticipates my intent and lunges toward me. I jump back, evading his reach, and run toward the phone. Not looking behind me, I grab the phone off of the phone rest and stick my pointer finger into the "0" slot to dial the operator. The intruder drags me to the ground and my finger rips from the dial. My head slams into the thinly carpeted cement floor and when I open my eyes, I see that he has put a knife to my throat. He tells me he will slit it if I make any noise. His entire weight crushes my body into the floor. I close my eyes, and my instinct to survive kicks in. I stop all resistance and the intruder rips my nightgown from my body, pulls his jeans to the floor, and pushes himself into me.

I tell myself to keep breathing. I count the steps to a new dance routine in my head. Though the attack lasts for a few minutes, it feels like hours have passed when he pulls out of me and slumps to the floor. He sits up with his legs crossed and arms resting on his thighs. His breath reeks of whiskey. He reaches into one of his jeans pockets and pulls out his wallet. He flips through the photo insert and shows me pictures of his wife and two small children. He tells me the children's names and says that the pictures are old; they are now in high school.

He rises, picks the knife up from the floor, and puts it into one of his pockets. He looks at me and tells me that I am a pretty little thing; that he would like to see me dance. I remain seated on the floor, having grabbed my nightgown for cover. I push all of my emotions as far inside of me as I can and glue my eyes to the intruder. I keep telling myself that I have to make it appear that all is okay. I tell him that his wife is pretty and nod my head in affirmation when he shows me pictures of his children.

I watch as he pulls his clothes back on. I can feel every inch of space between us. I do not want him to think that I am watching the door or looking to grab the phone. I wait quietly, breathless as he continues to talk about getting his car. What time is it? The sun is lighting up the apartment. There will be more pedestrian traffic on the street outside of the apartment, and also more opportunity to call for help. I think of mentioning that my roommate is expected back early in the morning but change my mind. I do not know how he would interpret a threat of being discovered. Surely he has some concern of being caught and will leave as quickly as he entered. He walks over to the door and, in an apologetic tone, comments that the door is okay and the lock is intact. With that, he opens the door, walks out, and slowly closes the door behind him.

I crawl over to the couch, pull the blanket down to the floor and roll up in it. One part of me says that I just had a bad dream and the attack was not real. But the primitive part of my brain has flooded endorphins into my bloodstream, making me shake uncontrollably. Waves of pain rip through my vagina, back, and abdomen. Morphine-like chemicals flood my brain, inducing tears that wet my cheeks and eventually bring on sleep.

~ ~ ~ ~ ~

Sissy fights the driving rain as she works her way through the streets. She inserts her key into the apartment door and finds it unlocked.

Deidre really must have been exhausted to have forgotten to lock up, she thinks. Once inside, she finds Deidre curled up in a ball of blankets on the small living room floor. Deidre is the most predictable person she knows, and Deidre never sleeps on the floor. Never!

"Deidre, wake up. Why are you on the floor?"

Sissy maneuvers herself closer. She cannot get Deidre to verbalize what is wrong. Is she sick? Has she taken an overdose of sleeping pills? Sissy walks toward the wall phone. "Deidre, I am going to call an ER nurse for advice in case you have mixed sleeping pills with something else."

I reel to my knees and scream. "No, don't do that! I don't want anyone coming here. No, Sissy!"

Sissy stoops and tries to look into my eyes, but I am covered with the blanket and avoid eye contact. "Okay, Deidre, I won't call anyone, but will you please tell me what is wrong? This is so unlike you!"

I blurt out. "I may have taken one too many pills. There was something going on outside in the middle of the night, and then those pills. Noise at the door...must have fallen asleep on the floor...so cold on the floor."

I keep repeating the same few phrases over and over again. But as Sissy listens, she cannot put together a congruent idea of what has happened. "Stay there, Deidre. I am going to get some water for you."

Sissy kneels and hands a glass of water to me. I accept the water and retreat under the blanket. Sissy realizes for the first time that I am more than hung-over from sleeping pills. She leans over to encircle me and holds me with both arms. For a minute I am back on the beach at Moran Manor being cradled by Aunt Catherine.

~ ~ ~ ~ ~

I walk into the rehearsal studio with seconds to spare. I tell myself that I have to move past what happened in the basement apartment. I deflect Sissy's attempts to make me open up. Rather, I immerse myself in the current dance production. This is the survival mode I have used all of my life, and it is a reflexive behavior that brings familiarity and comfort.

Bob, the rehearsal director, walks into the studio dressed in a black leotard and a black nylon fitted shirt. He faces the dancers. "We have work to do. We have exactly ten weeks before the opening of *The Nutcracker* and our holiday season. I want to start with the principals and then the secondary dancers. In between, I will choreograph the corps."

He points to the dance floor perimeter and impatiently waves the corps and secondary dancers to sit while he works with the principals at center stage. Bob points to Sissy and her partner. He intends to work through the dance sequence for the fairy dance. With no music, Bob briefly explains to Sissy and her partner how he wants this section to be performed. He does not seem to know exactly what he wants; rather, he experiments with Sissy and her partner by shouting out directions. When he sees movements that he likes, he yells, "That's it, remember that." Sissy and her partner are expected to repeat the series of favored movements from the many he has demanded of them.

Sissy grows increasingly tired from the rigor of Bob's demands and no rest time. I watch along with the rest of the seated dancers and wait for Bob to intersperse commentary about how he wants the dance sequence to communicate a particular emotion. Experienced dancers rely on the choreographer's insight during these brief lectures, but it also provides much-needed rest breaks. Bob walks into Sissy's personal space and asks her to repeat the sequence she had just done. Stepping backwards, Sissy begins the slow dance sequence and then projects her body on point and spins as if in a storm.

"Sissy!" Bob yells. "No, no! That is not what you did last time. You missed the transition between the slow sequences into the turns. Again!"

Sissy repeats the sequence, and once again, Bob tears it apart without providing specific direction on exactly what he wants. Sissy, wet with perspiration from her face down through her drenched ballet shoes, begins to stumble. Her male lead reaches out to her in a display of physical support. He signals toward a seated dancer and then gestures to the water fountain, silently requesting her to bring water.

"Oh for God's sake. Sissy, you are wasting *my* time." Bob moves toward Sissy, places a spread hand on each of her shoulders, and pushes her aside.

I bolt from my position on the floor and push all of my significant height into Bob's face. "What the hell do you think you are doing? Take your hands off of her!"

The veins in Bob's neck pop and his face goes scarlet. He stares directly into my eyes, but I do not back off. He thinks about escalating the encounter further, but there is something in my face that he has not seen before on a woman. He spins around and walks off of the dance floor.

Sissy grabs her dance bag, throws her coat on, and heads toward the stairs. I follow close behind, trying to explain the rage that erupted out of me. She turns and faces me.

"I don't need you to fight my battles. I have told you before; I can't afford to lose this job. I don't have an upscale house to flee to in Evanston so I can be taken care of by a wealthy aunt."

"But Sissy, I was just—"

"Why don't you direct your rage toward yourself and figure out why you have become so...so..." Sissy stumbles to find the right word. "So damn angry at the world!"

~ ~ ~ ~ ~

I follow the sound of a whistling tea kettle in Aunt's Catherine's kitchen. She hears my footsteps, looks up at me in surprise, and wraps her arms around me in a close hug.

"What brings you to Evanston? And before you answer, you know I love any excuse to visit with you, Deidre."

"Oh, you know, Catherine, the usual," I answer, eyes glued to my cup of tea while holding a cookie as if I don't know what to do with it.

Catherine is too observant to miss the dark cloud that I brought with me. She raised me from age eight, and while not my mother, she has acquired a mother's barometer.

"Let's get out of the kitchen and cozy up on the sofas." Catherine directs me into the spacious living room, complete with matching coral couches and footrests that I know well. Once settled in, Catherine sips her tea and patiently waits for me to disclose what is on my mind.

"I need to move. I mean, Sissy and I need to move out of our basement apartment into something that is... more secure. We don't feel safe there anymore," I explain. "And, of course, that is going to mean more rent money. Can you break the ice about it with dad when you talk to him again? I absolutely hate bringing anything up with him that concerns my life here in Chicago. He uses any opportunity to demand that I return to Cork and work for him." I pour out the words without taking a breath.

Catherine listens without responding; rather, she gazes at me with undivided attention. She waits.

"It makes me so angry that my own father—correction—my very wealthy father—does not want to see me happy in a life that I want to mold apart from his selfish needs. It isn't like he doesn't have the money. In fact, I'm sure that I have money from my mother somewhere, well-hidden by him. She would certainly want to help me build my own life if she was with us today, wouldn't she, Aunt Catherine?"

Catherine nods in agreement. "Yes, she would, Deidre. But knowing that does not help us today."

Hearing her response, I close my eyes and my entire body withdraws into a shell. My breath is fast and sometimes audible.

Catherine leans toward me. "Deidre, what is wrong? Are you mad about something?"

"Mad?"

"Yes, mad. You *are* mad, aren't you? Have I done something to upset you?" Catherine continues questioning to get me to open up.

"Hell yes, I am mad. I am mad at my father.

"Whatever for?"

"For not protecting me. For sending me away in the first place. Because apparently, I was in the way."

"It seems like you have been mad at him for a very long time. After all, he has supported your stay in Chicago financially even if done begrudgingly."

I consider my aunt's response and nod in agreement. "I have been mad at him ever since my mother died. He never talks to me about how she died, or why. I was left to figure that out piece by little piece. He could not be bothered with me." I am surprised at how much feeling pours from me.

"So you felt alone in that big house and unprotected by your father. But you weren't alone because Colleen was always there..."

"I still felt alone and unprotected," I push back, interrupting Catherine before she has time to finish her thought.

"At home. When my mother died. No one talked to me. No one

told me why she was so sick. No one talked to me after she died. No one talked to me when Colleen left with you for what seemed like an eternity. I was left alone in that old, rambling house with the family butler! We didn't even have a decent cook. One cook came in after the other, like a revolving door. No real school. No friends other than Cory, the son of my father's business agent. How could my father have thought that was acceptable? For that matter, how did Colleen think going away and leaving me alone was acceptable?"

My outburst pulled Catherine back to that summer at Moran when she and Colleen had tried desperately to push my father into seeing that allowing me to go with her was a better choice than allowing Colleen to leave. She also remembered that Colleen had reached her wit's end dealing with Patrick and bearing the weight of the responsibilities that had been placed upon her for decades. Something had to change to crack the status quo, even if that crack meant that the most vulnerable suffered.

"What else, Deidre?" Catherine said. "Are you mad at me, too?"

I look my aunt straight in the eyes. My throat swells shut and I struggle to answer. Eventually, I whisper, "No Catherine, I could never be mad at you. I am mad at my father. For giving me away. For not fighting for me."

"I am sure that is how it seems to you, Deidre. But trust me that your aunt Colleen and I were just trying to do what we both thought would be better for you at the time. We thought your father would be more cooperative. But in the end...well, you know just as well as I do what happened to get your father to see things differently and to send you here...eventually. I don't think either of us believed your father would live at Moran without Colleen."

"And, he really has changed. He was magic but that is for sure gone."

"What do you mean, Deidre? The magic is gone?"

"The magic is gone. At Moran. My father had the magic, Aunt Catherine." I whisper with head lowered looking into my mug of tea. "My father had the magic."

Catherine asks, revealing her curiosity. "Maybe it was the country of your birth, or Cork—a most magical place to grow up, for sure."

I shake my head to let her know she is wrong. "I know because it is the one thing I remember my mother saying. That father was magic. And he was. Before she died. His smile, his laugh, his stories about the history of our house, and our small country. He was the magic."

"Maybe your father is right when he says you should go home. Perhaps you will find something special there again to help you move forward in your life?" Catherine poses it as a question, but really, she is suggesting that those feelings are still alive.

"The magic died with my mother." My response is definitive. I take a deep breath that brings me back to more pressing issues. "Anyway, Catherine, to get back to my main worry today...Sissy and I really do need to move, and what we make at the dance studio is not going to get us a place much different than what we have now."

Catherine sits as if frozen, watching me. She is still back in Cork, thinking about what I have just revealed. She can't shake the image of her niece alone at Moran years ago. For all of these years, she believed that I had somehow coped well until her father gave in and sent me to the States. She wonders how she could have gotten it so wrong.

"Catherine?" I ask.

My aunt recovers and rejoins me from her daydream.

"Do you think that you will make more money after you are with the dance company a while longer?" Catherine is trying to be supportive yet encouraging. "That might help me make a case with your father."

"I am not really a main dancer. I am in the corps; the dancers who are never going to make it to center stage."

"Didn't you graduate from Northwestern with a business major? Why are you settling for a job that is outside of your major, and maybe outside of your real talent?"

"Because I may have to go home at any time. I don't really have control over my life, Aunt Catherine. This is what I can do that is easy for me until something else comes along." But my words ring in my ears. I am hiding from the real problem. I don't want to drop the pain from my attack onto my aunt. It is not fair to dump that kind of hurt on her.

"Something else?" Catherine asks me.

"I don't know. I doubt that I will be hired on for next season after what happened at the dance studio today. I am pretty sure I will be fired. I let my emotions and fears get the best of me, and I lashed out at the lead dance choreographer."

Catherine drops her eyes to her lap. She is wise enough to read that some event has triggered an eruption within me, an eruption that has been building for years.

"Deidre, let's do this. You and Sissy find an apartment that you can feel safe in. I will help with that expense until there is a good time to broach the topic of your allowance with your father. It is a temporary expense I can handle."

I leap from the couch, nearly knocking over Catherine's tea, and kiss her fervently on her cheek.

~ ~ ~ ~ ~

The holiday winter season slips by both Sissy and me. We keep in constant motion with barely a minute to wave a greeting between us.

Sissy stepped in as the principal dancer for half of the season. Ecstatic with the opportunity to star in her first lead role, she was relieved that *The Nutcracker* closed with sound reviews.

I drift. My dance assignments are not challenging, but I am content enough to be enveloped in the daily routines and hustle of backstage theater, and I am particularly grateful that I was not fired after my explosive outburst. I hustle to meet Sissy for an afternoon lunch date. "Hey, Sissy!" I warmly greet my sister-friend waving her down. "Don't you look like a Chicago model!"

I size Sissy up, as do others. She is cuddled up in a scarlet pink jacket trimmed in white rabbit fur. The voluptuous hood wraps around her shoulders like a fur shawl. Her long, toned ballet legs are outlined in black ski pants with straps on each leg that loop under her feet, keeping the pants taut, as is the rage in winter fashion this year. A pair of white, leather boots hug her legs and rest just underneath each knee. Two men sitting at the counter turn to watch the blonde as she walks across the room. Her hair is disheveled from being hooded, yet it bounces from one shoulder to the other as she struts to my table.

We hold hot chocolates in our hands and lean on the table to put our heads close together. A customer seated close by turns toward us when she hears me exclaim with joy. Sissy is truly overwhelmed with my reaction to the news that she has been offered a principal position with a start-up dance company. Sissy rattles off the sequence of events that brought her world into Andres' orbit.

"Deidre, this man came to my dressing room and introduced himself. He said he had come to three of my performances! The first time he came to the ballet as a dance reviewer. The second time, he came to specifically watch me, and the third time; he came to watch me in order to visualize how I would stand out in his start-up company.

He pushed through the bustle of backstage mania after our closing performance. He found my dressing room and unabashedly asked me to join his dance company as the lead female dancer!"

"And Deidre, within two days, I accepted! I have to confess that I feel guilty for not sharing all of this with you and asking for your input, but I really felt that I had to make this decision on my own. That way, no matter what the end result turns out to be, I will have to claim full responsibility," Sissy explains.

My eyes lock with Sissy's as I silently admire her strength. I am not surprised that someone has noticed Sissy's dance talent; it was just a matter of time. I have been dancing next to Sissy, and then behind her as part of the corps, for several years. But what really catches my attention today is the strength I see in my friend—her resolve to move in the direction of her primary love and do so under her own power. Was that strength always there, or was I so caught up in my own drama that I had simply missed it?

Sissy went on to enlighten me that, curiously enough, Andres and his small troupe of dancers had begun by working at a senior center. His dance group has become so much in demand among their clientele that they now rotate their performances among ten senior centers in the Chicago area. He has gained funding from the Chicago Arts Board and from various hospital foundations to pay for his dancers' time and a modest wardrobe budget. They rehearse at a vacated warehouse owned by one of the arts board members.

Whoever Andres is, he has gained strong momentum in gathering sponsors, financial backing, and, most importantly, a growing audience base. Sissy and I sit together and let the energy settle from sharing so much news that impacts her and me in ways that were yet unknown.

~ ~ ~ ~ ~

Sissy moves around our new apartment lighting the candles she has placed on the dining room table. I enter the dining room from the kitchen and am about to say something to Sissy when my eyes become glued to her dress. I thought we were preparing a casual supper. However, after eyeing up Sissy's evening dress, I suspect that there is another item on the agenda, an item that I either missed or that Sissy kept hidden during our conversation. As she turns toward the coffee tables with candles in hand, her bare back catches my eye. A black silk dress drapes over Sissy's small hips and leaves most of her legs bare. The dress is stunning and must have cost her an entire dance company check. I chose not to ask the obvious question at that moment in favor of observing the interaction between Sissy and Andres during dinner. Why bring a complication to the evening that might be all in my imagination?

The doorbell rings. I look in Sissy's direction, expecting her to approach the door to greet Andres, but all I hear is footsteps on the dining room floor as Sissy retreats to a back room.

"Hello, Andres." I greet the tall, handsome stranger. "It is so good to finally meet you after all I have heard from Sissy. I am sorry to confess that I did not catch your last name."

"Andres Soto, at your service."

He bows ever so slightly, extends a large bouquet of yellow roses in my direction, and flashes an easy, wide smile. He is six feet tall and has dark, wavy hair coupled with a hard, muscle-built dancer's body. He emits an aura of Hispanic testosterone that I rarely see in male dancers. I direct Andres to the compact studio couches that are now warmed by Sissy's strategically placed candlelight. I can't help but smile as I forewarn myself that there may be more on the dinner menu than beef stroganoff and wine. As Sissy enters, Andres jumps to his feet, moves in her direction, and kisses her cheek. With wine glasses in hand after a modest amount small talk, our threesome moves toward the dinner table.

Sissy volunteers to clear the main course and dishes. She strolls back and forth from the table to the small kitchen, her dress swinging and Andres watching her every move. I watch them as I slowly drain my wine glass. I reach to retrieve the wine bottle, knowing that Andres's attention is elsewhere, and refill our glasses. Sissy carries to the table a pot of dark coffee and dessert plates containing thick brownies topped with French vanilla ice cream. She plays with her dessert, eating very little, but that is nothing out of the ordinary. When Andres has made his way through half of his brownie, he directs his attention to me.

"So, Deidre, tell me, what do you see yourself doing, say, ten years from now?"

I had just filled my mouth with brownie and ice cream. "Mmmm, this brownie." I look up at Andres. "Honestly, Andres, I don't know. One thing is certain, though. It won't be as a primetime dancer. That is more Sissy's domain than mine."

"You have a business degree from Northwestern? And your family, that is your father, is in business in Ireland?"

"Yes, he owns hotels in Cork and Dublin. He wants me in Ireland working the family business. Truthfully, he doesn't want me working at all. He holds the patriarchal Irish view that women should work inside the home, doing whatever is needed by the family. He has offered to set up an office at Moran for me to conduct hotel business from there."

"Moran?"

"Our home in County Cork. It has been in the family for generations," I explain.

"Wow, that would be hard to leave," replies Andres.

"It's not that impressive. The manor itself is old, dark, and needs a ton of repairs. The hotels in Chicago are more glamorous than my family's estate."

Andres puts down his coffee cup. "So, do you see yourself returning to Ireland to do that?"

I start to respond, hesitate, and start again before admitting to both Andres and Sissy that I have been trying to find a way to tell my father that I will not be returning to western Ireland to work in the Moran Hotel business.

"Deidre, let me offer another possibility. I know Sissy has told you of my efforts at expanding my dance company. I put all my time into finding the best dancers, including Sissy. But I don't have a location for the studio. We currently work out of a senior center in North Chicago."

"That doesn't sound like a bad location for a start-up dance company," I respond, not all sure where he is taking this conversation.

"Deidre, the dance troupe has become so much in demand that we rotate our performances among ten senior centers in the Chicago area. But I am having a hard time managing all of the demands placed upon me. My heart is in dance choreography, not buildings, supplies, and budgets," he explains. "I need a business manager, Deidre. Someone who knows dance is a must. And, I need a financial investor. Would you be interested in investing in and running the dance company as an equal partner?"

I sit back in my chair. Obviously, Sissy and Andres have talked through the possibility of me joining the new start-up dance endeavor. I am not sure how I feel about either of them springing on me what seems like a plot when I have not met Andres until this evening.

"Wow, this is quite the surprise. I am thankful to both of you for your confidence in my ability to play such an important role, but I am not sure that it is a realistic move for me right now, Andres. And, as for a financial investment, I don't have that kind of money. In fact, I don't have any money at all!"

Sissy leans on me. "Deidre, you are blasé about your current role at Michigan Repertoire. This opportunity gives you the chance to stay close to the dance world and use your degree in business. What is unrealistic about that?"

Andres extends the proposal. "Would your father be a potential funding source? That would allow him to partner with you on a business project. I apologize for dropping this on you in this way. I understand your reluctance. Just think about it before outright declining. It could be an exciting path that would keep you in Chicago, and I am certain you would be a positive force to launch this company." Andres concludes, knowing it is time to say good night on a positive tone.

After he leaves, Sissy and I dress in our nightclothes and recline on the living room couches. "Sissy," I dare to say. "It is obvious from the difficulty you had looking Andres in the eyes all evening, and from the fact that he could not take his eyes off of you, that you have more than a business interest in him."

"I won't try to be coy about my relationship with Andres Soto," Sissy responds. "We have been seeing one another off of the dance floor for some time. I know what you must be thinking. That he is my boss and employer and that makes it complicated, maybe even foolish."

"But Sissy, you have been around dance for ten years now. We both know that very few of the male dancers are romantically attracted to women. Are you concerned at all about the Balanchine Effect operating with Andres?"

"I know about Balanchine," Sissy said. "I have thought about that, and somehow I managed to get the strength to confront Andres about that very issue, if you can believe it!"

I take in her response and continue to tread into her private life with care. "Sissy, have you thought about how devastating it could be if your relationship with Andres becomes more of a power struggle, or worse, if he isn't the man he claims to be? Or the most common occurrence with new relationships—that it doesn't work out and he calls it off, yet you are still working for him? And if I would agree to work with him, how do I know that I can trust him?"

"I know you are trying to protect me, Deidre, but I can't live my life being afraid of all of the what-ifs. At some point, I just have to be willing to take as big of a leap off of the stage as I do on it." She looks at me. "You know?"

Before heading to bed, I confess to Sissy. "I am jealous of how far you have grown, how strong you have become during this year. You keep taking really good risks and are building a life. I am so inspired by your courage. I have a lot of space to fill, Sissy."

"So come to work with us," Sissy begs.

"And if it doesn't work out? I will lose you, too!"

"I'm not going to be that easy to get rid of, Deidre Moran," Sissy quickly replies while giving me a goodnight hug.

I stand naked before my full-length mirror. Before me stands the reflection of a young woman with a trim waist that is toned from hours of dance and exercise. I place my hands on each side of my waist and glide them down over strong, wide hips. As I move my hands upward, I use them to massage my breasts. I am comfortable with my nakedness and believe it is the best way to size up my posture, to practice a standing pose for balance, and to watch how my body responds to the various challenges that the pose demands. I can hear Colleen's voice instructing the eight-year-old me to stand up straight because I would be a tall woman someday. I can also hear her instructing me equally often to slow down as I tore through Moran like a wild boar.

I look into the eyes of the girl in the mirror and whisper to her out loud, "You are still a girl alone in this world."

County Cork, Ireland, 1973

Patrick Moran pushes the back patio door open and steps outside. The dew wets the grass and morning birds call to find their mates. The scent of strong coffee permeates the musky air as Patrick walks to the garden table and sets down his hot mug and newspaper. On this August morning, his thoughts are on his daughter, specifically her upcoming visit for her twenty-sixth birthday. The hardest decision had been where to have the celebration. He would prefer the house. Isn't this where Deidre was born, after all? Colleen, on the other hand, argued for the Moran Hotel in Dublin to give the affair a more sophisticated allure.

Colleen maintained that they should plan a coming-out ritual combined with an air of homecoming. Patrick was well aware that this birthday was significant as she would officially come into the money that her mother had left to her; an invested inheritance that had grown into substantial wealth. Patrick recalled his surprise when he found that his American wife had the forethought to detail a will on her own for her sole benefactor, her daughter—their daughter. That would be unheard of in Ireland. The principle had accrued to a sizable amount, guaranteeing both security and independence for Deidre. But Irish law or at least tradition still held that the money was his to do with as he wished. And he did not wish that Deidre should have it. Not yet, anyway. He was not altogether certain if Deidre knew about the inheritance. He had made it a point to not discuss the subject of money with her. He maintained the Irish ways concerning money and women: silence.

Patrick drank the last drop of his strong brew and whispered the word "eighteen" twice. Eighteen years ago, he had sent Deidre to the States. He knew the old anger would surface again if he spent too much time recalling that morning when Colleen and Catherine had pulled away from Moran Manor in a cab to catch a flight to Chicago. Although it seemed like a lifetime ago, it never got any easier to remember how Deidre had wept as she watched the two women leave her behind. He felt forced to send the child to the States the following summer with assurance from Colleen that she would return to Ireland and Moran.

The air is muggy but cool as Patrick enters his Dublin hotel and makes his way to the ballroom on the top floor. Patrick looks inches taller than his true height. He is meticulously dressed in a beige summer linen tuxedo and matching Italian leather shoes. He is solo for the celebration, although he had contemplated asking any number of women to accompany him. At the last minute, he had decided that he did not want the responsibilities of an escort. He could devote all of his attention to his daughter. He needs to let Deidre see that he is trying to be a more responsive father, although, granted, some years late.

The ballroom is shoulder-to-shoulder with guests. A crystal chandelier with hundreds of intricate Irish cuttings hangs from the center of the room. As guests circulate and sit in any number of tucked-away conversation coves, their eyes are treated to a hundred crystal vases filled with yellow, white, and pink roses no matter which way they turn their heads. Swags of silk fabrics in purple and white hang from the ceiling, staged by carefully placed ceiling fans, creating a continuous aura of color and sensuous movement of fabrics.

Patrick is stunned by the visual impact the room makes upon him. He circles the perimeter, noticing that he is nervous, an uncommon feeling for him. It makes him uncomfortable. He shakes hands with invited business associates and family members, and he then notices that there are a number of young people he does not recognize. Turning his head to Colleen, he makes a slight hand signal to question the circle of young people across the room. Colleen smiles, turns her head, and ignores his silent request for identification. The room vibrates in a collective hum and he makes his way over to the corner where his sister stands.

A young woman walks down the platform of steps and into the sunken ballroom. Patrick's initial reaction is of curiosity. He thought he knew every gorgeous woman in Ireland. His reaction turns to embarrassment as he recognizes his error. Deidre walks slowly in his direction, a full smile on her face. When she is within a foot of him, his daughter stretches her arms wide open. "Father," she calls. "Daddy!"

Little girl she is not. Patrick smiles immediately and returns the gesture of outstretched arms. He hugs her close and then slowly turns her around to examine her Chicago-purchased birthday costume. Her strapless red silk dress follows the curves of her body and drapes to the floor. All he can see in front of him is skin. The dress is cut with a wide V down the center, which ends below her breast line and is banded underneath with a black silk ribbon. Her auburn hair is cut above her shoulders in a severe blunt cut. Large gold hoops swing from her ears. Wearing Italian stiletto high heels, she easily towers over him by four inches.

Patrick threads his daughter's arm through his and circles her around the room, seeking out family members first, one by one. Other guests recognize Patrick's intended pattern and wait patiently for their turn. As the evening wears on, Patrick realizes he still hasn't learned who the group of young people is that he had spotted earlier. He excuses himself to Deidre under the premise of getting her another glass of champagne and gathers up Colleen to identify the circle of interlopers. Once he is armed with the information he needs, he makes his way back to Deidre, who is in the midst of the group laughing and exchanging short conversations.

"Here he comes, the tiger protecting the den," Cory says, speaking under his breath to a male friend. He directs his attention to Patrick who is approaching the group. "I bet he wonders how we undesirables managed to get an invite to Deidre's shindig." Reacting instinctively, like a defensive soccer player, Cory steps in front of Deidre and lightly catches her elbow with his hand.

"You haven't forgotten me, have you, Deidre, my dear?" he teases, catching her by surprise. "Dance?"

Looking directly into Cory's eyes, Deidre counters as if she is giving an announcement for the benefit of the assembled group. "Cory McInnis," she says, "I was wondering if you would work me into your busy social calendar to help me celebrate."

Cory waltzes Deidre around the floor with a strong lead as they make a full circle. "So, I hear you traded horses for another kind of arena," he says. "You spend a lot of your time on the Chicago dance stage and are no doubt tangled up with the dance community as well. I guess it's just another way to rebel against your father and aunt's efforts at trying to shape a proper Irish lady out of the wild child." He teases, casting his eyes in Deidre's direction. "Sure you have high enough heels on there, girl? You know we Irish men are not known for our statuesque height. Oh, but I guess you have pretty much horse-traded Irish men for the American brand, then again?"

Deidre does not fall prey to the back-and-forth banter for which Cory is known. She meets his bright eyes with her own and breaks into a full smile, still not able to resist the charms of Cory McInnis.

As the waltz finishes, Cory secures a commitment from Deidre to meet up with him. He walks Deidre back to the circle of his Cork friends and crosses paths with Patrick, who is headed toward Deidre.

"Hello, Cory." Patrick nods, curious that Deidre would have anything in common with a childhood friend that he thought she had left behind years ago.

"Hello, Mr. Moran," Cory responds with a full smile. With a strong, calculated gait, he walks past Patrick and away from the group of young Cork locals.

~ ~ ~ ~ ~

I slip out of bed and part the drapes to gaze down at the 100 steps that grace the front of Moran Manor and lead to the sea. No matter how often I gaze at it, I can never get enough of this spectacular view.

A soft knock at my bedroom door serves to remind me that I am not in Chicago. There, I have one day, Sunday, away from the dance studio to dress, make a light breakfast, or do nothing other than just lounge in a silky baby doll pajama until late afternoon, when I finally dress and go out to meet friends.

Here at Moran, things have remained the same since my baby feet scampered the floors. A maid knocks each morning and enters to prepare me for the day ahead. While never stated aloud, it's clear that lounging around in see-through nightwear is not to be done at Moran. I recall the conversations that Aunt Catherine and I have had over the years regarding the rigid morning rituals at Moran. But unlike my Aunt Catherine, I do not mind this particular adherence to the past. I enjoy the comforts of being attended to as I was all the years of my girlhood.

I wish the young maid good morning, and set her to the task of finding my riding clothes. A few hours later, I pull my worn but reliable Jeep through the gate at Schull Stables. I swing my knee high boots to the ground just as a stable boy saddles up two golden-haired quarter horses and leads them out to Cory. This morning reminds me of earlier days when Cory and I would escape our parents and ride horses as fast as we dared while still remaining in any kind of seated position. Back then, our rides took place under the watchful eyes of the Moran's stable master. We rarely talked while we were riding and today is no different. I relish the time to escape into the wild Irish countryside and become a part of it. Today, Cory has chosen an out-of-the-way stable in rural Schull. It is on the seacoast and just a short drive south of Moran.

Cory greets me in his usual fashion. "I am a bit surprised to see you here, girl, after that shindig last night. Thought you would still be tucked under a pile of blankets. Are you ready to make a run of it?"

"Am if you are. I think you had a later night than I did from the looks of those Bantry buddies you brought along with you."

"Hope that wasn't a problem," Cory answers seriously. "Your dad raised his eyebrows once or twice in our direction."

"No, not at all. I told you to bring along whomever you liked. After all, it was my party." I flash a big smile in his direction.

"Well then, let's get on with it. Hope you can keep up. If not, I will circle back and collect you," he teases.

We raise ourselves into our saddles and I follow Cory through the gate to the open summer fields before us. I match each of Cory's moves with my horse as he slowly posts into a gentle trot and then leans forward to execute a full gallop. The fields of summer clover blanket the ground underneath my stirrups and my senses take in the warm sun and the gentle breezes off of the Atlantic.

As the ride progresses in intensity, my brow becomes wet with perspiration and my hair drips with the mist still rising from the fields. Blood rushes to my face, caused by the exertion of my thighs, hips, and calves pounding against the quarter horse underneath me as I work to stay astride. My confidence may be high, but my body tells me it has been awhile since I last executed such a challenging ride on top of a horse that is conditioned by daily jaunts through uneven fields. My heart rate rises and my cheeks radiate heat. The stress trapped inside my body melts into the Irish air.

Cory leads our horses through their paces. After what seems to be hours, but is really just twenty minutes, he calls out to the horses to slow their gait. We take a gentle walk to cool down the horses and ourselves. He directs the horses to an open field dotted with a cluster of high oak trees that is just yards from the ocean. Halting his horse and dismounting with one full swing of his legs, he approaches my horse and grabs the reins.

I look straight into Cory's eyes, reading his body's every move. I have done this dance with this man before. If there is one thing that I remember about Cory McInnis when we were growing up, it is that Cory does not waste muscle energy. Every movement is deliberate. I jump to the ground and step toward him. Without either of us saying a word, he grabs me around the waist with one arm while his other arm reaches for my riding helmet. He removes it and tosses it into the air. While grasping my head in his hands, he pulls my mouth to his and we drop to the ground as if in a familiar choreographed dance that we have rehearsed time and time again.

Protected by the privacy of the tall grasses that encircle us, Cory places his jacket down to make an outdoor bed. I shed my riding clothes one piece at a time and use them as another cushion against the field's prickliness. I lie on top of my clothes and pull Cory down on top of me. He straddles me and pulls me forward, then places one of my legs on each of his shoulders. I am as athletic when making love as I am on the dance floor or riding a quarter horse. Matching my movements to Cory's energy, we execute a series of motions that result in maximum penetration and ecstasy for us both.

I am exhausted and wet, and so is Cory, who has collapsed over me in such a way that I am pinned underneath. Content to remain intertwined in one another, we listen to the wind as it brushes the long grasses and blows over our heads. Sleep comes to both of us as gulls, terns, and swallows add their songs to the murmur of the wind on its way toward the ocean below.

"Deidre, Deidre, Deidre," Cory whispers as he wakes me from my nap. "Marry me, marry me. You belong here. We belong with each other," he pleads. I look into the eyes of the wild Irishman whom I have known all of my life. A large part of my heart wants nothing more than to merge with Cory's heart and build a life with him in Cork.

"It would be so easy to say yes. You know I do love you, and I always will. But I am in the middle of something in my life right now, and if I interrupt that process, that energy stream, I would blame you forever." I try to explain to Cory, but his shoulders tighten and he looks over my head.

"Deidre, you would have a new and different energy stream— whatever the hell that is—here, in the world that you belong to and belong in. Why can't you see that?" There is frustration in his voice.

"I can't make that commitment and feel as though I am doing the right thing by you."

"You can't make a commitment to *me*, you mean. Why don't you just say it, Deidre? Your father has drummed into your head since you could walk that you can play with the hired help but you can't really bring them into the fold. Isn't that what it is really about?"

I look at Cory while gently shaking my head in disapproval. "Let's not spoil this beautiful morning by the sea. I want to remember it just like this for the rest of my life." With those words, I pull Cory back down into our grass bed. And for now, he is content with that.

~ ~ ~ ~ ~

"Patrick, be reasonable. Times are not changing that fast in Ireland. We have some challenges right now with staffing the hotels in Cork and Dublin, but things are bound to improve. Putting women behind reception and concierge desks is not the answer." Michael, the general manager of the Cork hotel, looks at Patrick Moran in an attempt to judge whether his message got across.

Patrick shuffles the stack of papers that holds the most current accounting report. Room bookings and catering reservations are on a downhill slide so Patrick hired an on-site consultant to study the Cork and Dublin hotels. The expert strongly suggested that the Moran Hotel chain needs to reach out to a more progressive traveler, which means visibly incorporating women onto the hotel staff. Another serious limitation of the Moran properties, the consultant reports, is the chain's reliance on old booking and advertising methods. The Moran staff is unmotivated to move into marketing strategies that target national and international travelers. Patrick had anticipated some of the consultant's recommendations, but the general manager had not. Michael is a dyed-in-the-wool Irish Catholic conservative who sees nothing but bad omens from moving women from the home to the workplace.

"Besides," counters Michael, "It is against Irish law for women to work outside the home."

"Not single women," Patrick argues. "The consultant says Irish law is about to change allowing Irish married women to work. It will be a slow transition and the law will likely require some heavy enforcement as it is likely to be resisted. In the meantime, he recommends employing college-educated single women. According to the report, many Irish girls have gone abroad to US universities to study business, accounting, and hotel management. They have degrees from some of the best American colleges. What we need to do is get them back home to Ireland and use their education here in the country of their birth rather than in the States or in London, where most of them are working now. What I really need to do is get my daughter to move back home where she belongs. She has everything in place that this consultant talks about."

Michael lets loose into the air at the idea of hiring women, and Patrick endures the storm of insults. When Michael grows tired, Patrick lifts his coffee mug before bringing the hammer down on the issue. In an understated fashion, he informs Michael that he has already made the decision to go ahead with all of the recommendations in the consultant's report. He has signed a contract with an employment agency in New York that also has offices in Boston and Chicago, three metropolitan areas where substantial numbers of Irish nationals live and where many prestigious colleges and universities are located.

"If Deidre comes to work for me here, Michael, it will soften things a bit. She will get a better reception because she is a local girl. You can teach her what she needs to know to begin to make some of the changes we need if we are going to grow and remain competitive."

Michael holds his breath as he stalks out of Patrick's office. It is the only way he can control his anger and not push back at the other employees as he heads for the door. What he had wanted to say to Patrick is that Irish men will never accept women in roles they feel are the rightful place of men. His instincts tell him to go back in there and tell Patrick to walk around the Cork and Dublin hotels so he can count the number of men employed and see the roles they hold successfully running the hotels. Each one of those men reports to another man, who in turn reports to the man who heads each department. Whether checking guests in, handling luggage or ordering cabs—each and every single one is a man.

He tries to imagine how the male employees will behave if he tells them that they will soon be working side by side with women and, God forbid, that a woman could eventually be their boss, even if it is Deidre Moran. Michael imagines that the employees would think it nothing short of an insult at best, and at worst, a direct assault on their masculinity. Imagine the conversations that would take place in the pubs after work and the anger the men would bring home with them! He shudders when certain faces come to mind; these men already have a reputation for taking their bad moods out on their women. It would be natural for these same men to unload on their own women because of "professional" women who get beyond themselves and above their expected role in Irish society. And, there is one thing that Michael knows for sure. Any woman thinking she is going to replace a man at work in Ireland, including Deidre Moran, is sure to experience retaliation in some unladylike ways.

Patrick reaches for the phone and calls Moran Manor. Colleen picks up. He lets her know that he wants Deidre to eat in with him that evening, alone, with no company. He puts the phone back on its cradle and once again scans the consultant's report. He has to admit that the pattern is indisputable. Women are becoming a force with respect to the travel business. Whether he is ready for such a dynamic change or not, it is clear he will have to make some changes to make his hotels competitive. Rather than hiring a woman from outside to be the female face of Moran Hotels, he thinks it best for Deidre to be that face and work with the transition. It is time for Deidre to come home for good and use that expensive education he has paid for to benefit Moran Hotels.

~ ~ ~ ~ ~

I walk down the three flights of stairs that are still covered with the original wool carpets. Each flight has a room-sized terrace landing, which provides plenty of room to gaze down the foyer for signs of my father or Aunt Colleen. My hands slide down the familiar oak banisters as I continue my descent, all the while thinking of how perfect Irish summer days still remain. My face flushes, adding to the hint of a sunburn, as I recall how unrestrained my behavior with Cory would seem to some women my age, to say nothing of what my father would think if he knew. My eyes light up with the memory of the afternoon, and I can't help but smile.

I proceed through the main foyer, looking for signs as to whether dinner is to be in the formal dining room or in the smaller breakfast room. I see lights in the breakfast room and move in that direction. The drapes are still open to expose the hills and the blue-green bay. I sit down at the table and think how pleased I am that we are to have an informal dinner in the small, cozy room that my American friends would call the kitchen, although this room is far removed from the food preparation room on the ground floor.

My father's footsteps go undetected as he walks across the foyer's thick, worn carpet into the small room. He catches me staring out at the bay with my chin cradled in my hands.

"A drink precedes a story?" he asks, looking toward me as he slips into his usual seat at the table. He pours me a glass of Cabernet, an American habit I have acquired from living abroad. "You are lost in your thoughts, or maybe a dream?"

I blush, which does not escape my father's attention, and I apologize for not greeting him. "I am going to have a hard time returning to Chicago after such a glorious party, followed by riding through the fields of Schull on a quarter horse in its prime."

My father raises his eyebrows, "You rode alone?"

"I confess I did not. I met Cory McInnis and we revisited many of the riding paths from when we rode as children and teens."

"I saw Cory at your party. I did not recognize him at all. Then, I don't see him like I used to when he was a boy and his father worked for me. He would bring him to the house with him. I had forgotten that you and Cory were *a chara*. In case you don't remember, that's Irish for 'fast friends.'"

"I remember, Dad. I have not been away so long that I have forgotten the Irish ways."

Aunt Colleen enters the room along with an assistant from the kitchen. They both carry dishes to the table. Aunt Colleen slips into her usual seat, allowing the assistant to continue with the task of aligning the dishes on the table and scurrying back and forth to the kitchen with more serving plates and bowls filled with steaming food.

"I can see why the Americans love their small eat-in kitchens. You can just about lean over and pick up a dish from the counter or a kettle from the stove," Aunt Colleen chats as she looks to me for affirmation. "Don't know why we don't convert some of the unused first floor into a modern kitchen like Catherine has in the US."

"I have told you time and again that I don't understand why you insist on serving food both at breakfast and suppers, Colleen. You hire sound kitchen help and I pay their wages." My father reprimands Colleen lightly, with a smile on his face. "Stubborn Irish woman that you are, Colleen Moran."

We finish our supper quietly as we watch the sun fall over the horizon and seemingly into the bay's glassy waters. Aunt Colleen gets up to flick on the chandelier light, which has only recently been changed from gas to electric. She excuses herself, allowing some private time between my father and me. There has been little of that from the moment I arrived.

"You have been gone a long time, Deidre. Are you homesick for Ireland?" my father asks.

I lean across the table and look deep into my father's eyes. I know when he has something on his mind, and I know his Irish way of circling around a subject before hitting upon it directly. I wait for him to elaborate. Sensing that I am not going to answer the question or push him further, he begins to make his case. He describes the hotel consultant's report and his awareness that Moran Hotels has to become much friendlier to women travelers, both business and leisure.

I wait to hear more. I had thought much the same during my short time at Moran Hotel-Dublin and during my observations around Moran Hotel-Cork, and I feel the same way about Irish businesses in general. Ireland is fifty years behind the times when it comes to women's roles, and especially women in the workplace. Every time I step off of the plane in Dublin, I am reminded that I am stepping back in time.

"I need you to come home, Deidre. To work for me—for the family business at Cork and Dublin." He pushes a copy of the report across the table to me. "I trust you to begin the process of opening up the hotels to women, both as employees and as travelers. You have that fancy American business degree that I paid for. I think it is time for us to put it to work."

I move my food around on my plate as my father's words sink into my consciousness. I am not surprised to hear that he wants me to come home as he has said that plenty of times over the past several years. And as for Moran Hotels being the family business, I know that is not truly the case. The family is Patrick Moran. If there had been a son in the family—if I had a brother—we would not be having this conversation about me joining the business.

"Dad, I am not sure that I heard you correctly," I respond cautiously. "I am really honored. First, that my father would have enough confidence in my abilities to do what we both know is going to be one hard turn to the left, and second, that you are futuristic enough to see that the Ireland of old has to wake up if it is to be competitive."

I reach for the bottle of wine on the table and refill my glass, biding my time. I am still reeling from the suggestion that my father would be one of the first businessmen in Ireland to deviate from the men-only workplace standard and forge a way for women to work outside of the home. And, I don't want to alienate him. I have my own agenda item to put on the table with him tonight.

I pick up the consultant's report, glance over the list of recommendations, and see nothing that I had not learned as part of my business degree at Northwestern. The consultant is right on.

"You're right, Dad. But you have the wrong person in mind for the job," I say. "I am a dancer, Dad. Not a hotel management professional." I see him wince at my words as he attempts to disagree with me, but I don't give him that opportunity. "Yes, I know you are going to say that I have a business degree and that I have lived in the States and I am up on all of the women's issues. All of that is true, Dad. But I love the dance world. I want my own dance company, not a hotel."

I lean back in my chair and bring the wine glass to my lips. I watch my father's face, searching for a sign that he will open up to me as I admit to him and to myself that I want to be a part of the dance business, not the hotel industry. My father shows little emotion or reaction to my words. I know he is used to people agreeing with his position and complying with his expectations, particularly women. That is what makes this moment uncomfortable. I wonder if he will launch into one of his famous temper tantrums and once again reduce me to being the child.

"I'm sorry, Dad," I say. "I can't leave Chicago. But I do know some women grads from Northwestern who would jump at the chance to transform Moran Hotels from the old to the new. And they are not just names, dad. These are women who are prepared to do just what this report says that you need."

I continue to whisper words of gratitude and assurance, but my father still does not respond. He looks over at me.

"I see my daughter that I sent away so many years ago, and I cannot help but wonder if this is part of the price I am paying for thrusting her out of her home at such a young age." He finally smiles at me, reaches over the table and takes my hands in his.

"I'm not ready, Dad. I'm not ready to come home," I whisper apologetically.

"What's this idea about you running your own dance company?" he asks.

"Just that, Dad. I have an opportunity to be the business director of a start-up dance company in Chicago. I want to buy in on the ground floor. Aunt Catherine mentioned that mother left me a sizable inheritance payable on my twenty-sixth birthday. I could use most of that to buy in as a co-owner. The company needs capital, and I have learned from you that owning a company gives you leverage in all kinds of ways that being an employee cannot."

Patrick unclasps his hands from his daughter's and leans back in his chair. "I am afraid your Aunt Catherine is mistaken, Deidre. The money is tied up. I put it to work in the Moran Hotels rather than have it sit idle over the years. More the reason for you to come home and use your business degree in an investment that you already have."

I stare into my father's eyes to see if I can read any signs that he is not being truthful. I see none.

I go in another direction, trying to find a bridge between our common interest in business. "What about helping me with a business loan that uses my inheritance investment as collateral?" I ask.

"That doesn't get you back here working for the Moran Hotels, does it?" My father looks straight into my eyes.

I watch as a housemaid approaches and then quickly changes direction when she sees my father and me deep in discussion so late at night, a highly unusual occurrence. Taking a cue from her, I rise and say to my father, "I'll get the names of a few women who can handle the changes you need. Good night, Dad."

The old childhood feelings of isolation and unworthiness swirl around me once again. I am sick to my stomach. There is no point in remaining at the table with him—with a father who still sees me as a young girl to control. I feel trapped and alone as I climb the stairs and cross each of the three terraces to my room.

Chicago, 1976

I sit behind a long oak table that I rescued from an Evanston library. My papers are stacked in neat piles and surround the electric typewriter that dominates the middle of the table-turned-desk. It has been two years since I left Ireland without a penny of my mother's inheritance. I connected Brenda Garlind, a friend in my business program at Northwestern, with my father and, remarkably, he hired her. After his deep disappointment in my refusal to work at the Moran Hotel in Cork, I had not expected him to take even the tiniest bit of advice.

Andres knocks on my office door and, since I provide no discouragement, he opens it. He pushes his head through, catches my attention, and then slowly walks through the door. *Just like a dancer would do*, I think.

"Here is the dance poster, including the mission statement you wanted, Deidre." Andres edges the poster towards me.

I turn from the electric typewriter I have been glued to for most of the day. I peer at a brightly colored photograph of five dancers posed in a complicated body maze. I silently read the bold, black statement. I nod and read aloud to Andres, as if he is unaware of what he wrote on the poster. "North River Dance Company brings artists, the arts, and dance together to enrich, engage, educate, and transform so that the

Company may change lives through the experience of dance." I gaze at Andres over my narrow readers and sigh. "Oh my. That's very good."

Andres, whose official title is Founding Dancer and Artistic Director, flashes a broad smile. Well into our second year of collaboration, he constantly reminds me that I am exactly what he needed to grow his company—and I remind him that it is *our* company, a notion that it still one step above his comfort zone.

While he never admits out loud that I am easy to work with, he pronounces time and again to both Sissy and me that my work has been critical in helping the company connect with audiences and make solid ties to funding sources. All he wants to do is focus his attention on the art and craft of dance so he is amazed at how quickly I filled a diverse board of directors: bankers, North and South Shore landowners, and people from the traditional Chicago arts community. I was quick to see the importance of hiring a cultural programming director whose job is networking within the region and country to expand the dance company's cultural taste buds. I made it clear to the new CPD that if I see her at the dance studio office often, it means she is not doing the job expected of her: traveling to New York City and other major dance venues across the country.

"I'll see you tonight at the board meeting," Andres responds, pleased that I approve of his mission statement. "Did you want to catch dinner with Sissy and me before the meeting? It would give me a chance to lay out a plan to connect with a broader array of Chicago artists before presenting the idea to the full board," he explains, adopting a tone that suggests he needs my read on it.

Later that night, I slip out of the cab and saunter the short distance to the restaurant's front door. I remain uninfluenced by the current Chicago fashion, which favors long, loose skirts. Instead, I wear a silk black pencil skirt that hugs my hips and reaches my ankles. A matching jacket hugs my waist and is highlighted with elongated white stripes down the sides. My ensemble screams model, and maybe business, but I don't care. After all, I am in the dance world and not the hotel business.

Dinners with the three of us, when they do occur, tend to be orchestrated by Sissy. She speaks to the waiters and inquires about food options that we (dancers) prefer, leaving Andres and I to pour over the company agenda. Tonight, we are in the middle of our first major disagreement with no compromise in sight with the board meeting just a couple of hours away. After a lot of head-nodding and hand-waving, Sissy quietly suggests that we merge the better of our two approaches into one workable strategy. She hates that the two people she cares for most are increasingly confrontational and attracting the attention of early diners.

"Look, Deidre. I am determined to expand our current efforts and spend company resources to network with the Art Institute of Chicago. I want to create a spin-off company, North River Two, to focus on professional development efforts for teachers, university dance programs, and affiliated health professionals," Andres states for what seems like the hundredth time.

I reply, "That idea is brilliant, and it connects perfectly to the dance company's mission. My concern, Andres and Sissy, is that an American focus tends to be provincial. And in this case, the province is Chicago."

I detail the advantage of directing the company's five-year plan toward forging an international pathway. My point is to not think exclusively American, but rather to explore lesser known themes. I push hard toward gaining inspiration from international art museums, perhaps in Paris or London—or Ireland, for that matter. I argue that the European masters' work at the Louvre or exhibits highlighting the African continent could provide inspiration for the company's dance choreography and future programs. "Why not merge your conceptualization of American modern dance with European influence to create a fresh, innovative American style?" I extend my arms into the air and put my fingertips together in a steeple fashion to stress my ideas.

Andres's head of long hair shakes violently. His voice becomes louder and louder, emphasizing his Cuban accent. His dark mood draws the attention of a steady stream of diners who are being seated. His frustration with my inability to accept his point of view has reached the boiling point, and I know that he is running scripts in his head about the company being *his* dance company and that as a Latino man, he is the one who makes the final decisions. I recognize that restraint on both of our parts is critical to avoid destroying all the scaffolding we have built together.

"This is an American dance company, Deidre. Establishing deep roots within Chicago and the United States was my first priority when I began North River. Dance has become stagnant and dated because it has been choked by adhering to traditional European ballet. Your strategy to rely on the traditional European artistic influence is just more of the same constraints," Andres argues. Then he lowers his voice and adopts a conciliatory tone. He tucks his head and moves toward me, denoting a desire to increase the privacy of our exchanges and turn the focus in another direction. He says, "This company cannot compete if it is to adopt the transcontinental lifestyle that you have been accustomed to all of your life. A split focus will put a drain on our resources and both of our energies. We need to focus in one direction at a time, Deidre."

My outward appearance is as calm as I can make it, but my emotions churn in a tidal wave. I have witnessed my father during heated business meetings at Moran as well at the hotel in Cork. I have watched him become calmer and quieter in order to lower the volume on a disagreement as the tone grows hotter.

"I appreciate your position, Andres. I really do." I let out a small laugh. "And yes, I do see how you would worry about a novice North River Dance Company shuffling itself between two or more countries." I smile as softly as I can. "And, my family arrangement has taken a certain toll on my life."

I lean back in my chair and assure Andres and Sissy that putting the dance company on an international performance schedule is not what I have in mind. I pull myself up in my seat and lean toward Andres. "When I joined this company, we agreed that as the executive director in charge of business and planning, I would make the business decisions. I have made up my mind about this. North River's number one priority for a period of five years will be to establish international themes and connections with the art world in order to inform its dance choreography at the Chicago studio."

Dishes clatter in the background, and when a waiter eager to do his job as he was trained approaches our table, Andres waves him away.

"I hate to play the money card, Andres, but I did manage to get a substantial amount of money to invest in the company—money that came from my Aunt Catherine, money I will have to pay back. I am taking a financial risk here with my aunt's money." I wait for a response from Andres. Seeing none, I continue. "Andres, you are the artistic director and founding dancer, and as such, you will continue to enhance North River's connections. We can work together on the line items later, but for tonight's meeting, I would ask you to report to the board that we are working on a very exciting plan for North River Dance with more details to follow soon."

I can't help but notice the wounded and angry expression on

Andres's face. I take another move from my father's playbook. I know that I have to soften my tone and reestablish a bridge between our two positions. I say, "Andres, let's not argue the strategy anymore. Sissy and I need your talent and vision right here in Chicago doing what only you can do. I assure you that as we move forward with an international strategy, we will revise our course of action if it looks like I have taken on more than the dance company can handle."

I reach across the table and cup Andres' hands in mine. "Friends?" I plead.

Andres relents. "You are right about the money. The company has progressed to the extent it has due to the influx of Catherine's money. We will remain friends no matter the difficulties we are forced to settle. If we don't stick together and we lose the dance company, Sissy will have to find another company to dance with, I will have to find another job in choreography, and you, dear Deidre, will have to go home to Moran and hear your father say you should have listened to him all along. That thought should motivate all of us!"

London, 1976

My cab pulls up to a building in the Bloomsbury neighborhood in central London. I climb out and look up at the Georgian brick townhouse that will serve as my home base as I investigate possible international dance themes for Andres. He remains convinced that my time in Europe will be a colossal waste of time away from the dance company in Chicago—something it can ill afford.

I love the fact that my London rental is in the notorious neighborhood of the renowned circle of writers known as the Bloomsbury Group, who had lived just around the block during the 1920s. Within the same neighborhood stands Bedford College, the first college dedicated to educating women, specifically those who would teach at institutions of higher education. I did not learn that the College would be one of my neighbors until after I rented the flat. It is as if I have a ready-made friend.

During my undergraduate days at Northwestern, I devoured all of the novels written by Virginia Woolf, the most famous member of the Bloomsbury Group, as well as those by her predecessor, Jane Austen. The curriculum at my suburban Illinois college was similar to that at most universities worldwide: students read and studied the works of men, which were obviously written from the point of view of a man's experience.

I had stumbled quite by accident upon a female professor at

Northwestern who specialized in literature written by women. I experienced a sense of shame that I had not known of the brilliance of Woolf, Austen, and other women writers and felt appalled that their contributions were not part of the required college curriculum. It altered me profoundly and made me appreciate the freedom I now possess, which was earned by the women who came before me.

It has been a three-month whirlwind since my feet first touched ground in London in April. I have sent letters to museum directors notifying them of my arrival and the purpose of my visit. My days consist of combing art museums and a small sample of the numerous British historic homes. So far I have found Chatsworth to be my favorite. One could spend a year just studying the art, Old Master drawings and neoclassical sculptures at that estate alone. I booked a private tour with the head of collections and heard the back stories of how particular pieces came to be at Chatsworth as well as the not-so-known tales of the dukes and duchesses who resided there for sixteen generations. My house at Moran Manor is a humble cousin when compared to Chatsworth.

And, I have managed to get myself on the invite list for the Pompeii Exhibit reception at the British Museum. During one of our daily phone calls, Andres had mentioned that the exhibit is *the* major hit of the year. The reception promises to host the most important people from the art, archaeology, and music worlds, exactly the connections I have pushed our dance company to explore.

I choose to walk the short distance from the townhouse to the museum, which is also tucked into the Bloomsbury neighborhood. I applaud my decision to wear an off-white linen pantsuit as the spring air is made decidedly cooler by strong winds. Before leaving my apartment, I traded my high heels for a pair of two-inch, chunky-heeled pumps. I carry my red wide-brimmed hat to avoid a chase down Montague Street in case a gust of wind puts it in flight mode.

I turn the corner on Great Russell Street and approach the museum. I have one hand on my hat and the other on a small clutch bag. I turn my head down to the sidewalk for just a moment and inadvertently walk dangerously close to the edge when a cab door suddenly opens. I startle and lose my balance. A tall man emerges from the cab. He reflexively catches me by the arm to secure me from a probable fall and catches my hat before it hits the ground. Once righted, I apologize for my inattention while the man does the same. After reassuring one another that we are not responsible for the near collision of cab door and walker, the man introduces himself, as do I. He hands me his business card and insists that I allow him to buy me a drink later in the day for escaping my near misfortune.

Meeting male strangers is not something I make a habit of doing, but this one catches my eye. Perhaps I am allowing myself to be influenced by the power of male persuasion because my guard is down and I am not immersed in my business identity. I look down at his business card, address him using his first name, and agree to meet him at the cocktail bar next to the museum at seven o'clock that evening. Flashing a warm smile that once again catches his attention, I continue on my way, walking slowly until I am out of his view. I am well aware that he is most likely watching my exit.

Clutch bag in hand, I enter The Museum Bar exactly at seven o'clock. "Missing your red hat after my grand rescue?" Steven asks as he rises from a stool at the bar that is made from cherry wood and runs the length of the room.

"I had someone run it home for me since all it seemed to be doing is causing me trouble," I explain while giving him a wide smile.

"My...a private ride home for a bonnet. I am not speaking with someone terribly famous that I have failed to recognize?" Steven teases.

"No, not famous. Just a woman not paying careful enough attention to her belongings. A bad habit of mine, I am afraid," I counter.

"Let me buy you that drink I promised."

The bartender begins mixing the drinks and Steven suggests we move to a more comfortable booth tucked in a corner. We settle in and, given that we are the accidental couple, engage in comfortable small talk during which we exchange brief autobiographical information. Steven then settles back and watches me as I sip my drink, allowing a period of quiet to drape over us. I sigh, smile at my new suitor, and sink back into the leather booth. This man is so appealing to me—or is it just that I let my guard down earlier in the day and am now more open to the natural chemistry of attraction? It has been months, and more accurately, perhaps a few years, since I met a man that draws me out of my head and into the moment. I am surrounded by beautiful men and women in the course of my life in Chicago, so meeting another tall, dark, and handsome man is not a unique experience for me.

When we finish our drinks, Steven says, "I don't always invite unfamiliar women to walk in parks with me during the evening. I know you would think I was making a well-practiced pass at you if I said that you don't feel like a stranger to me. But there is a quaint neighborhood park just a block from here with landscaped English gardens. It is still early, and if you will allow me, I would love to walk you home, Deidre."

I nod in approval and admit that, indeed, I have had similar offers that I considered to be pick-up lines. But somehow, tonight, coming from Steven, I do not care if it is.

As we walk from the Museum Bar through the streets of the charming Bloomsbury district, we exchange questions and reflections

on our work and lives. I explain that I hope to bring back an idea or
two on how my Chicago dance company could take on more of an
international perspective in its programs. Unexpectedly, Steven stops
on the street and turns to face me straight on.

With a serious look on his face, he says, "Deidre, you are an
amazingly self-sufficient and ambitious young woman. However, you
should know this about men. A man needs to know that he is needed
in your life. If you are so strong and work-oriented, a man will not be
able to see that he has a place in your life or that he can fulfill a lasting
need for you."

Steven looks deep into my eyes and asks if I understand what
he is trying to say. I am caught off guard by the sudden shift of his
conversational tone and the intimacy of his advice. I quickly smile and
dismiss his concern with a laugh.

He continues to escort me to the picturesque Bedford Square.
Steven explains that the square had been built by one of the Dukes of
Bedford during the late 1770s. He shares that a number of distinguished
Londoners have made their homes at Bedford Square since its earliest
construction, including Lord Eldon, one of the longest-serving Lord
Chancellors of Britain.

"Bedford Square's most singular feature is the preserved Georgian
architecture of the buildings. It is as if the square has been frozen in time
since the structures today are still as they were then," Steven explains in
a tour-guide fashion.

As we peer inside the fenced-in garden, Steven turns to face me. We
stand in front of a sign that reads, "private property, no admittance." He
pulls a set of keys from his pocket and inserts one into the iron gate that
keeps out city walkers. I listen as the antique lock gives off a loud click,
signaling it has opened, and Steven leads me into a world set aside by

time. It does not escape my notice that this man seems to have access to the most private of gardens.

Steven escorts me under the rows of tall pines that line both sides of the expansive walk leading toward a collection of estate homes. Perennials of every variety and rarity stand entrenched in their beds. As we walk further, I see garden gazebos and palatial private outdoor buildings where walkers or residents can sit, read a book, or seek protection from a summer rain. I am no stranger to living on an estate with a legacy of European gardens. Nevertheless, I find the immense garden unique, both in its beauty and its architectural symmetry.

As the sun drops in the sky, hundreds of miniature outdoor lights turn on automatically, throwing a sunset glow over the garden walks. The garden lights signal sundown and with them the return of a damp chill in the quiet outdoor air.

"It is later that I thought," I say. "I am happy you offered to walk me home as it will be darker on the streets once we get out of these amazing lighted gardens."

I suddenly come to a stop as we head back to the Bloomsbury neighborhood. "I hope you are not going to tell me that you are related to the owner of this garden and estate? I am not sure why that would matter that much to me, really; it is not as if I have never met men of great wealth before. But this garden and estate and their historic footing really take my breath away," I confess, nearly in a whisper.

"Not to worry, Deidre," he answers. I am not next in line to inherit the Bedford Estate. But, I am a friend of the Duke and am currently living in one of the houses on the estate. It is a small cottage that has been empty for some time. I am in the British military as a medi-vac administrator. When I am not heading up medical operations in any number of locations, I home base here at Bedford. The Duke and I were together at Oxford years ago and became instant close friends. Now, we are more like brothers. I entered the military after medical school, same as the Duke."

Steven escorts me to my flat and asks to see me the following evening. As I close the front door, I take his card from my clutch bag and place it in the small crystal bowl on the entryway table where I collect business cards, a practice left over from the Victorian home-calling rituals that the flat owner still honors. I am on my way up the stairs when I reconsider, walk back down the stairs, and retrieve Steven's business card from the bowl. I examine the full name printed in bold gold ink: Steven C. Whitney; Royal Medical Corp. I hold it in my hand like a teenager swept off her feet with a first crush and retrace my steps to my living quarters.

Another month evaporates from my calendar as my well-ordered life is turned upside down. I see Steven every day, and we are often together from morning to night. He avails himself to me as I continue building an artistic network by taking in as many special events as I can. At Steven's insistence, I set aside days to spend with him. We seek out guesthouses in rural London, take the train to Scotland, ride horses in the Welsh countryside, and trample through the literary homes of Shakespeare, Austen, and Woolf. When I mention the Pompeii Exhibit, Steven announces that he can do much better than a stuffy afternoon in a museum.

He pulls up at my townhouse just as I walk down the steps with a small overnight bag slung over one shoulder and a purse hooked around my neck. Steven rescues me from the luggage as I slide into the front seat.

"Where are we off to, if I may ask?" There is a smile on my face as Steven pulls away from the curb and merges into the London traffic.

"To the airport. A pilot with my organization will fly us to Naples. I hope you are comfortable in a small Cessna. I think you will get more out of seeing Pompeii in all of its archaeological glory with your feet on the ground. Judy Knight, a friend and the best tour guide I know, will meet us at the airport. She is originally from Dublin and was a history and archaeology major at Trinity College. She was completing a graduate degree in Rome—Italian archaeology and history—when she met her future husband. She has been in Rome ever since."

"You are amazing. How perfect is this?" I lean over and hug Steven's arm.

Judy Knight pulls up in a Jeep at the Naples airport, catches Steven's eye, and waves. To avoid the traffic on the main highway, Judy chooses a longer route that hugs the Mediterranean and provides us with spectacular views. Once in Pompeii, I am immediately overpowered by the scents of laurel, rosemary, and Spanish bloom. Acanthus, pomegranates, and red poppies carpet the ground and surround us as we follow the paths around the amphitheater. We walk on oversized paving stones where the wheels of ancient carts once traveled. Judy points to the region around the amphitheater, most of it still untouched by excavators, and challenges Steven and I to imagine how the ancient town must have looked surrounded by fertile farmland. As we pass the back part of the old city wall, Judy points to a plaque inscribed with a quote from a letter written by the Italian patriot Luigi Settembrini in 1863:

They have been dead for eighteen centuries, but they are human creatures seen in their death struggle. This is not art, this is not imitation, these are their bones, the relics of their flesh and their clothing mixed with plaster, and the pain of death that regains substance and form.

The words send shivers up and down my spine. Images of dancers in a death crawl across a stage shoot across my brain.

Judy guides us through the temple of an imperial family and the ancient temple of Zeus. We walk through the badly damaged forum buildings and view tapestries and paintings depicting Pompeii before and after Vesuvius erupted. I am shocked that much of the art we view in the temples and palaces is pornographic; some is so outrageous, Judy informs us, that it was removed from public view and hidden.

Judy stops, turns, and faces us. "Close your eyes and imagine that it is August twenty-fourth in 79 AD. You are now among the villagers who live in Pompeii. You are going through your day, either outside or perhaps tending to life inside of your dwelling. Mount Vesuvius erupts, burying all of Pompeii in a layer of small volcanic stones that swim down the mountain in rapid streams of white-hot gas and liquid. This stream moves at the speed of several hundred kilometers an hour and kills all life, including you. When it finally settles, it hardens over your body and encapsulates you into a solid form. You, along with all human life in Pompeii, are overcome by the white gas and are killed within minutes."

Judy takes a breath and instructs us to keep our eyes closed, then continues with her narrative. "And then imagine for a minute two young lovers hiding in a cave above the city of Pompeii. They watch as Vesuvius erupts and buries everyone below. The young girl has been forbidden by her parents and family to be seen with her young lover, as he is suspected of being one of the few Christians living in seclusion in Pompeii at a time when Pompeiians still worshipped the pagan gods of Rome. They survive. See them as they climb down the mountain, elated that they have survived. But their joy turns to horror as they walk among the bodies of not only their families but absolutely everyone in the village. They see the complete ruination of the only life they have ever known."

We stand in silence, as if attending a graveside burial. I am stunned into inspiration.

~ ~ ~ ~ ~

I pour through my traveler's closet, not at all sure what I am looking for. Steven has invited me to his house in Bedford Square for a cocktail party with the Duke and a few other close friends. He advised me to dress chic. I pull a violet dress from a hanger and draw it over my head. Standing in front of a full-length mirror, I inspect the form-fitting dress with its deep "V" neckline and check the above-the-knee hem to make sure it is intact. I pull my hair off of my neck then allow it to drop back to my shoulders. Thinking chic, I brush and pull my hair into a variety of styles before settling upon a tight French twist adorned with a jeweled comb.

I slide into the car Steven has sent. He normally picks me up, but today he had muttered something about a tight schedule. After a few minutes, the cab pulls up to Steven's two-story brownstone cottage at the edge of the Duke's estate. It reminds me of the estate manager's house that stood at Moran until my father had it torn down. Architecturally, Steven's cottage looks like it predates the 1800s.

A butler opens the door before I have a chance to use the knocker. Once inside, I hand over my sweater cape and he leads me into a small reception room that houses a variety of upholstered chairs. A large ottoman holds stacks of books, papers, and magazines. The room is devoid of a television set, record player, or even a radio. Within minutes, the butler brings me a small glass of Jameson without bothering to ask me for a drink preference. I sip the whiskey and look around the room, wondering whether Steven has arrived yet and, more to the point, when the other guests will arrive.

Just then, Steven enters the room dressed in a full tuxedo. "Good evening, my love," he greets me. "Come. Let me give you a private tour of the house." He leads me from room to room, making comments on the obvious age of the décor, or the lack thereof. We end up in a quaint but formal dining room. The oval hardwood table is laid out in fine crystal, china, and silver.

"Setting for two?" I ask in a surprised tone, eyeing up Steven.

"I decided against inviting others. I am not ready to share you with anyone just yet. There will be plenty of time for that." Steven smiles, lips closed, and his eyes follow my face. I lock his eyes with mine and try to read any hidden messages there but find none.

The butler appears again. He looks at Steven, who nods but does not say a word. The butler brings a starter course of camembert and brie spreads to the table along with tall flutes of champagne. Steven raises his glass, "A toast to you, Deidre. You are stunning tonight, just as I had expected."

I smile, not quite sure what to say as I am still adjusting to the announcement that there will be no other guests. I slowly gather the cheeses on my crackers. Catching Steven's eyes, I smile. "Does the butler come with the house or does he come with you?" I tease. A warning goes off in my brain triggered by the apartment invasion I survived. I tell myself that if I need to alert the butler for help, I will.

"He comes with me. He has been taking care of me for some years now. I find that my unpredictable work schedule requires both a butler and a cook, and William is able to do both. I rely on him like a wife." Steven smiles and winks.

William collects the first course and sets a small Caesar salad in front of us. He returns with a bottle of chardonnay and two more wine glasses.

"Your butler does not like to crowd the table with too many glasses, I take it."

"I must confess, that is my preference. I like neatness and space and having dishes removed straight away when they have outlived their purpose. Another reason why William continues to stay in my employ. He adopts my idiosyncratic preferences without expecting an explanation."

We turn our attention to eating our salads and sipping the white wine.

"Steven, I have to ask. Why didn't you call and tell me that you had changed your mind about having guests tonight? Why lead me on and surprise me? I would have dressed in something more comfortable."

"And that would have definitely been my loss." He smiles at me and offers no more. It is apparent that Steven is a man who is in complete control of his life. Another warning signal fires from my brain.

William reappears to collect the salad plates and wine glasses and then, minutes later, brings two dinner plates filled with Châteaubriand steak, a shallot sauce, and a mushroom side dish. He places the plates on the table, exits, and returns with an unopened bottle of Merlot and two more glasses. He places the wine, an opener, and both glasses in front of Steven.

Steven stands to gain leverage as he attaches the wine opener to the bottle. He quickly pops the cork and then pours the Merlot into the glasses, filling each precisely half way. He resumes his seat at the table and extends one of the glasses to me.

"You look as though you have done this a thousand times. Do you always open your own wine when your butler could do it for you?" I ask.

"Usually not. But I did want to show you that I am capable of doing something for you. It is my way of assuring you that I can be helpful to you. Remember what I told you when we first met? A man must be able to do something for you in a manner that you can depend upon and enjoy."

We continue with small talk as we finish our dinners. William enters, Steven nods, and the butler clears the table once again.

"And now for the best course," Steven announces. William brings two Irish crystal cocktail glasses filled with Bailey's Irish Cream and a tray of truffles. "I don't have to explain the crystal or Bailey's to you, but the chocolate comes from Charbonnel et Walker of London, the chocolatier of the House of Windsor." Lifting his glass, he toasts, "To the best Ireland and Britain have to offer to help bring the best of you and I together."

I take a bite of a truffle. My eyes widen as I sip the Bailey's and nod my approval. Smiling at my dinner host from across the table, I make my own move.

"Steven, I am going to turn the conversation in another direction, and I apologize up front, but how old are you? And why have I not heard anything about your family or personal life other than your friendship with the sequestered Duke?"

Steven puts both of his elbows on the table, leans in my direction, and replies in a soft tone. "I am forty-three," he says. "Yes, that makes me fourteen years older than you. Does that bother you?"

"Forty-three and single? Any children or adult children?" I ask.

"Yes, single. And no; no children. My life with the medical services in the military is not conducive to a scheduled or commitment-based lifestyle. You must be able to relate to that somewhat. After all, you are twenty-nine, never married, and childless yourself. And, you travel alone. Probably more rare for a woman in your situation than for me, wouldn't you say?"

I put down my half-eaten truffle and take a final sip of Bailey's. I feel checkmated and unsure of a response, either verbal or nonverbal. Should I thank him for a delightful dinner and make a move to end the evening? But before I have made up my mind, Steven stands and makes his way to the back of my chair.

"Let's lighten up the atmosphere. I have some terrific jazz in the next room. Come, join me." And with that, we walk to yet another room that William no doubt had softened by lighting candles and putting Steven's favorite jazz album on the stereo system. Steven holds out his arm, directing me to dance. We dance our way through the vinyl jazz record without whispering another word.

Another month in London disappears. I visit the remains of the Billingsgate Roman Bathhouse and devote the better part of a week of afternoons at the British Museum to study in detail the ancient relics from the city of Pompeii. The curator in charge of the Pompeii exhibits gathers a pile of research and photographs of the exhibit for me to carry back to Chicago.

Steven is in and out during much of the time. His work requires him to be on call with little notice. While it would be ideal if he could be with me for some of the days and at least in the evenings, I understand the pull of a demanding profession. You go where you are needed and do what is required.

~ ~ ~ ~ ~

Earlier this afternoon, Steven arrived without prior notice. It is a quieter afternoon than usual at the townhouse. Steven and I rest in our favorite chairs, which we each acquired by habit. With my feet elevated on a footrest, I close my eyes and am beginning to drift into a nap when I see Steven standing in front of me. My brain sends out an alarm bell but dissipates with Steven's familiar voice.

"Deidre," he says gently. "A snack for your favorite time of day? I hope you don't mind that I raided your kitchen."

I open my eyes to a view of a handsome man standing in front of me, his hands filled with frosted biscuits and hot tea.

"Now this is a view I could get used to," I tease.

Steven sits on the empty footrest, directly in my view. I can see that his mood has altered. I warn myself that the past months have been too good to be true and prepare myself for what I feel certain is to be a change of his heart.

I set down the plate, tuck my hips firmly into my chair, and wrap my hands around the teacup to extract its heat, as if to build a reserve of energy. I try to calm the panic sirens that have begun to activate within me, all the while thinking he is going to say that he is leaving me.

Steven begins gently. "I have been thinking about how I am going to say what I want to say to you. But all I can think of is Virginia Woolf."

"Virginia Woolf?" I respond with brows lifted and scrunched together, and a look of total confusion on my face.

"Yes, Virginia Woolf. When I first accepted the Duke's offer to make Bloomsbury and the Bedford Estate my temporary home, I set out to read everything I could find about the neighborhood. I gathered quite the collection from the British Library. I didn't get far before I discovered the Bloomsbury Group of writers and intellectuals, and specifically Virginia and Vanessa Stephen, who moved to the neighborhood after their father died."

Steven's segue into the neighborhood's history adds to my confusion, but I remain still, waiting for him to make the connection between our relationship and his library searches regarding the area's history.

"Virginia Woolf's most notable early publication, *A Room of One's Own*, is about every woman's need to have a private room within her home that is for her use and hers alone. I was struck by how revolutionary her idea was to me when I first read it. It never occurred to me that a woman may not be so happy living in a home provided by her husband in which all of the rooms are cohabited, with the possible exception of a study or office for the man of the house."

I continue to observe Steven, still not clear as to where the conversation is going. Reading the confusion on my face, Steven reaches over to me, removes the cup of tea from my hands, places it on the floor, and takes both of my hands in his.

"All Virginia Woolf wanted while she lived in this neighborhood was a room of her own, probably sensing the freedom that came to her as she lived away from her father for the first time in her life. Deidre, not only do you have a room of your own, you have a family estate in Ireland, an income of your own, and a lifestyle that looks more like a man's than a young woman's."

I begin to tremble as Steven's words hit me. Here is his retreat, his rationale for turning away from our relationship. I am a woman who lives like a man. I am not a real woman that he could hold in his arms forever. Instead, I am more like a temporary lover.

"You have no idea how amazing of a woman I think you are for a life that gives you the freedom and the room to grow and change in whatever direction it is that you decide. But, Deidre, I am going to take a huge risk here and ask you to do something just for me."

Steven tugs his footstool even closer to me. "Will you marry me, Deidre? Will you allow us to find a home we can share? I promise you now that we will find one that has an entire floor just for you." Steven pleads with the softest of expressions while gluing his eyes to me.

My sensory system has not caught up with Steven's dialogue and proposal. I am still hearing his words. Every cell in my body is on high alert for another of the emotional traumas that it knows only too well. Unsure what to think of my delayed response, Steven quickly repeats the most important part of his message. "Deidre," he says. "Will you marry me? Can I hope to make this most extraordinary woman my wife and the mother of my children in whatever house or rooms she cares to have?"

I smile and, with a tear slipping down my cheek, I throw my arms around Steven and pull myself to his lap on the footstool. We exchange a deep, passionate kiss and Steven suddenly releases me.

"Does this mean yes?" he teases with a coy smile.

"Most certainly a yes, and even Virginia Woolf would approve," I whisper with a smile of complete happiness on my face. Then, sensing it is my turn to be coy and reassert my confident demeanor, I inform Steven of yet another change in my life.

"But Steven, I have to update you on the status of my 'house of her own'. There is a new start-up jazz studio in the neighborhood. The studio owner spoke with the townhouse owner about needing rehearsal space. The landlord offered to rent the first floor of the house to them as a rehearsal studio. He warned me that the house may take on the look of a brothel with the coming and going of musicians, given the bourgeois dress style most of them wear for navigating their daily lives. I have been giving some thought to finding a different location for me."

A loud laugh escapes from his belly. "I could have saved myself a lot of beating around the bush with that never-ending proposal if you would have told me that yesterday. Well, I am happy to have solved that problem for you. I mean...with you," Steven corrects himself and lifts me off of my feet, twirling me around in a full circle.

~ ~ ~ ~ ~

Soaking in a sea of bath bubbles, I reflect on my head-over-heels love affair with Steven. While a week has gone by since his proposal, I continue to think about his warning of making room for a man in my life and allowing something from him that I need. Our first night of intimacy did not come in the evening at all, but during my favorite time of day: late afternoon, when I invited him to stay for tea. I sit back in the bath and re-live the series of events that led us from the tea table to my bedroom.

I was in the middle of a sandwich and was drinking tea spiked with a flavored brandy. I had talked intensely about my family in Cork, Sissy in Chicago, and the struggles Sissy and I endured as beginning dancers. I also described my initial foray into the dance business world. While I continued on with my rambling story, Steven stood and moved toward me until he was just inches from my chair. He pulled me to my feet and led me to the bedroom. Once there, he combed through my hair with his hands and then slid them over my shoulders, under my chin, and down along my waist. As if the slow pace of his movements were his way of asking permission, I smiled and gently stepped out of my clothes when he unbuttoned my long cotton skirt and lifted a summer sweater over my head. I stood in a sheer bra and panties, and he stood back to gaze at me in admiration. Steven held out both arms to me in a dance position and said but one word: "Waltz?"

We waltzed. Without music to guide us, we drew upon our rich experience of having danced the waltz hundreds of times with a host of dance partners. Steven then grew impatient and moved the dance to my high bed.

Our lovemaking was slow but intense. My passion had been locked away but his no doubt had been regularly expressed, so his strength and experience were all at my disposal.

After that memory passed, my mind traveled back to the afternoon of Steven's proposal. I criticized myself for going down my well-rehearsed road of doom, anticipating the worst rather than expecting the best. I now recognize that my reaction was a hard-wired pattern that came from my own childhood story of loss, and perhaps it was also a residual effect of the attack in my apartment. I need to forgive myself for assuming the worst and silently thank whoever watches over me for sending Steven across my path during that fateful afternoon walk in London.

I question myself on how fast my relationship developed with Steven. Neither of us has predictable lives. We live and work in two different countries and that alone increases the need for us to push our relationship ahead. And, we are not naive to the limitations we both have with respect to forging a traditional relationship. Neither one of us is that.

I stand up in the bathtub and wrap a towel around myself. I look into my full-length mirror and say to the young woman who stares back at me, "He has such a great need for me. I have waited so long to be needed in such a quiet and intense way."

~ ~ ~ ~ ~

Late afternoon on the day after the proposal, a long-distance operator puts a call through to Sissy in Chicago. Steven sits in the first-floor reception room that will soon be converted into a jazz studio. I open the conversation with my surprising news. Sissy let out a scream of happiness, which is followed by, "No, no, no!" She does not approve of my plan to get married within one month. But I explain that Steven needs to return to Vietnam.

Next, I call my father and Colleen, knowing it will be emotional. After breaking the news to my father and providing assurances that Steven and I will visit Cork within a week, Colleen takes ownership of the telephone for the remainder of the good-news call. I compromise on the one thing that Colleen insists upon: I have to marry in Cork rather than London or it will break my father's heart. As I listen to Colleen's emotional appeal, I know she is right. Marrying in London would seem like retaliation for my father's lack of support for my intent to remain in the States. I do not want to reinforce conflict and create more distance between my father and me.

County Cork, Ireland, 1976

Colleen took the lead from my father and put into play all of the key arrangements for a late summer wedding. We arrived at Moran Manor just one week after my call home.

My father had been certain that I would choose either London or Chicago for the wedding. He could not bear to ask about my plans. To his surprise, I not only asked to be married at home but also told him that I wanted the marriage to occur within the walls of my family home rather than at a church in Cork or Bantry, the closest village to Moran Manor.

I float through my home, intentionally trying to connect with my girlhood feelings. Swishing the bare wooden floors with my violet silken nightgown and robe, I walk in a slow rhythm, placing one foot at a time on the ancient floorboards. Pressing the soles of my feet against the well-trodden floor, I conjure memories and sensations from all of the times I had run from my bedroom to the flight of steps while Colleen called to me from one floor below or above. Now I walk a slow pace, reaching out to the invisible ghosts of the past as if to engulf them in my arms and hold them close to my heart.

While I admit that my mother's face comes to me primarily from family albums scattered around Moran rather than from my own memories, I had experienced a sudden recollection of her voice a few times during my life. Her voice first surfaced when I was in the bathtub during one of my college visits. It had been a particularly lonely time in my life when I felt disconnected from both Chicago and Cork. I had closed my eyes while engulfed in a hot bath and heard my mother's voice chanting, "Everything will be okay. You are okay." Now, with Steven at my side and with all of the excitement of introductions and wedding planning, the natural exuberance I'd had on a daily basis when I was a young girl at Moran has magically returned.

As I walk the hallways in the quiet of the early morning or just before Steven and I join father for tea on the patio in late afternoons, I can hear her laughter. I can also hear her loving voice say, "I don't need a wild pony because *you* are my wild pony." The memory of my mother's laugh surrounds me and anchors my heart to my Irish home once again.

Patrick sipped a second cup of strong Irish coffee outside on the garden patio and sat in quiet contemplation. He had purposefully declined to accompany Deidre and Steven on their many visits to her friends or on their walks of the Moran grounds. He had, however, invited Steven to take two of the quarter horses for a gallop around Moran's riding trails. Patrick wrongly assumed Steven would be an experienced rider since he was a seasoned military man. When Steven enlightened him that he was foremost a medical man with a military assignment, Patrick altered the pace of their ride to a walk or, at most, a slow trot. His afternoon spent bonding with his future son-in-law provided no reason for Patrick to regret Deidre's choice. On the contrary, Patrick found Steven to be extremely likable.

Still on the patio, Patrick walked to the sidebar and traded his coffee for a Jameson over ice. He kept telling himself that there was every reason to feel exuberant with Deidre's upcoming wedding. But he could not get over the remorseful belief that if he had kept Deidre in Cork rather than sending her away, he would not have lost seeing her each and every day as she grew up. He would never get those years back. At the same time, Deidre's world had opened with opportunities that he would have either squashed or at least seriously persuaded her against. He chided himself for how selfish he may have been and still was. His efforts at keeping Deidre's inheritance from her and trying to force her to return to Cork had failed. He was losing her again. This time to a man with whom he could not find a single fault.

Chicago, 1977

The cab arrives in the circle entrance to the high-rise building where Steven and I live. I stretch out my long legs and reach the vehicle before the driver has a chance to park, eliminating an unnecessary delay to my already over-scheduled day. The ride to North River Dance from my building overlooking Lake Michigan is short enough for me to drive my own car, but the traffic drains my attention and energy.

On this October morning, I toss my leather planner aside and settle back in the cab to think about Steven. I reflect on the sacrifice we are both forced to make because of his commitment to the British Medical Corp and the international travel it requires. On most days, I am able to cope with our separation. I know there are hundreds of other couples who suffer the same fate, particularly soldiers and their families.

I encourage the driver to take the long route to the studio so I can extend the internal conversation I am having with myself. When Steven and I married, I glossed over the complexities that would come with his responsibilities to the medical corp. And, I confess to myself, Steven did not disclose how his military schedule would impact our personal lives.

When I think back to the first months of our marriage, shame-generated heat comes over my face. I had been naïve about the actual events overseas, especially Vietnam. My association with the Vietnam War was linked primarily to the hundreds of antiwar demonstrations that were staged in downtown Chicago as I went to and from one dance studio or another. To me and Sissy, Vietnam was about navigating the streets by moving around the demonstrators, the squads of police controlling agitated marchers, and the crowds of equally agitated observers. Sure, I was aghast at the nightly newscasts that ran video footage of soldiers and helicopters under fire. Reporters embedded with troops on the ground provided the first live images of what journalists had covered from a distance during previous wars. Both Sissy and I tended to side with the antiwar position that the United States needed to get out of a war that we could see no real purpose in and that was taking the lives of thousands of young men in a foreign country where we had no connection.

Marrying Steven catapulted me into the category of those who feared for a loved one's safety; consequently, I became far more invested in international hot zones. Steven's role as an administrator of the British Medical Corps requires him to make frequent trips into war zones that England supports financially but has no military investment. I was horrified when Steven confessed to me that he had been in Da Nang during the last week of the American occupation, and especially the very last day in April the year the United States pulled out all of its remaining troops. He described the sheer terror he and his team experienced in loading military transport aircraft carriers with seriously injured soldiers, Vietnamese patriots, families, and orphaned children in the last dark hours of the American presence in Vietnam.

I had pictured Steven in a safe and orderly office moving medical staff and supplies from one point to another by signing orders and contracts but not actually with his boots on the ground in medical operations. I felt both relieved and angered that he had not divulged the dangers that came with his job. I quickly learned that marriage entails protecting one's spouse from having unsettling information that would only cause worry and pain—at least, that is what Steven told me to justify withholding the imminent danger of his field assignments. And, the fact that I still do not know in what part of the war-torn world he heads off to when he leaves does not contribute to my peace of mind.

I cue to the cab driver that I am ready to be dropped off at the studio. I gather my belongings and tell myself I need to focus on *Pompeii: The Best of Days*, a production that North River Dance will premiere in just a week. The production has proven to be the gem Andres and I needed to glue our visions together and form one solid creative team. Selling Andres on the idea of choreographing a dance production to tell the story of Pompeii and its disaster was easier than I imagined. I had wrongly assumed he would reject every creative production idea that I presented in retaliation for upstaging him on the company's five-year priority plan, but I was wrong. I had sold Andres short and his boundless drive to create a stand-out dance production for Chicago.

When Steven and I visited Pompeii, my immediate reaction had been that I wanted to tell, by way of dance, the human story of the volcanic disaster that buried Pompeii. But I had no idea where to start. Once I was home in the Chicago office, I laid out the materials and artifacts that Judy Knight had collected for me. As Andres poured over the exhibit artifacts laid out on the office planning table, numerous story plots poured out of him. He centered most of his ideas on a Pompeiian narrative of Romeo and Juliet, substituting the poison scene for the volcanic burial scene.

Andres tapped into his Chicagoan network of writers, artists, and playwrights, hosting a week-long series of meetings that lasted from morning to night, until he settled upon a creative team for the project. Deferring to his position as head choreographer and artistic designer, I sat in on the Pompeii development meetings as the financial advisor and contract negotiator for the endless list of talent Andres insisted on hiring: dancers, set designers , historians, and Italian music experts. Once I saw how energized the entire dance company was in bringing the Pompeii story from the dance floor to full production, I gave Andres the benefit of the doubt regarding costs.

Andres suggested that the Christmas tradition of staging *The Nutcracker* be substituted for *Pompeii*. He argued that while Christianity had not yet taken root when Mount Vesuvius engulfed the town of Pompeii in 79 AD, the production writers could incorporate Saturnalia, the Roman fall and winter feast celebrations that honored the deity Saturn. He said that Christians borrowed the Saturnalia activities of gift giving, banquets, and dances that the Romans used to celebrate their holiday that they called "the best of days."

But in my usual fashion, I balked at the suggestion that the studio should showcase the Pompeii ballet instead of the traditional *Nutcracker* performance. After all, I warned Andres, Chicago was in the middle of the Midwest, and the Midwest was known to resist pushing aside tradition in favor of modern interpretations. *The Nutcracker* was sure to make money, and lots of it. *Pompeii* was a significant financial risk. I had pushed to slate the *Pompeii* production for the spring season.

And once again, Andres resisted. "*Pompeii* is exactly what you had in mind, Deidre, when you insisted on the international five-year plan. Now that it has blossomed right in front of us, you want to retreat back into the safe and conventional holiday program? This time I get to play the heavyweight. I say we go forward with *your* plan to push the envelope and produce a production that is fresh, international, and culturally rich. It will hoist North River Dance onto a national stage one way or the other, successful or not. We are certain to get good press coverage as dance reviewers are eager to critique something they have not seen a hundred times."

I relented.

~ ~ ~ ~ ~

Steven lifts my mink fur from my shoulders and hands it to the coat clerk. We arrive for the production's opening night just thirty minutes before curtain time. Andres has instructed me to stay front and center in the reserved section set aside for VIPs and supporters. My presence there is far more important than my appearance backstage. He reminds me that I do not belong backstage given opening night jitters and hysteria. After all, he politely adds, I am no longer a dancer but a dance company co-owner and business manager.

I slowly turn my body so I can look to either side, and then lift myself out of my seat to scan the upper balcony. Andres has assured me that the opening performance is sold out; however, I am concerned that the season ticket holders will fail to show up at the opening. Creating buzz and conversation after the event is nearly as important as being in attendance.

Sensing my nervousness, Steven moves his head close to mine and whispers, "Looking for your lover in the cheap seats, my dear?"

I crunch my eyebrows together and throw Steven a disapproving glance, misreading his deliberate attempt at lightening my mood. "It's a huge risk leading with a nontraditional production during the holiday theater season, and the money invested in this is huge," I whisper. "All I can think about is the thousands of dollars of my Aunt Catherine's money, and if this fails, my father gloating that I should have followed his advice."

"The money has already been spent," Steven says in a matter-of-fact tone meant to be agreeable and supportive. "I suppose if the whole thing is a miserable failure and the company is shunned by theater-goers left and right, you can always retreat back to Cork and Moran Manor and hide."

"You are a terrible man to tease me so at a time like this," I quietly say, smiling. "You will be severely punished just as soon as I get you out of this audience."

I settle into my seat and remind myself how lucky I am that Steven and I have found one another. He provides me with the one thing I cannot seem to find on my own: acceptance without conditions.

When the curtain rises, my anxieties return and heighten with the appearance of each dancer—especially so when Sissy enters center stage. I have come to know them all so well. But as the story emerges, the juxtaposition of ballet and Pompeiian Italian-Greek culture with modern dance to portray the human conditions of celebration and catastrophic loss is brilliant. I forget my investment in the production and the audience's reaction to it. I am under the spell of a story told by the voices of ballet, classical music, and modern dance.

The last curtain call is finished. The only thing left to do is to wait for the moment when the reviewers' words hit the press and are distributed throughout the city during the hours between midnight and sunrise. Andres has thoughtfully arranged for the post-show sit-in. Snuggled together in a private room at a neighborhood bar, Sissy, Andres, Steven, the core production staff, and I anticipate the "rag reviews," as they are commonly called. Andres assures the group that if the reviews are solid, Deidre can build an effective holiday sales campaign. However, if there is just one devastating review, it could signal a deathblow and lead to closing the production early.

A bar bus boy brings the first review tabloid into the back room and holds it high in front of him with a questioning look in the group's direction. Sissy, first to read his intent, jumps from her chair and grabs the paper. Flipping through and tracing her fingers down one page and then the next, she scans the columns quickly, looking for references to the North River Dance Company or *Pompeii*.

"Here it is," she announces. She races through the review silently. With a blank expression on her face, she cries out, "Oh, my God!"

I nervously watch her flip to yet another page and trace her finger down the columns before exclaiming once again. Sissy reads from the print pages. "Oh...my...God! 'Compelling human story told in a fresh performance this season...inspiring, creative art form.' Oh my God! 'Amazing and spell-binding.' Oh, another. 'If you see just one just performance this season, let it be *Pompeii: The Best of Days.*'"

Sissy squeals with delight as Andres grabs the paper from her and devours the critiques in silent intensity. "Not so fast, Sissy," he says. "In the *Tribune*'s Chicago Entertainment and Theater section, Robin Wright, who we all know as a top tier dance reviewer, writes '*Pompeii: The Best of Days* may have had its best day last night and is noteworthy in its attempt to offer something new to the Christmas entertainment season. But it does not satisfy and delight like the traditional fare. Best to look elsewhere this season.'"

After what seems to be hours, Andres quietly put his hands on top of the opened tabloid pages and looks directly into my eyes.

"Mixed reviews, yes. But now is not the time to give up."

"I'm not so sure, Andres. We could lose the company if we continue."

"I know you have more invested in this company in terms of money than I do, Deidre. But if we put our heads together tomorrow and figure out how to promote *Pompeii* by playing on those good reviews, I think we can sustain the production."

Andres sees me in a dejected state and does not want me to make a final decision tonight. "Let's sleep on this and talk more tomorrow."

Andres and Sissy stand up and Andre gathers the reviews before they head toward the door. I will my body to stand, still stunned by Wright's lack luster review which will carry weight in the arts community.

I struggle to stop my emotions from cycling into sadness and depression. I had hoped to celebrate *Pompeii* with Steven late into the night, but when I turn to find him, he is on the phone by the bar engaged in heavy discussion. Soon thereafter, he is on a jet headed back to London and I am in a cab going home in the cold to a lonely Lake Michigan high-rise.

~ ~ ~ ~ ~

Sitting around the table during our weekly planning conference following the end of the holiday season, Andres loses no time in pushing for his agenda. His strategy of continuing the production and calling in all the favors owed to us in order to promote *Pompeii* had paid off. The production enjoyed solid attendance and finished its run with a sold-out performance. Andres's vision is to use *Pompeii's* success to catapult North River Dance on a national tour. He is keen to double the company's size. I hold back, reluctant to dilute the budget or spread Andres and the dancers too thin.

"Deidre, this is the time to accelerate the rest of the priority plan for North River. I give you complete credit for the creative intelligence that led you to pursue an international collaboration with the art world in order to inspire our dance production. But, now is the time to capitalize on your vision, the company's financial success, and its emerging national presence."

"You mean create a North River Dance 2 to tour?" I ask, but I already know the answer.

Andres tucks in his chin and looks me squarely in the eyes. "Do we really have to go down this road, Deidre? You know exactly what the mission and priority action plan look like. Why, after the courage I saw in you to pursue the vision that has landed us so much success, do I see this reluctance in you to push forward?"

There is not a single word in Andre's pitch with which I could disagree. I can feel my body pull back, and I sense a wrench in my gut that warns me to get ready for a fall. My life pattern has taught me to expect a hard blow after a run of good days. I know it is irrational, and projecting doom and gloom onto the dance company's success is simply not fair to any of us.

Andres grabs my hands in his. "Deidre, let me take the lead right now. You have had an incredible amount to deal with in the past five years. You have to be exhausted by transitioning yourself from dancer to Dance Financial Director and co-partner, wife, and international traveler. All of us revert to old patterns when our reserves get low. We are dancers, Deidre; we both know that we can push and train and demand only so much before our bodies start to yell out and scream from the tip of our brains to our little toes. If you don't slow down, Deidre, your body will slow you down. Let me lead now. Sit back. Enjoy the ride. Hassle me about the financials. Keep the bills paid. But let me do the work to put North River Dance on a national stage. Can you do that?"

I take a deep dancer's breath that both of us recognize. Trading smiles back and forth across the table, I nod in agreement and confirm that I can do what he requests. It is indeed time for me to let go.

"You know what would really help me to let go, Andres?"

He peers into my eyes, detecting that the direction of the conversation has abruptly changed.

"Writing my Aunt Catherine a sizable check toward repaying her loan to the dance company."

~ ~ ~ ~ ~

Andres walks into the suite of office rooms that comprises Deidre's domain. "Is Deidre in?" he asks the young assistant at the reception counter. A large vase of pink and red roses sits on one corner of the counter. He does a quick gaze assessment and raises his eyebrows. He has not been in Deidre's business quarters for some time. He looks up at a huge oil painting of female dancers making their way across a wooden floor. *An original*, he thinks.

"What can I do for you, Andres? I am in a rush, trying to hire additional staff to support your university and school dance programs for the summer."

"I guess I did not realize the extent to which your operation would expand due to our voyage into education programs," Andres comments.

"It's an avenue that is all new to us and to the Chicago community. We need to send first-class advertisements and glossy brochures to selected schools. It's an entirely new venture and it means specific professional expertise."

"So, low key Deidre is once again in full drive?" Andres asks.

I look up at Andres, tuck my chin, and open my eyes wide, not saying a word. Andres recognizes the nonverbal cue.

He picks up a draft design of a dance brochure, surveys it, and puts it back down. "Is Steven coming home for a month soon? You probably want to get your staff in place before he arrives so you can take some time off."

I put down what I am doing and stand up. "Why do I get the feeling that you do not want to see me at the studio on a full-time basis, Andres? A growing dance company with the scope that ours has does not run itself. I thought you would have a better understanding of how important the business side of the company is by now." I draw my eyebrows together and shake my head in disbelief.

"Look, Deidre, I'm sorry. I did not mean to be so unappreciative of your work and the results you get. Sissy sent me on a mission today to get an idea of Steven's travel schedule so we can plan a few fun things together. I got sidetracked when I saw all of the activity going on here. And by the way, the office décor is classy. Who did the painting that hangs over reception?"

I relax and give Andres a full smile to soften the conversation. "It was done by an art student here in Chicago. Seems to me the company should support students' artistic efforts by purchasing their work, particularly with our expansion into the student realm." I smile at Andres, sure of his approval.

A knock on my office door interrupts our conversation and the reception assistant informs me that there is a London call coming in.

"That may be the answer to your question about Steven's schedule. I will catch you right after this call."

Andres leaves my office while I sit in my leather chair to settle in for a long conversation with Steven. Andres is not the only one that has been mulling over Steven's schedule.

~ ~ ~ ~ ~

The secretary notices Deidre's line light up, and then Deidre buzzes her. *Unusual,* the secretary thinks. Her boss never buzzes her; she always gets up and speaks with her directly. The secretary knocks on the door and waits for Deidre to address her. After several minutes of waiting, the secretary leans close to the door and asks if she can help. A few moments more lapse without a response. Then the secretary slowly opens the door to find her boss slumped over her desk.

Deidre pushes a piece of paper in the secretary's direction and the secretary looks at the note, which is a list of things marked "urgent." She looks up at Deidre for an explanation, but Deidre shakes her head. The secretary backs out of the office and closes the door.

Andres answers the knock at his door and looks up to see Deidre's secretary. "I think you would want to see this," she says, pushing the list across Andres's desk. "I hope I am doing the right thing in showing it to you."

Andres bounds from his chair. "Call Sissy. Tell her to get here right away," he instructs before heading for Deidre's office.

He finds her frozen behind her desk. He moves a chair close to her, sits down, and reaches out for one of Deidre's hands. He pushes the note in front of her, looking down at the list:

Get plane ticket to London for today.

Pick up travel bag in closet.

Check for passport in bag.

Funeral

He holds his finger on the last item.

"Deidre," Andres says, "What happened? Is it Steven?"

He waits for Deidre to respond, thinking that she would be flying to Cork if it was her father who died.

"He's dead, Andres. The small airplane he was on crashed somewhere in a jungle. Aviation fuel explosion and fire. Both the pilot and Steven burned to ashes."

Deidre speaks to Andres as if she were a news reporter summarizing the death of someone she did not know. Andres observes Deidre closely. She seems to be in a frozen trance. He moves in closer, puts both of his arms around her, and holds her tight.

London, 1977

The rain falls in heavy sheets. Fog rolls through the streets without any promise of lifting. A small contingent of my family and friends climb the steps to St. George's Church in Bloomsbury. I hold Sissy's hand while Andres loops his arm through mine. My father follows in the back with my aunts, Colleen and Catherine.

As I stand in the receiving line inside the church, I chide myself for not knowing more of Steven's life and for not spending more time with him in London. As I extend my gloved hand to the small group of mourners at the funeral, I press back feelings of guilt and shame, although I am uncertain where those feelings originate. My legs give way once or twice so I lean on Andres and my father even more tightly, wishing for a quicker end to the service formalities. Just as the reception line thins, I look up to see a tall young man walking towards me. Is my mind playing tricks on me? A man who appears to be Steven's identical twin reaches his hand out to me.

"Mrs. Whitney—Deidre—I am..."

But I don't hear the rest of the young man's introduction. Both of my legs buckle at once and my world goes black.

County Cork, Ireland

A small charter plane glides over the Irish Sea and touches down at the Shannon airport without a bounce. I step down and clutch my father's arm as he guides me to his waiting car. We ride in silence to Moran. Colleen wraps me in a long hug and directs me to my room. A hot tub waits. I dismiss the maid who appears to assist me, saying I prefer to be alone. I lie back in the hot water and allow it to cover me. Gazing around the familiar bathroom, I feel relieved to be home, yet I am once again on emotional territory that is too familiar: dealing with death, loss, and the feeling of being adrift and alone.

This day, after I have been at Moran for weeks, Colleen knocks on the door. "I'm still in bed," I say. "Please come in and sit while we talk."

She enters my room and I continue to speak. "I miss him so much already, Colleen," I say. "I'm not at all sure how I am going to get along without him. And, I am still in shock over the fact that Steven has a grown son he never felt the need to tell me about."

"He may have been waiting for just the right time," Colleen quietly answers. "He may have wanted to focus on grounding his relationship with you before introducing his son." But Colleen can see that I remain unconvinced. We both know that I do not need to be saved from difficult moments or placed in a simple life scenario.

"Tomorrow, then? During dad's morning coffee. I need you there," I remind her.

Colleen nods and quietly closes the bedroom door. She takes a moment to compose herself and heads downstairs.

Patrick Moran sits in the breakfast room and stares through the large glass window at the thin layer of mist blowing across the inlet bay and wetting everything in its way. He breathes the aroma of the strong coffee sitting before him. Patrick is stunned and glazed over, and he cannot force the analytical part of his mind to fire up. Nor is he able to think about the pain his daughter suffers. He lost Deidre's mother at about the same age that Deidre is now. Was it necessary for the pattern to be repeated?

Deidre's unannounced presence interrupts his thoughts. Upon seeing her, Patrick rises to his feet and insists she sit down while he walks to the buffet to pour her some coffee and dish up a plate of scrambled eggs and a generous slice of Irish soda bread. Sitting across the table from his daughter, he observes her carefully. There are black circles under her eyes, and her face looks as if it has been pressed with white powder.

"Were you able to get any sleep, Deidre?" he asks gently.

She nods and lifts her eyes to her father, forcing a smile onto her face. They sit together in silence, eating their breakfast. The rain slows then stops as the clouds gently roll across the bay, revealing a bright morning sun. The changing weather soothes their battered hearts.

Colleen greets her brother and niece as she sits down alongside Deidre. "I see you both got a head start on me," she says. "I am going to rest here a minute and watch the sun burn off the mist before I help myself to some breakfast."

The three sit and absorb each other's presence. A few more minutes pass. Then Deidre breaks the silence. "Dad, I have something to tell you. I think you will be pleased."

Patrick looks at his daughter with raised eyebrows. "I was waiting until I saw Steven again in person before I told him," continued Deidre. "I am expecting a child in about seven months, Dad."

Patrick lets the words sink in. As they do, he is pulled into his life once again. He immediately stands and, with eyes smiling, he agrees that the news could not be better.

"It is very sad that Steven did not share in this good news," Patrick says. "At some level, it may have changed some things for him. Maybe the knowledge that you were expecting would have altered his work destinations a bit." Seeing the sadness return to his daughter's face, he quickly corrects his statement and says that it could also have made just the opposite impact. Then, just as quickly, he apologizes and says he just needs to be quiet as he does not know what he is talking about. Patrick does not want to drape her news with tragedy; she has experienced enough of that. When he looks at Deidre with remorse and discomfort, she suddenly breaks out laughing.

"It's okay, Dad. I don't think any of us know what we are doing today."

Turning to Colleen, Patrick says, in a heightened state of anticipation, "We will convert one of the rooms upstairs to a nursery immediately. The old nursery was turned into a pool room years ago. It is about time that room is restored and set to a purpose."

Deidre sits back in her chair to relax her body and then takes a deep breath. "Dad, I will be returning to Chicago in a week or so. I plan to continue working at North River Dance, the company I helped build into a success. I will deliver the baby in Chicago, Dad."

Patrick could not believe Deidre's words. Just when a light had appeared in this terrible storm, it was quickly extinguished.

"Deidre, that is ridiculous. This is your home. You have family who love you here and who can take care of you and your baby. Your baby will be an Irish citizen if it is born here; yes, I know it will have Irish citizenship anyway, but your baby needs to be raised on Irish soil," Patrick argues firmly. "Bring the damn dance company home to Ireland. I will free up some of your inheritance so you can do whatever the hell you want. You cannot deprive your child of his or her Irish heritage. Morans have lived in southwest Ireland for over three-hundred years. This is simply crazy—and what for? To make your point that as a woman of the 1970s, you can do whatever the hell you want?"

Deidre straightens her back and pushes her shoulders together, moving her shoulder blades toward the center of her back. In a weak voice, she reminds her father that the baby is Steven's, too, even though he is dead, and the baby will have its father's roots, too. She has to admit that she does not know the exact nature of those roots, given the surfacing of Steven's son. Deidre is thankful that her father did not jump at that remark in an attempt to solidify his argument that the baby should be born in Ireland.

Deidre rises to her feet and puts both of her hands on the table to stabilize herself. "We can talk more about this later, Dad. But I won't change my mind. I am not eliminating the possibility of returning to Ireland one day, but for right now, my life is in Chicago. I am going back upstairs to lie down for the rest of the morning."

Colleen and Patrick watch as Deidre walks from the breakfast room. "This is all your doing!" Patrick scowls while setting his eyes directly on Colleen. He shouts, "I never should have listened to you about sending her away when she was a child. I lost her then, and now I will lose her again. I will also be unable to watch my only grandchild grow up." He stands, slams his coffee cup on the table, and storms out of the room, leaving Colleen glued to her chair.

Colleen gazes out on Bantry Bay in its entire splendor and reminds herself that it is the nature of the bay and ocean to change without notice. *Human storms are natural, too,* she thinks. She can excuse and forgive her brother's eruption. Colleen knows Patrick well enough to see that he is beside himself at accepting such a string of serious events, but yet it is not his responsibility to make this decision. She will continue to give Deidre the support that she needs to build a life best suited to her. She does not want to be contrary to her brother, with whom she has lived with all of her life and who has seen his own severe storms and losses.

But Deidre is different. Her security blanket was pulled from underneath her as a child when she lost all that was familiar to her. Yet Deidre thrived. Now, barely thirty, she faces yet another crisis with the loss of her husband. She faces a difficult road ahead, and Colleen intends to support her every step of the way.

~ ~ ~ ~ ~

I pull my car into the dock parking lot and survey the vehicles lined up near the water. As I step onto the wooden dock with my riding boots, I realize that one does not wear boots sailing. I swing a large canvas bag over my shoulder and hear someone calling my name behind me, then turn to see Cory ambling toward me with a slow, stretched-out gait. He has a wide smile on his face.

"If you aren't a sight for sore eyes, I don't know what is," he says. He reaches out, wraps both arms around me, and holds me to his chest. I feel the rhythm of his chest muscles as he breathes. "I don't know what kind of sailing you expect to do wearing those boots, though," he teases, as is his long-established pattern.

"I was just thinking the exact same thing. I am so glad you called me, Cory."

Cory reaches out to stabilize my balance as I step off of the dock and into the waiting sailboat. "It's just you and I, Deidre. It will be a leisurely float in the bay around the perimeter of the Atlantic coast."

"You would think that I would have learned at least the basics of sailing after going out on your boat for all of these years," I say.

"Has never been something I thought you needed to do, Deidre. I just like looking at you out on the water and far away from Moran. As you know, it's not very formal out here, but I do have a plate of sandwiches and some great Schull cheese below deck. I thought you could use the sun on your back and the roll of the water to relax and soothe you."

He steps around me, tending to the motor rather than the sails, as motoring requires less of his attention. Once he has the boat in order, he turns to face me. "When you are ready, give me the long story of what happened with your husband. Don't hurry. We have nothing but time out here," Cory assures me.

I gaze over at my longtime friend and handsome former Irish lover. I am grateful for his ability to kidnap me from my adult life and bring me into his world of play. I peel off my cardigan sweater and reveal the tank top underneath. Then I pull the tall riding boots and socks from my feet, stretch my ridiculously long legs, and allow the sun to warm my bare skin.

I have barely begun to tell the story when Cory urges me to stop. He goes below deck and retrieves a tray of sandwiches, then puts them next to me. He grabs the ends of his white sailing shirt with each hand and draws it over his head. He stands before me and I can see his tan, athletic chest, which is layered with dark hair that curls and circles his stomach below his navel. He says, "We're ready, Deidre. Make the story last until the sun goes down."

I spend hours telling the narrative of Steven and me. My skin becomes cold, and it isn't until I grab for my cardigan that I realize the sun is low in the sky. Cory has navigated the boat into the calm bay. He drops the anchor overboard.

"I can make you some hot fish chowder and crackers to warm you up. Have to confess the chowder came from the Schull deli, but I am good at turning the knob on the boat stove."

Cory extends a hand. With the other, he bends to pick up my boots. I smile at the effortless way he takes care of me, which has been a longtime habit of his. The cabin is lit with small lights that are strung around the ceiling. Cory puts on a CD by a local folk singer and makes his way to the small refrigerator. Within minutes, two bowls of hot chowder sit before us, along with two mugs of strongly brewed Barry's tea, the only tea Cory drinks when forced to drink tea at all. We sit listening to the music, eating the chowder, and sipping tea. I look around the cabin and comment that it still looks pretty much the same as it did the first time I sailed with him. We talk about everything and nothing in the way that close friends do. More importantly, at a time of grief and sorrow, we are comfortable with not saying anything at all. Cory leaves his thoughts and reactions unspoken. This is a sign that he accepts all that has occurred and all that I feel.

Soon, Cory leads me into the boat's small shower. He helps me out of my clothes, turns on the hot water, and hands me soap and shampoo. Naked himself, he lathers shampoo into my hair and sprays it clean. He takes body wash and, with a bath sponge, carefully lathers my front and back, being careful not to engage in any sexual overtures.

Once we are out of the shower and dry, he coaxes me to lie down in the cabin bedroom. Using cedar massage oil, he gently applies heat to my neck, shoulder, back, and thigh muscles. Guiding me to my back, he gently massages my temples, my forehead, and the front of my long shins. He then tucks me under the sheets and blankets and returns to the outer cabin to check that the boat's exterior lights are on before sliding into bed alongside me.

Cory gathers me into his arms and puts my head under the crux of his arm and shoulder. His shoulder is wet and I realize that I have been silently crying. The waves rock the boat in a gentle, rhythmic pattern orchestrated by nature. Sleep comes to both of us.

At some point in the middle of the night, I awake disoriented. I turn toward Cory and see the moonlight that falls on his face through the port window. Waves of emotions move over me. I snuggle down next to him and nudge him like a rider nudging a horse to walk out. Cory awakens on cue. I roll underneath him and draw my arms around his shoulders. I wrap each of my legs around his waist and hook them together in a leg lock.

Without questioning, Cory enters my body and eases his way to a rocking that simulates the rocking of the sea. His approach is slow and light. After a few minutes, I push my legs up higher and wrap my hands around Cory's neck. He rolls over to lie next to me and catch his breath, but I do not need a break. I straddle him with my arms locked on either side of his hips and raise my back long and tall. I keep my eyes closed and think only of what I am doing at this moment in time. My heart races and my skin becomes drenched in sweat. I lift Cory up into me and continue to rock him up and down, even long after he is spent.

My legs won't hold me upright any longer and the tops of my thighs scream in pain. I release my grip on Cory and roll over onto my side.

Once our breathing slows and our hearts calm, Cory once again gathers me into his arms. I place my head, wet from sweat and long strands of disheveled hair, on his chest. Deep sleep comes to us. The sun is high in the sky before we wake.

~ ~ ~ ~ ~

Cory admits to himself that he was nervous about accepting Deidre's invitation to a family dinner at Moran. Granted, a week has elapsed since their time together on his boat and as a grown man, he certainly is not guilty of any impropriety. Yet none of that makes it any easier to look Patrick Moran in the eye.

Cory stands up from the comfortable seat directed to him by the maid. When Deidre enters, he has just taken a sip of the cold beer that was brought to him, allowing her the chance to get in the first words.

"Thank you for the beautiful flowers you sent to the house, Cory. And the Irish proverb you wrote on the card was quite romantic: *Maireann lá go ruaig ach maireann an grá go huaigh.*"

"So, you remember it then?"

"'A day lasts until it's chased away, but love lasts until the grave.' I told you, I did not leave the best of Ireland behind me."

Cory smiles widely in acceptance of her appreciation. "It has been a long time since I have been inside the house where you and I played as children at least once a week. Not much has changed," he notes as he looks around at the first floor rooms.

"You said a lot there, Cory. Nothing has changed. You and I are not children anymore, but as far as my dad is concerned, he seems to have not taken notice of that. So you had better mind your P's and Q's." I smile as I issue the warning.

Patrick shows his very best side during dinner and warmly converses with Cory. He makes sure wine and whiskey are on the table, offers Cory the first serving, and sees to it that his plate is filled a second time. Colleen carries the conversation well and asks just enough questions of Cory and his life in Schull.

I dismiss myself from the table and leave Cory and my father to talk about the Irish economy and how each of them is getting by. I catch Colleen in the kitchen.

"What is going on with my Dad, Colleen? He is being way too nice to Cory, and I know for a fact that he has not approved of me spending much time with him since I reached adolescence."

Colleen looks at Deidre with her chin lowered to her chest and her voice in a whisper. "He knows you have had a fondness for Cory since both of you were children. And, he also knows you did not come home one night last week after telling me you were going sailing with Cory. I think he is taking a new look at Cory now that you are pregnant and widowed. He also knows that Cory would never leave Ireland, not even for you."

The two women carry the torte to the dining table, one bringing the dessert and the other the whipped topping. The cook, who would usually bring all of the food to the table, is behind them carrying a pot of coffee. She knows that the women need an excuse to have a private conversation away from the men and she chuckles to herself. The men would hardly notice such efforts at concealment.

Cory stands up from his seat on the overstuffed couch when he finishes his torte, but my father and Colleen remain seated and are in no hurry to finish their coffee and dessert. I follow him to the front reception room.

"This may be goodbye until my next trip home, Cory. I plan on returning to Chicago soon. Too much pressure from my father to move to Moran permanently."

"I can't say that I haven't been thinking the same thing, Deidre," Cory confesses in a low whisper. He takes both of my hands in his and pulls me close. "We are so good together, Deidre. Marry me, marry me. I can take care of you and this baby."

I look at Cory. I am not surprised by his proposal as he has reissued it many times over the years, but I do not know how he learned of my pregnancy. Seeing my surprise, Cory says, "Your father mentioned it while you were retrieving the dessert. You can't really blame him for playing the one card he and I have in common."

Cory steps in closer to me and wraps his arms around me. "What is there to think about, Deidre? You have your success and you have your own money, which I am more than comfortable with." He teases me with a broad smile on his face. Then he says, "I would love to raise your child with you and be a father to her or him. Don't overthink this, Deidre. Just say yes."

"I wish I could let myself say yes, Cory, but I am still so insecure about molding a life here in Ireland that would be accepted or even tolerated. And as open as you are now to an Americanized Irish marriage, you may grow to feel as though you have been cheated out of the traditional woman-man relationship, which is still very much the norm in Ireland." I whisper to prevent any lurking ears from hearing.

Cory gently squeezes me. "Like I said, Deidre, don't overthink this. Just trust me. Trust my love. I have known you my whole life. Don't you think I have noticed that you are not the traditional Irish Miss that most Irish men covet? I am not in love with an idealized image of some Irish Miss. I love *you*."

I step back from Cory so I can look into his eyes. "Cory, I need some time to get my feet back on the ground. My entire focus has to be on having my baby and coming to terms with Steven's death. But will you make me one promise? Will you ask me one more time?"

Cory places his hand underneath Deidre's chin. "That is the easiest promise anyone has ever asked of me. Granted, my lass, granted."

Chicago, 1980

The long grass sways back and forth in the gentle, morning winds that blow off of Lake Michigan, making my lawn look more like the fields of Moran than a yard in suburban Chicago. With a large mug of hot tea in my hand, I walk the perimeter of the yard in my bare feet, examining every new plant that has sprung up overnight, and notice how the property seems to have been taken over by a host of bees, butterflies, and ladybugs. I smile to myself as I recall the effort it had taken to hold my ground with the lawn care man. I told him I did not want any chemical treatment on the grass and I wanted the lawn to be mowed just once every two weeks. When he shrugged and warned me that such lax cuttings would result in the lawn looking more like a field, I told him that was exactly the effect I had envisioned.

The back door opens and then slams, and a small girl flies out onto the grass. Barefoot like me, my daughter carries a piece of toast in one hand and a hair ribbon in the other. She lies in the grass, her full, dark head of hair spread like a fan, and holds her toast in midair.

"Macy, whatever are you doing?" I ask.

"Keeping the toast away from the bugs and bees that will want to eat it. It has strawberry jam on it." My three-year-old's voice is serious.

I observe my child with new wonder each day. Macy seems to live in a world of her own creation, ignoring the usual routines such as sitting at the table for breakfast. Just as quickly as Macy had stormed from the house to the grass, she rights herself and runs through the immense field of white daisies that the gardener planted. The flowers blanket the ground until it meets the sand beach that leads to the lake.

"Just to the end of the flower field, Macy. Then turn around and come back. Don't go to the beach alone," I call out to warn her. I remember the first time that Macy had looked at the grass-and-flower field and said in her baby-talk language that it was just like Grandpa Morn's. It had taken me a minute or two to decipher what Macy meant: that this field buttressing Lake Michigan was like Moran Manor with its 100 steps and its grassy field that gently slopes to the ocean-fed bay.

Like me, Macy had begun transcontinental trips from Chicago to Cork, but at a much earlier age than I did. But unlike my trips, Macy's are joyful delights where every minute is orchestrated by her grandfather and Great Aunt Colleen to spoil and dote upon her, an only grandchild.

I watch Macy's hair fly into the wind as she races through the flower field on her return run back to the house. I can't help but engage in my daily ritual of doing the Macy body-soul check. I watch for any signs of disruption in her development or signs of insecurity, but I never see a thing. I also make sure that Macy knows her father was a brave man who died doing an important job. I had whispered it to her when she was an infant while I swung her in my arms, dancing to a lullaby. I said it again when she sat in my lap while we were reading a storybook that included a father. And I answered Macy when she would look up from her lunch and ask me, as if she had just noticed that she did not have a father around, "Where is my daddy?" I would repeat that she had a daddy who was a very brave man but that sadly, he had died doing an important job.

So when Macy's preschool teacher shared an incident that had happened, I was caught off guard. She thought it was important for me to know what Macy had shared in class about her father. I smiled at the teacher as I was sure that she would repeat my explanation.

"Macy told her classmates that her father was brave and that he vanished."

"Vanished? Are you sure that is how she put it?"

"Very sure," responded the preschool teacher. "You can imagine how some of the other children reacted. There were a lot of questions about how her father vanished. One child asked Macy what 'vanish' means. Macy raised both of her arms into the air and said, 'Poof...he vanished.'"

I observe Macy as she races through the grassy field. She is sweaty, dirty, and imitating a galloping pony on a sunny spring day. I had read that young children are unusually spontaneous and given to amazing displays of creative play and imagination. When I checked in with Macy's pediatrician after the preschool incident, she encouraged me to keep reinforcing that Macy had a brave father but that sadly, he had died. The pediatrician assured me that as she grew older, Macy would come to accept that her father was indeed dead and that, unlike something that can vanish one moment and reappear the next, her father would not return.

Macy and I had just gone inside when the back doorbell rings and is followed by a spirited voice calling hello. I turn around to see Sissy drop her purse on a corner chair.

"Sorry I didn't warn you ahead of time, but thought I would drop by to see Macy. It seems like it has been such a long time since I have seen my one and only godchild."

Sissy scans the kitchen for a pot of coffee. "Any coffee left? It's probably too early for wine."

"You know you don't need an invite to stop in, Sissy. But you are just the person I need to see. Now that you are here, I want to run something by you. I am wondering if I should talk to Ramona—you remember; the therapist you accompanied me to some of my sessions after the attack? Anyway, something has been going on with Macy."

I summarize Macy's teacher's concern and look at Sissy with my face scrunched up. "I can't imagine what I said to her, Sissy that could have planted the idea that her father just vanished in thin air. I ran it by Cory the last time he was here and..."

"And, what did Cory say?" Sissy interrupts. "By the way, before you answer that, just so I get this on the table for us to discuss in case we get sidetracked, Cory has been on a regular visitation schedule from Ireland, hasn't he? I think that is really curious as you have always said how crazy he thought it was for you to make the 'transcontinental Irish jig,' as he called it," Sissy spouts.

"Yes. To answer your second question first, Cory has been a regular visitor to both me and Macy. He seems to enjoy Macy's company as much as mine." I respond with a full smile. "As for Macy's version of where her dad is, Cory does not say much at all other than that the Irish have a way of dealing with the uncertainty of important things in life by placing them into the Irish mist. He says it is a way of preserving the most important things. He continually reminds me that Macy is Irish and has been brought up around all things Irish no matter that she happens to live in Evanston," I explain.

I have no more than finished my last sentence when Macy comes storming from her bedroom and flies directly into Sissy's arms.

"Aunt Sissy, Aunt Sissy!" the child screams with joy.

"Oh my!" Sissy reacts with delight. "This is indeed the greeting I love to get from you, sweet girl."

I open the refrigerator and pull out a variety of containers, including milk and a cold bottle of white wine. While I have my head in the refrigerator digging for lettuce and veggies to add, Sissy pulls placemats from the sideboard drawer, opens the kitchen cabinets to gather plates, glasses, and silverware, and proceeds to the set the dining room table for three. Macy skips and twirls around us in a manner suggesting that a spontaneous meal is an ordinary occurrence in all three of our lives. Seated at the table and enjoying our late afternoon meal of warmed leftovers and salad, we watch Macy primarily for the joy the child brings to us. But we also watch due to the concern that I have once again described.

"As far as your earlier suggestion about talking with Ramona, I don't think it could hurt, and she probably can shed some additional light regarding You-Know-Who," suggests Sissy.

"Who is You-Know-Who?" the precocious child asks.

We look at each other and erupt in laughter. Our laughter travels to the small Macy, who imitates me and her adopted auntie and matches our laughter. This brings Sissy and me to tears and creates more laughter, which Macy matches and then easily exceeds in enthusiasm and drama. Exhausted from laughing and crying, Sissy and I finally run out of steam and focus on taking sips of wine.

"Macy, honey, why don't you go to your room to ride your horse for a while and let Mommy and Auntie Sissy rest for a bit."

Macy climbs down from her seat at the table and runs to her bedroom at the back of the house.

"About the other question?" Sissy nudges Deidre. "The Cory question?"

"It has been three years already since Steven died. It seems like a year or less; so much has happened with Macy's birth, the purchase of this house, full-time work at the dance company." I pause and a shy smile comes to my face, an expression that Sissy does not see on me often.

I look at Sissy and see the girl, now a grown woman that I have confided in since we went to elementary school together. There is no one that I trust like Sissy.

"I am going home, Sissy," I nearly whisper.

"What? No!" Sissy counters. "Leave the dance company?"

"Let me start over again, Sissy."

I take a deep dancer's breath, which Sissy recognizes as her cue to do the same. We settle our bodies into our chairs and reach for our unfinished glasses of wine.

I begin. "Let me do this in order. Three years ago, when I was at home at Moran, Cory asked me to marry him. I know what you are going to say. Nothing new—he always asks me to marry him. But Sissy, this time was different. Steven had died. I was pregnant and determined to leave Cork and raise Macy here, and my father was as determined as any hard-headed protective Irishman could be to change my mind about staying in Ireland and raising my child at Moran, where I was raised...where he was raised."

After a moment, I continue. "Cory put forth a similar argument, in a much softer manner, granted—but it was the same message. He reminded me of how similar we are and how strong our connection has remained over the years. He made a very convincing proposal, and I was extremely tempted to say yes then and there. But, Sissy, I knew I would regret making an impulsive decision because it was what my father and Cory wanted, obviously for different reasons."

"Regret? How?" Sissy asks. She is well aware of the passionate connection Cory and I have maintained for all of the years she has known me.

"It was too easy. I could not run away from all of my feelings and allow Cory to step in and be the father that Steven was robbed of being. And say nothing of just walking away from my dream of building the dance company to where it is now. I knew deep in my heart that it was not the right answer. It was not the right time."

"When I hear you say that, Deidre, I am reminded of the old me, who would do just exactly that. Do what someone else wanted me to do," Sissy says. "And, because I accompanied you to some of your therapy sessions, I can hear Ramona's voice quietly asking, 'What is it that you really want to do, Deidre? If you don't really know, then do nothing.' That advice has really stuck with me."

I nod in agreement at Sissy's reminder and go on. "So I told him to ask me again. I needed time to grieve, to deliver the baby, and to go down a different path alone for a while. He was pleased with my answer, Sissy. And, he has been a steady presence during the past three years, on the phone and in person, never bringing up the proposal again. That is, until his last visit to Evanston."

Sissy sets her wine glass on the table and pushes herself to her feet. She takes one long step over to me, locks both arms around me, and squeezes me for what seems like an hour. We are both in tears. I try to explain further but Sissy hushes me into silence.

"I have always known, Deidre, maybe before you did, that you would eventually return to Ireland. I learned your story in small bits at a time, first why you appeared in school in Evanston and then, later on, why you continued to stay in what was looking like a permanent living arrangement with your Aunt Catherine. I also saw how painful it was for you to convince yourself that the arrangement was just a temporary one. When it became apparent that you would continue to be raised by your aunt and schooled in Illinois when all you ever wanted was to return home, I watched as your insecurity grew and enmeshed you. It was your strength of mind that has pushed you forward over the years. You are going home, Deidre. No words of justification are needed. You are going home."

~ ~ ~ ~ ~

I enter Ramona Hancock's clinical office, inspecting the rooms with a critical eye. It has been years since I visited this space, both on my own and accompanied by Sissy. Ramona crosses the reception area and envelops me in a warm hug.

"I wish this was just a social visit, but of course you already know it is not. You probably received notes from the assistant who made my appointment," I say. I summarize Macy's unusual behavior with respect to her explanations about her father.

"Deidre, why do you believe your daughter has devised this particular father scenario?"

"I think there may be something to Cory's explanation that vanishing is a common storyline in Irish culture; fairies vanish, woodland goddesses appear and then vanish. It certainly influenced my imaginative play as a child growing up there."

Ramona listens intently and then asks, "Deidre, can you describe Cory to me so I can form a picture of him in my mind?"

I snuggle back into my chair and begin at the start, describing Cory and me as children running through my family home. "We would run through the kitchen and grab whatever food was handy and then run up and down the flights of stairs, down the back staircase and outside, down through the stables, in and around the horse stalls to be herded out of the way by stable workers, and then inevitably down the 100 steps toward the bay. As we grew older, we would tear off just enough clothes to bare our legs and feet and take on the persona of Irish quarter horses. We'd gallop along the beach until we both were so exhausted that we fell into the sand or grass."

Taking in the image I have just painted, Ramona asks, "Deidre, how were you and Cory the same during those childhood years?"

I respond immediately, rather enjoying reminiscing about Cory's and my early years in Ireland. "We were wild—wild as the wind, wild as Irish ponies let out of the stable on a spring morning. We ran like there was going to be no tomorrow. And the next time Cory showed up, we would do it all over again."

Ramona smiles as my eyes light up and my face radiates light while recalling those magical moments of my Moran childhood. "How did you stay connected with him once you left Cork for Evanston, Deidre? Usually childhood friends, especially those divided by the Atlantic Ocean, grow apart."

I nod and begin by asking Ramona if she has ever had a friendship that continues uninterrupted even when she doesn't see her friend for months or years at a time—like Sissy and me. Yet, I acknowledge that such a connection is somewhat rare between women and men, probably due to another significant relationship of either the man or the woman. Old relationships change, or perhaps dissolve altogether, in order to protect a new bond.

As I articulate to Ramona how Cory and I have stayed glued together so strongly, another thought comes to me. "Maybe it is because Cory never married. That may be why our relationship never cooled. And even after I was married to Steven, we both knew that the chemistry was still there. We just needed to make sure we did not ignite it. But it has always endured."

Ramona looks at the clock on her desk and notes that the session is more than half over. She turns the conversation to Macy. "Your daughter has a precocious nature, and that is combined with her exposure to Irish culture that is steeped in stories of fairies, magic, and romanticism. When in Ireland with her grandfather and others at Moran, she no doubt has heard others refer to events where people have vanished, as if in thin air, and she has heard other colorful Irish legends."

Ramona reminds me that children have a far greater propensity toward imagination and the ability to create a multitude of endings for stories. "Perhaps Macy's insistence on her father vanishing is a way of keeping open the possibility of her father reappearing to her."

Ramona continues, "It is a significant positive that Cory, as a future father, is someone she already knows." Ramona smiles when she hypothesizes about what is obvious. "He will be able to keep that sense of wonderment open for her until she can come to terms with not having had a chance to get to know her father. That is probably what has vanished for Macy."

As I walk from Ramona's office to my car, I mull over what we shared during my session. I had not considered the need for Macy to hang on to the hope of someday meeting her father and creating a way for that to happen. Certainly, being exposed to Irish fables for all of her life had provided my daughter with the ability to create a comforting father fable of her own.

I could not gather the courage to confess to Dr. Hancock that I had sensed my deceased mother's spirit and heard her voice at Moran before I married Steven. Like my daughter, I had fulfilled a need of my own by willing my mother's voice to reappear and be with me.

County Cork, Ireland, 1980

The caravan of vehicles eases its way along the narrow roads, going from one canopy of heavily wooded oak trees to the next. With the passenger's side window rolled down, I watch as the branches reach into the car window. It seems to me that the lushness of County Cork is reaching out its long arms as if to welcome one of its own back home.

I settle on an indirect route once we load up the vans at Cork Airport. I yearn to see the West Cork country in the ripeness of late summer. I am happy to escape the hurried Chicago lifestyle with its hot highways void of anything that looks alive and its elevated trains packed with sweaty travelers in the summer heat. I want to drive to the ocean and see the ships at Kinsale Harbor, then head further south to the village of Skibbereen. Its brightly colored storefronts have been rooted in the same place for 100 years, nestled in a line on narrow village streets.

Rather than turn north from Skibbereen to Bantry and Moran Manor, I instruct the lead driver in the van ahead to go south to the Atlantic, where we will spend the afternoon tucked away in the oceanside village of Schull. I long to see the wind fill the sails on the boats that dot one of my favorite harbors. And, I want Macy to visit the Schull stables where Cory and I spent so much of our youth. Once there, I will boost Macy up on a quarter pony for a turn around the riding rink. So much of what I treasure about my home in West Cork has to do with the sweet smell of leather saddles, the breeze off of the ocean, and the serenity of a slow afternoon.

Sissy and Andres, who drive the lead car, squirm a bit when I say I want to spend the night in Schull at a Georgian retreat house. Cory had found the Schull hideaway during my short visits home when we were in need of a private place away from my father's long arm and vigilant eyes. I assure Sissy that we will enjoy the stop-over before we head north to Bantry, but more importantly, I want to relish time alone with Macy before we all are encapsulated by my Moran family and its vigilant staff. I yearn for a simple life, one I hope to build with Cory. As the line of vans circles through Schull on its way to the retreat house, I am eager to snuggle Macy in one of its bedrooms, where the staff is minimal and the beds are high and deep with pillows.

~ ~ ~ ~ ~

Mist settles over Bantry Bay the night Cory makes an unannounced call at Moran. He walks to the front of the estate and looks down the terraced lawn, which leads to the 100 steps and the home's domineering position on the bay's southern shore. Low on the horizon, the sun throws scarlet waves across the bay as if a painter had filled a brush with red and blue paint and pulled it across the landscape. He stops to gaze down the ancient stone steps that were laid by Patrick Moran's ancestors in the early 1600s.

Cory is no stranger to the legend of the Moran Estate. Long ago, a male Moran relative had warned the British of the arrival of an invading French fleet. The bay proved to be a perfect launching spot for enemy soldiers. As a reward for his vigilance, the King of England awarded the ancestor the title of Baron and later elevated it to that of an Earl. Along with the peerage came gifts of land and money, which enabled the new Earl of Moran to build the manor and purchase nearly all of the land that surrounded it. He created magnificent gardens, the 100 step staircase to the bay, and five stone walls with attached gates to surround the interior grounds. Because of its strategic location to Bantry Bay, Moran Manor continued to be an important observation point for the British during both World War I and II. More than once, the military had occupied a wing on the first floor of Moran. But tonight, Cory is reminded in particular of the significant affiliation Moran men have had with the military.

Cory is also fascinated with the arched stone stables that sit toward the back of the estate. Like the estate grounds, the stables are surrounded by soaring stone walls with a number of gates and decorative arches. Thirty individual horse stalls are carved out within the protection of its walls. Before the advent of the automobile, it was not unusual for fifty to sixty horses to be in residence. Cory shook his head just thinking about what some of the stallions must have looked like during the era when horses were more valuable to an Irishman than gold in his pocket. *It was a different time*, Cory thinks as he circles around the estate to the front door.

The butler smiles as he greets him. Cory stands before one of the reception room's windows, facing the bay and catching the gas-lit view of the stone staircase. Patrick enters the room with a strong stride. He closes the space between Cory and himself and extends his hand.

"What a welcome surprise this is, Cory! I was feeling a little sorry for myself tonight. I had expected the house to be filled with Deidre and her friends' voices and my granddaughter's feet running all over the

place, like you and Deidre used to do. When I heard they were staying
at Schull, I was a bit glum, if you know what I mean."

"Yes, sir, I was feeling somewhat the same. Seems a shame to have
all of this space at Moran and decide to camp in at some old village inn.
But that daughter of yours is not a predictable woman."

Patrick directs Cory to the formal sitting room. He points to an
over-sized upholstered chair, walks to the sideboard nearby, and pours
two whiskeys, one over ice and one neat. He hands the neat whiskey to
Cory and takes a seat in a matching chair across from Cory.

Patrick has years of experience sizing up men who are in a
celebratory mood, as Cory certainly could have been given that Deidre
has agreed to marry him and return to Ireland. Patrick has even more
experience at appraising men when they have something on their
minds and cannot find a path into the conversation. Patrick notices
Cory avoiding eye contact and then diverting his attention to his boots.
He watches Cory swirl his drink in the glass as if he could create just
enough energy to make the liquor evaporate on its own, along with
Cory's anxious state. Patrick predicts that Cory will only relax if Patrick
creates a conversational bridge from the familiar and nonthreatening to
whatever is on Cory's mind.

"Cory, it as an old man's prerogative to repeat himself, but as I
said a bit ago, I am pleased you stopped by. I have not had a private
moment with you since you and Deidre shared the news concerning
your future marriage." Patrick takes a generous gulp of his drink and
glues his eyes to Cory's. "I know you and I have had a somewhat rocky
relationship over the years, and particularly when you were younger.
I was not encouraging of your visits to Moran to see Deidre when she
came home when she was in high school and college."

Patrick watches Cory's body for signs that he is easing into his chair and relaxing against its back. To the contrary, Cory moves his shoulders to the front and rests his bent arms on his knees. "A lot has happened for both of you since those earlier years," Patrick continues. "I am extremely proud of what my daughter has been able to accomplish with growing a dance business, something that I don't know a thing about. But equally, that she bloomed in a foreign country and dealt with all of the obvious and not-so-obvious challenges of being a young woman on her own. I confess to you, Cory, I still have guilt and regret over my decision to send her abroad at such an early age."

Patrick paused. "I am not sure how to say this to you, Cory, but I think you can understand when I say that I really thought she was happy with Steven. From what I saw of them together, he made her happy. And that is all a father wants for his daughter: to be happy."

Patrick watches Cory, anticipating a reaction, but he is silent as he continues to hunch over his drink and alter his gaze from his glass to the floor and then back again. So Patrick continues. "Life has a way of pushing up a small mountain or two along the way, and Steven's death was certainly a mountain for Deidre. But I guess all of us have had to climb that mountain of sadness and grief in our own way. In the middle of the pain, some unexpected blessings rise up as well. God knows Macy was the best treatment for Deidre's broken heart that could have been offered. And, I have to say this to you, Cory. I was silently praying that you would renew your courtship of Deidre. I also will confess to you that I did so for selfish reasons. I wanted Deidre and Macy home in Ireland, and I believed you were the only person that could make that happen."

Cory smiles at Patrick and is a bit embarrassed at having put his future father-in-law on the offense for making him anticipate the nature of this visit. He relaxes into his chair. "Mr. Moran," he says.

Patrick interrupts to correct him. "Cory, I think it is time you call your soon-to-be father-in-law by his given name."

"Patrick, then. I debated whether I should come here tonight to talk to you about a matter that has been on my mind or if it would be best just to let it ride until after Deidre is settled back at Moran. Or, if I should just let the whole thing go," Cory discloses.

Patrick sits back in his chair and waits for Cory to flesh out the details of his concern. He does not want to interrupt his train of thought that is obviously troubling him.

"The thing is, Patrick, one of the guys has been talking in the pubs in town—a Dublin pilot with the British Military. When a plane goes down in a blaze, it creates a lot of interest in the details of the event. And those pilot guys are a close-knit club. There's talk that Steven is not dead. That he survived the crash. I returned to the same pub after finding out the name of the bloke who was telling the story the night before and confronted him. He repeated the same story, insisting that the scenario had more to it than just a good pub tale. He backed off when a friend told him who I was. He asked what my interest in the event was; I told him. He said he did not want to make trouble but that I should probably check it out before getting too far down the aisle with another man's wife."

Patrick's eyes squint so much they nearly close as he takes in Cory's words. He wishes he could emphatically tell Cory that the story is ridiculous because such absurd things do not happen in the modern military world. He wants to say that soldiers do not live in the jungle for a lifetime, waiting for a war to end the way lone Japanese soldiers did during World War II, nor did men like Steven just walk away from a crash and reappear alive after several years. But he could not say it because he knew of incidents, bizarre as they were, that turned out to be true.

"Cory, you did the right thing bringing this to me before telling Deidre. And, of course, she has the right to know. Let me see what I can find out. I think my name may still carry some weight with the British military higher-ups, or at least that Moran Manor on Bantry Bay may ring a few bells."

He stands. Cory, thinking Patrick wants to put a quick end to the unpleasant conversation, does the same. Patrick steps over to Cory and puts his arm around the younger man's shoulder, something that Patrick is not in the habit of doing with other men. Patrick confides, "I am not sure I would have been as strong as you or willing to take the risk of losing the woman I have loved all of my life, but you are right that such a secret would stand between the two of you like a bad taste in your mouth, whether it is true or not."

Draped in darkness and showered by a light mist off of the bay, Cory walks from the manor and through the grounds to his car. He has often differed with Patrick Moran, finding him irritating and disagreeable on a multitude of occasions. But tonight is not one of them.

~ ~ ~ ~ ~

The minivan caravan winds along the quarter-mile drive to the front of the manor house. Sissy and Andres lead the way. A second van, driven by a hired man, follows close behind with Macy and me in the backseat. Behind us are two additional vans crammed to the brim with luggage of every variety. Two young men that we hired in the village of Bantry sit alongside of the driver. Their job is to unload all of the vans and disperse their contents to wherever Colleen and the butler direct.

As the entourage comes to a stop, Colleen emerges from the front door with the maids close behind her. Edwin runs out of the house wearing a scowl instead of his dignified countenance. Somehow, the others have beat him out of the door, and while the protocol puts him in the lead, younger staff do not adhere to the traditional roles that he still expects to be honored.

My father catches the first glimpse of the vehicle train from a second-floor perch and slips out of a side door. As each van passes, he waves it on and into the arms of Colleen and the waiting help. By the time he gets to the front of the house, there is a general rush of confusion, hugs, and rumbling luggage. In the midst of it all, Macy escapes from the vehicle and heads toward the field of grass and the 100 steps. I call out to my racing child to slow down and not to step one foot near the water alone, but before I can be seriously concerned, Colleen walks at a fast clip behind the escaping child.

Colleen knows that I prefer informality to the known habits of the past, but this is one occasion when she is determined to assert her authority. She directs my group into the prepared drawing room while acknowledging that we are at the end of our long journey and no doubt need a short rest, drinks of some kind, and a chance to put our feet up before going off to our assigned bedrooms upstairs. I quickly obey Colleen's directives, which brings obvious pleasure to the house's seasoned acting mistress. My total compliance comes as a surprise to Colleen as she cannot help be reminded of the younger me who fought against all decorum. I thank Colleen profusely, throw my arms around my straight-backed aunt, and drop into the nearest chair in anticipation of a hot cup of tea.

Sissy finds a chair next to me. She examines the room, which is antiquated but lush. She rests her head on a tapestry pillow and tips her head to the ceiling. A stunning Irish crystal chandelier catches her attention.

"Wow, Deidre," Sissy exclaims as she continues the visual survey of her surroundings. "I knew you were raised in the lap of luxury, but this is simply breathtaking. What was it like growing up here?"

Deidre smiles at her sweet friend. "It was just home, all I ever knew. You know how it is when you are a child. You go from moment to moment and one afternoon to another, having fun. I did not really pay much attention to all of this," Deidre explains as she sits back and scrutinizes the room as if she were seeing it for the first time. "But honestly, Sissy, I still remember the very first time I visited your home and family in Evanston when we were in grade school. It made such an impression on me. The closeness of your family members in your small home made me feel so secure. Sometimes it feels like this is more of a museum than a home." I look up at the Waterford chandelier above my head.

"I can't tell you how happy I am to have you and Andres here with me at this time, Sissy. I want you to treat this house as if it is your home away from home because that is exactly what it is. I am sure Colleen has made it her task to assign you both a perfect room, if not rooms. It is the custom for wives and husbands to have their own rooms in this house, Sissy. So just a heads up so you aren't surprised to find your luggage spread between two rooms."

I rise to my feet and excuse myself as fatigue slips over my face. I creep up to my waiting bedroom to give my body and mind a chance to settle the swirling energies from the long trip before putting my feet back down on Irish home ground. I think of all that waits for me— decisions to make as to when I will marry and where we will live—but my dancer's body tells my head to be still. I lie down on my familiar bed and fall into a deep slumber while the sun slides behind the Caha mountains.

~ ~ ~ ~ ~

A series of mornings and evenings arrive and glide away as Moran
Manor bustles under renewed energy. The manor takes on the aura
of earlier days when Deidre was just a toddler and her mother was the
mistress of the house. The kitchen staff grows in number as full dinner
meals are planned and placed on the table at exactly six o'clock in the
evening. Breakfast is set up on the sideboard by seven o'clock each
morning and kept warmed and filled until nine. Lunches are ready by
noon and served depending on the schedule provided by Colleen. A
housemaid or butler brings tea each afternoon between two and three,
along with sandwiches and sweet treats. When he is given the tea task,
Edwin complains that the job is more in line with a footman's duty. Patrick
reminds him that footmen were eliminated when the family decreased
in size. After Suzanne died, Patrick had stopped using the house to
entertain. Thus, the butler and everyone else simply had to adapt.

The number of horses stabled at the manor increases from three to
ten, and three additional riding hands are employed to take care of the
horses and provide riding instructions for Sissy, Andres, Macy, and any
guest who happens to appear at the estate to visit the Americans. Music
is set up outside to provide relaxation in the afternoon and is brought
into the largest drawing room for dancing in the evenings. Deidre's
friends and acquaintances are invited to the manor to meet her special
family and to dance in the halls of Moran. The house and estate seem to
expand, and it rises to the occasion for which it was originally designed
to serve: hospitality, grace, and fun.

Patrick departs to London at the height of the festivities, assuring
Colleen and Deidre that he will return in a week. Business calls and
there does not seem to be a better time to slip away than when his new

family is distracted and deep in fun and exploration around the estate and West Cork. It is understood that Cory's role is to play the host during Patrick's absence and to ensure Deidre's happiness and peace of mind.

Patrick waves down a taxi at Heathrow after the short flight from Cork to London. Carrying a small valise and no luggage, he jumps in the back seat and directs the driver to St. Ermin's Hotel. The taxi initially heads toward Buckingham Palace and the Houses of Parliament before making a turn toward St. James's Park. It stops in front of a block-long, Queen Anne building complete with a full courtyard. Patrick is aware that the hotel was used by the UK's MI6 Secret Intelligence Service during the WWII but did not realize that the SIS still maintains its operational base at the hotel.

He steps off of the elevator and approaches a reception desk. A woman in a long-sleeved navy-blue dress asks how she can be of assistance. Her clothing looks like it came from the 1940s, and her hair is pulled back in a severe French twist. Before Patrick can take a seat to wait, another clerk invites him to follow her down a hall to a private office.

The Secret Intelligence Service's Deputy Director rises from his desk and introduces himself summarily. He briefs Patrick as to Steven's role in the intelligence arena, particularly as it relates to foreign activities. He works off of the request for information that Patrick had filed with the British Medical Corp, which routed the RFI to the MI6.

"Steven Whitney did not work for the British Medical Corp; he worked for us in intelligence. Before you ask the obvious question, it is not unusual for our employees to build another identity concerning the nature of their work, and, of course, all of our agents have a constructed life made for them when they sign on as an agent. However, Steven was not an agent; he did not engage in covert intelligence. He was a field representative, and his work regularly required him to travel to foreign destinations."

The director sees that Patrick is about to interrupt with a question and cuts off his impulse by asking him to hold any questions until he finishes his full briefing.

"Steven was on a small military plane that crashed and burned in Southeast Asia. Our investigation team on the ground reported that both Steven and the pilot were burned beyond recognition. We reported the same to their families. That report was wrong. Steven managed to escape the burning wreckage. Villagers brought him to a civilian hospital. He convalesced in Vietnam for several months. Why he did not contact us as soon as he was well enough to do so, I don't know. But I will tell you that as soon as we found out he was alive, we sent both a telegram and a military escort to his home to let his wife know of the change in his status. That would complete our obligation with respect to updating family on any changes in the status of a soldier or, in this case, an intelligence employee."

"But his wife, my daughter, Deidre Moran Whitney, was not informed about the change in his status," corrected Patrick.

The deputy director looks down at his papers then directly into Patrick's eyes. "The name you just gave me is not the name of the woman that Steven had indicated as his wife." Without any hesitation, he adds, "It is not unusual for personal information to be outdated— divorces, death, that kind of thing. Intelligence people have their own unique way of dealing with their personal affairs. They tend not to be as diligent as ordinary citizens."

"I attended a funeral service with my daughter for Steven in London. Who arranged that? An adult son of Steven's attended. There was a military representative at it as well." Patrick looked at the deputy looking for some kind of explanation. The deputy remained silent.

"Deidre visited Steven's house on the Bedford Estate. She said the house was nearly empty. His butler had made all of the arrangements for his possessions to be packed up and dispersed according to Steven's written wishes he had left in the event something happened to him in his line of work."

The director states he has nothing additional to share and that the best route for Patrick is to speak with Steven directly. With that, he pushes a small notecard across his desk in Patrick's direction.

"That's as much information as I have on your request for information. Unless there is something more that you have not made me aware of, I suggest you follow up with the information on this card," the director advises.

No sooner had Patrick Moran closed the door to the Deputy Director's office than the director reached over and dialed the phone. When his call was answered, the director reported that Patrick Moran, formally Earl Moran from a very long line of British titled Morans, had been at his office asking for information regarding Steven's status. He ended his curt update with one brusque directive: clean up your mess.

Patrick steps off of the elevator and looks at his watch. The meeting had taken exactly ten minutes. Once outside, he surveys both sides of the street and finds what he needs. He sits down in the dark bar, orders a double whiskey, and stares at the notecard with Steven's contact information on it. His return flight is the next day. He has plenty of time to make one more visit in London. He signals for another drink and ruminates for the rest of the afternoon on how the newly disclosed information will impact Deidre and all of them. Legally, Deidre is not a widow, nor had she been a legal wife to Steven.

~ ~ ~ ~ ~

The rain pours in sheets from a grey sky as Patrick sits on the plane waiting for takeoff. He stares out of the window at the water accumulating on the runway, thinking he would not be bothered if the small commuter flight was delayed until the rain abated. He is in no hurry to return to Moran.

Patrick conducts his affairs along a strict line of decorum. He does not immerse himself in others' problems unless the problems affect him either financially or personally. While he admits that Steven's reappearance does directly alter his personal life, he knows that it will be Deidre's primary dilemma. More than once, he had found himself on his way to the address provided by the Deputy Director with the intent of confronting Steven in person. Each time, he instructed the cab driver to drop him off at a pub so he could go over things more precisely in his mind. But he never made it to Steven's. How would he justify to Deidre that he had decided to take things into his own hands before informing her about Steven's status? He lets the weight of his head drop on the headrest and is sound asleep before the plane reaches its full ascent.

He awakens to the rustling of passengers and luggage as the plane descends in preparation for landing in Cork. As he walks out of the airport to locate his car, the sun beats on the top of his head and the back of his neck, relaxing his muscles and dissipating some of the stored anxiety caused by his trip to London. He dreads returning home and is thankful that he chose to drive himself to the airport and back rather than using his driver. Solitude is what he needs most.

Colleen hears the front door quietly open and close. She is sure the butler is unaware of Patrick's return, but Colleen, who holds a vigilant lookout, knows the moment of his arrival. She senses that something serious has disrupted Patrick's schedule. He never travels spontaneously, especially for business, as his routine is to have his associates do the legwork and resolve issues directly. In the event that Patrick's physical appearance is required, he makes careful preparations well in advance. Colleen has also noticed Cory's unease whenever a question or comment arose about Patrick's departure or return. Whatever has pulled at her brother and caused him to make an uncharacteristically hasty trip to London, Colleen is sure that Cory is somehow involved.

Colleen surveys the entryway hallway and finds Patrick's valise and coat thrown over a chair. She walks back into the kitchen, buzzes Edwin, and sends him upstairs to check on Patrick. Within minutes, he returns to the kitchen and indicates that Mr. Moran wants a supper tray brought up to his room with a small flask of whiskey and whatever is readily available to eat. Colleen quickly heats a left over lamb stew and loads a tray. Edwin does not make another appearance in the kitchen.

Colleen sits at the large oaken table that has been in the kitchen for decades. She has no appetite, nor is she thirsty, so she has no reason to remain there. She tells herself she should go up to her own bedroom and get ready for bed. But the kitchen is an island of safety. No matter the trouble, it contains everything she could possibly need to provide comfort: hot water for tea, a hearth, a fire or oven to cook and bake, and cold water to drink. Perhaps most important of all are the familiar sounds and smells that predict the nurturing of life: a teapot whistling, soups simmering, pots clanging, and women talking in any number of different voices and demeanors. But Colleen finally gives in to her exhaustion. Whatever the next move is to be, it will have to wait until morning.

Startled by a vigorous but quiet knock at her bedroom door, Colleen rises from her bed to find Patrick still dressed in street clothes.

He utters an apology for awakening her in the middle of the night. Colleen, saying nothing, opens the door further and Patrick steps inside. Within minutes, Patrick has summarized the purpose of his trip and the outcome. He apologizes to Colleen for involving her ahead of Deidre, but he justifies his action because he needs Colleen's help with orchestrating the following day given that his granddaughter, Sissy, and Andres are in the house. He needs several hours in the morning with Deidre, and she will need privacy following the ill-fated news. He confesses to Colleen that he wants to shield the information from those not directly involved as much as possible, but as soon as the words escape his mouth, he and Colleen both know how unlikely that will be.

~ ~ ~ ~ ~

My lavender silk robe sweeps over the floor as I stroll into my father's study, cupping steaming tea in my hands. I take a deep breath and inhale the smell of the lemon oil that the maids use to clean and polish an oversized desk and wall bookcase that have inhabited the room for over one hundred years. I run my hands over the desk, following the wood grain as if saying hello to an old friend. Then I stoop low to inspect the small space under the desk where, during childhood, I hid from my father and the other "adults," as I then referred to them. I sit back on my haunches as I stare into the nest-like space. I am sure I can still see a small child hidden safely away from any perceived threat or nuisance. Heavy gold-gilded photos of male Moran ancestors hang from wire picture hangers on all four walls. Two brocaded, forest green couches are still in the same exact positions they've been in for as long as I can remember.

As I peer into the portrait men's faces, I wonder what the women who actually ran the house must have looked like. If I were to insist that all of the wives of the wall-mounted men be included in the study, how much wall space would they take up? Everything at Moran, I came to understand as I grew up, had a story—a very old male story. I wonder what it would take to restore a sense of accuracy to these walls by including the story of the Moran women.

I turn in a half-circle to face the door as I hear my father's footsteps on the corridor floor and then watch him join me in the study. He is shaved and dressed in dark corduroy slacks and a light-blue knit dress shirt. Nevertheless, he looks as if he has been up all night. I scrunch my eyebrows together. I am not accustomed to seeing my father look old and weathered. I know he and Colleen have maneuvered the early morning schedule so my father and I can have some private time, and my first reaction to his appearance this morning is that he is not well.

I put my tea down and circle my father with both of my arms, hugging him as tightly as I can while pushing away thoughts that suggest that my father is in any manner at risk. He points to one of the brocade couches that sits in front of a large window and is bathed in morning light. We sit father and daughter huddled together, and bask in the warmth. I enjoy this moment in time that is void of a single problem even though my instinct tells me that is about to change.

Gathering my courage, I pull my head from my father's shoulder and ask, "So, Dad, as lovely as this special morning attention is, is there something on your mind?"

My father smiles at me and recognizes a trait that has not changed since I was a little girl running the floors of Moran. I have never been able to sit still for long.

"Deidre, I am feeling like a father who once again has failed his daughter," he says, missing some of the syllables in his words. "Since the moment you arrived in this house, all I have ever wanted for you is happiness and security."

Puzzled, I cannot predict the source of my father's concern. It does not sound like an opening for a conversation about his health so I think perhaps there has been a dramatic downturn with his business. Possibly Moran is in financial jeopardy, as any number of homes and estates in Ireland have sold off or closed entirely.

"There is no easy way into this conversation, Deidre. I wish there—"

"Dad! I'm a big girl now. I'm not nine years old and without a mother. I am a mother of my own three-year-old daughter. What could possibly be so wrong? Unless, of course, you are going to tell me that you are extremely ill and—"

He interrupts to assure me that his health is entirely sound. With that assurance, the energy once again turns in my direction. We sit in silence for a few moments more until my intuition gradually cracks open the one possibility that would put my father's emotions in such a tailspin.

"It's about Steven, isn't it?" I ask.

My father looks directly into my eyes. Without saying a word, he confirms my feeling. He pulls energy from deep inside and proceeds to relate in sequential order the events that led him to London and to the office of the British intelligence. He keeps his sentences short and to the point, imitating the Deputy Director's communication style.

"Deidre, the initial findings substantiated that both men had lost their lives in the small aircraft crash. But after a few months, word came back from a hospital in Vietnam that Steven survived the crash, was rescued by local residents, and was brought to a hospital."

I try to interrupt him but he ignores me and proceeds with the rest of the story. He slows his phrasing and proceeds. "Steven is alive."

My face lights up with unanticipated joy and hope, which prompts my father to shake his head.

"Deidre, the British intelligence notified Steven's wife—the wife Steven listed on the personnel information file. He is married and was already married when you were wedded to him here at Moran."

The fire in the stone fireplace, burning since early morning, has produced a pile of white ashes. The log collapses and makes a hissing sound in the study's otherwise tomb-like silence. My father watches me as the reality of his words sink into my consciousness.

"Dad, can you repeat what you just said?"

I wince as if someone has pricked me with a hidden object and then I shake my head slowly, as if I'm trying to balance something valuable on my head. I repeat what he said and my nearly inaudible words float in the air. "Alive? Steven...alive...married? Steven is married?"

Large tears glide down my face. I am not a widow. I was not married, and Macy does have a father who vanished—one who is very much alive and on the earth. My tears run fast and furious, my breath becomes irregular, and I gasp for air.

"How could I not have known? Or did I know on some level but refused to examine the man with whom I fell so quickly and deeply in love? I never asked him for names of the people he worked with, but I did try to ask him about his personal life, his upbringing in London—if, in fact, he grew up in London. He ignored most of my questions and always maneuvered the conversation to some other topic. I chose to retreat into a child-like role, trusting in his maturity and his love."

I wipe my face with the handkerchief my father provides and then I reach for my tea, which is on the table. I lean back on the couch and inhale until my lungs are filled. "There were clues all along, Dad," I say.

"I had a sense during our courtship in London that something was out of place, but I talked myself into ignoring it."

My father says nothing.

"I knew, Dad, when Steven's son appeared out of nowhere at the funeral that the Steven I thought I knew turned out to be someone very different. How could he have not told me that he was a father of a grown son? I had asked him at one point before we were married if he had been married or had children. Looking into his son's eyes in London and hearing that his son knew very little about me as well, I knew then that the man I married was someone very different indeed. But he was dead, so what did it really matter to dredge up his past and personal history at that point?"

My father reaches for my hands and clasps them tightly inside of his. He does not know how to contain the pain that he sees enveloping and invading me. He whispers in a soft voice that nobody had any inkling of Steven's deception, and he chides himself for not taking the liberty of carefully checking Steven out.

He does not tell me that he had an investigator in place to do just that but then reluctantly changed his mind. If he had learned something that concerned him, how could he be certain it would have had the same impact on me? Worse, I would have known that my father did not trust my own judgment regarding my private affairs. He had warned himself that an investigation could widen the gulf that had already formed between us due to his decision to send me to the States.

My father rises from the couch, walks to his desk, picks up a large envelope, crosses the room, and faces me. "When I was in London, I launched a full investigation immediately after I left the Deputy Director's office. I have put together typed notes of what I know for sure about him. Keep in mind that this is just the beginning, and I typed the notes from updates I received while still in London and by phone last night. There is not a lot here, but it is a beginning, Deidre. It is not for me to make any decisions about what you should do at this point."

The sun has risen higher in the sky since my father and I first entered the study. Now it is bright and bold, as if making its own contribution to shedding light on this dark revelation. I take the envelope from my father and turn to walk from the study, but I reconsider and retrace my steps back to the couch.

"I can't tell you how grateful I am to you for pursuing this, Dad. I know this turn of events has to be tearing you apart. You did the right thing by bringing this to me so I can get ahead of it. It was sure to come out publicly anyway. That would have been much worse."

I give my father a kiss and ask him to spend the day with his granddaughter and the others. "I am okay, Dad. I will work this out. It will take some time, but I will choose the best path for Macy and for myself."

Within the secluded safety of my father's study, I try to rise from the couch. Pressure builds in my heart. It grows heavier, which decreases its ability to expand and decompress. I raise both hands, palms open, cross them, and lay them on my chest as a human bandage. The pain is intense and robs my body of the strength to pull myself up, much less walk from the study. Once my father spoke of Steven's willful deception, it made real what my head had been trying to signal to me all along.

I am not prepared for the deep-rooted feelings of abandonment and betrayal that crush me and catapult me back to losing my mother. A gasp of air expels from my lungs as my body pushes into a flight or fight mode. I have been unconsciously holding my breath and my body is fighting for a fresh supply of air. My years of dance training take hold.

I give up any effort to rise from the couch and collapse into the deep cushions as I draw in more air and slowly expel the old. As childhood pain and injuries bubble up, my brain yields to its emotional center, ceasing to process language in order to release feelings, old passions, and fears from thirty years ago that I have unknowingly held within me.

Colleen tiptoes down the thinly carpeted hallway that leads to the study and presses her ear to the heavy door. After just a few moments of listening, tears began to stream down her face as she takes in the gasps for air and the moans of pain and suffering that travel through the oak. She turns in retreat, providing the privacy for Deidre to grieve alone. Retracing her steps on several occasions to check on Deidre, Colleen gently pushes the door open to find Deidre sound asleep in a chair by the window. She retreats and returns yet again with a maid. The women wrap a lamb's wool throw around Deidre's shoulders and lift her to her feet. Between them, they lead the exhausted woman through the long hallways and up the terraces and stairs to her second-floor bedroom. Colleen pantomimes additional directions to the maid, who immediately departs the bedroom but returns with a pot, two mugs, a newspaper, and Colleen's sweater.

Colleen had lacked courage and the knowledge of how to help Deidre when she was a little girl at Moran faced with losing all that she knew and loved. Maturity and wisdom have come to Colleen as she had aged. She listens to Deidre breathing slowly and steadily. At thirty-minute intervals, she gently awakens her patient and brings warm tea to her lips before tucking her back into her childhood cocoon. Colleen knows that Deidre will recover fully and be stronger than ever—that is, if she takes the time now to mourn and heal and do little else.

If Colleen had known the importance of releasing grief and administering emotional nursing in addition to tending to physical needs when Deidre was a little girl, she may not have been in such a hurry to send her across the Atlantic Ocean into a world of strangers before she was ready. Colleen settles back into her chair, which is alongside the bed that has been in the room for two lifetimes. She lowers her head in a prayer position and tells herself she is grateful to have another chance. She will do better this time, for Deidre.

London, England 1980

Bedford Square lies in a covering of autumn snow and resembles a film set from the late 1800s. Dressed in a black wool pencil skirt, cropped jacket, and tall riding boots, I climb out of the taxi. Randall, my father's attorney and now mine, pays the driver. We walk briskly in silence, past the wide paved walks and the collection of Georgian stucco buildings once inhabited by private families but now occupied by one corporate nonprofit or another. We walk past garden shrubs recently clipped of their faded fall blooms. Late-flowering plants are still weed-free and stand upright. Walking through Bedford on this early November afternoon, I recall the summer evening when Steven introduced me to both the Square and the gardens that encircled it. Now, I focus my thoughts on the nature of the day's visit with both anxiety and trepidation: Steven. Once I had emerged from the shock of learning Steven was alive and married to someone else, I relied on my father's investigators and Randall. Randall had contacted Steven on my behalf. I ruled out Moran or any location in Ireland as a place for us to meet. I voiced my concern about meeting at Bradford Square, but in the end, I agreed. It is private and holds few emotional ties. Randall made it clear that the first visit is simply to lie down the conditions of further personal interaction and limitations where Macy is concerned.

I directed Randall to point out to Steven that I do not need him to provide explanations for his behavior.

I stop in front of the familiar Bradford residence and tuck my leather bag tightly under my arm. The last time I was here, William had finished the task of packing house contents into boxes. I draw in a breath to compose myself. Randall, who has slowed his pace and fallen behind to provide me with time to gather my thoughts, catches up to me.

"Deidre, remember what we talked about. Steven has seen the preliminary set of stipulations. Don't let him start to talk to you about any of them. He may try."

"I understand your concerns, Randall. I will do just that. I know the reason behind this meeting is to see for myself that Steven is alive."

"I will wait right here for you. This should not take long. If you need to at any point, tell Steven your attorney is right outside of the door or simply leave. If you don't leave this residence in thirty minutes, I will assume you need me to take some kind of protective action."

I nod in agreement and proceed toward the residence. I grab the iron door knocker and rap twice. William appears and directs me inside. He gives no indication that we have met. He says, "Would madam like a drink of any kind?" Then he takes my coat and hat.

I am in the middle of asking for water when Steven enters the room. I am taken aback by his strikingly handsome appearance, but I also note that he looks tired and much older than I had remembered. Instead of his usual preference for black dress slacks and a crisp shirt with a stiff dress collar, he wears a pair of relaxed jeans and a navy cotton sweater.

"Bring two glasses of water and two glasses of Jameson neat," Steven instructs William. He turns toward me, says hello, smiles slightly, and extends his arm in the direction of the sitting room located down a short hallway, one that I had previously walked when Steven and I were dating.

My plan stalls. I sit frozen staring at the man I thought was dead. Despite all of the preplanning for this encounter, my attorney was right; it is harder than I imagined and could have prepared for. My heart rate quickens and heat spreads across my face and travels down my neck to my chest. My eyes well up with tears and I struggle to retrieve any words. A deep sense of betrayal and shame hits me hard. How could I have been so easily taken in by this man?

"I have to say, Steven, I am glad to see you well and alive after..." I stop my words dead in their track. I have already stepped across my own carefully constructed boundary.

"Thank you, Deidre. I don't deserve your kindness." With that, he reaches toward an end table, picks up a white envelope, and hands it to me. "I don't want to break our preset rules, but I am asking you to take this letter with you and consider it. I am giving it to you now because I don't know how this time together will work out between us."

His move reminds me that once again he is one step ahead of me, pushing me off balance. I take the envelope from his hand, open my bag, and tuck it inside. I retrieve a large envelope of my own.

"I have an envelope for you, too, but I am guessing mine contains communication of a different sort. None of this is negotiable, Steven. Nothing. Especially the paragraph pertaining to Macy, our daughter, the daughter you have never met. If you respect me at all, you will honor my wishes and not go around me."

"Deidre, I did not know until recently that you had a child—that we have a child."

"How could you? I thought you were dead. That was what I was told, and you never corrected that score. You were dead to me and to

Macy. You are still dead. Although I will never be able to sort out why the good and happy life I thought I had with you is a fraud. That you are a fraud. The last time I was in this house was after your memorial service—an empty house. William was in charge of clearing things out. You seem to move in and out in fast form."

Steven produces a wince at hearing my words, but the sincerity of his reaction is impossible to detect. I lock my eyes with Steven's, trying to see if I can find answers to some of the hundreds of questions I have asked myself since learning of his identity and status. I wait for him to provide some compelling reason for his behavior that will unravel this mixed up puzzle. But Steven sits frozen and indifferent to my distress.

I stand, signaling an end to our meeting. As I approach the door to leave, I turn to face Steven. "Macy needs time. I need time. Four years is not unreasonable for all of us to acclimate to our new lives as two people, unmarried, who have a child together. She will be eight then, the age of reason, or so they say."

I turn my back to Steven and as I do, my head begins to spin throwing my body into an equilibrium tail spin. Randall, who was waiting outside on the pavement, steps up to the concrete landing and catches me by the arm. We reverse our direction and head down the walkway designed for leisure and views of the gardens without experiencing either. I leave Randall at Bradford Square and get into a waiting cab assuring him that I am okay. I close my eyes and will my body to take me away from Bradford Square and deliver me to London's Heathrow airport.

Draped in large, dark glasses and a soft woolen scarf, I force my way through the teeming crowd of people. I am intent on making a straight path to the Aer Lingus terminal. Once on board, I can order a stiff drink. More than any other international airport that I have traveled through, London's Heathrow never fails to entertain me with its costumed international nomads or the hundreds of conservatively suited businessmen conducting their livelihoods. But this is no ordinary flight. At the Aer Lingus check-in, I push my passport across the tall desk, answer yes or no to the few questions the agent asks, and walk outside to the boarding zone for my flight. Once on board, a flight attendant approaches me and tells me there is a change in my seating location. She directs my attention toward the back of the plane. I squint and see a blonde woman standing and waving her arms over her head. I feel my body let go and a smile makes its way to my face.

Sissy squeezes her way up the aisle in between passengers loading the plane and reaches out to grab my carry-on luggage. "You didn't think I was going to let you fly home all by yourself, did you?" she says while stashing the suitcase overhead.

"How in the world did you manage this?" I ask in a shaky voice. "You can't know how good it is to see you."

"One word: Colleen. By the time Andres and I found out what was going on, Colleen had a travel itinerary in my hand with instructions to land at Heathrow, deplane and re-board as soon as possible. We are seated back here in this two-seat row, close to the ladies room and service area. Plenty of wine—or something stronger—is just a foot away."

We have barely settled into our seats when the stewardess brings glasses of wine. Sissy raises her glass to me with a toast to hard times: "Though they may be inevitable, may the hard times be short in duration and accompanied by true friends."

For the following half hour, I try to find some kind of order in a life that has fallen apart. "As you know, Sissy, once Steven and I were married, we lived an international marriage. I made every effort to support the flexibility Steven needed. Yes, now that I look back, there were warnings that surfaced from time to time about Steven, but like a lot of women, I think I chose to ignore them."

As I continue the story and Sissy chimes in by adding an unflattering word or two to describe Steven, our mood lifts in the way that sadness can so often erupt into laughter. A few more drinks ease the pain. As the small jet begins its descent, we brace ourselves on the back of the seats in front of us for the touchdown's inevitable kick-back. We look at one another and break into laughter. We are last to walk off of the plane, and Sissy thanks the stewardesses for their indulgence as she wraps her arm around my waist.

The attendants watch us teeter down the steps to the ground below. They know from taking care of every kind of traveler and from catching bits and pieces of our conversation that I am traveling in pain. They could see that Sissy had lightened the journey and eased my hurting, at least for a while. They watch until Sissy and I walk through the Cork airport doors, then they turn to each other with raised eyebrows. One of the attendants puts her open palm across her heart. The other nods in agreement.

County Cork, Ireland, 1980

Rain falls in heavy sheets for the fifth consecutive day. Four-year-old Macy runs from room to room, climbing on the window seats to peer outside. She screams an order at an invisible person outside to make it stop raining before running to yet another window to make the same demand. Traffic to the house has trickled to an occasional visitor; the Irish are content to stay inside and wait out the wind and rain by piling on woolen sweaters and baking brown bread.

I think about how Chicagoans respond to rainy, stormy days. They are impatient for the weather to change so they minimize their efforts at accommodating to it. I smile as I realize I have become one of those impatient Americans demanding speed and change instead of enjoying the moment in rain, fog, or sun. I want order and peace restored to my life. I want my heart to be healed this instant.

Christmas of 1980 is upon us. I have told Colleen and my father that I would really love a small and quiet holiday season, foregoing the customary Christmas celebration at Moran. My father is in the habit of throwing the house open the week following Christmas, inviting any and all. I appeal to my father that I cannot muster the necessary energy to play hostess as I know I would have to do, even though he assures me it would not be necessary. In the end, and with Colleen's persuasion, we have reached a compromise: open house at Moran for one day rather than a week. This is no small accomplishment as "the way it has always been" is still the standard my father uses to govern his life.

The estate gardeners set up large pine trees in the front entryway and in each drawing room on the first floor. Open house or not, Colleen is making sure that all are strung with the Moran family collection of antique lights accumulated from decades of previous Christmas seasons. After all, she confides, it is her Christmas too. Wreaths are hung on all of the floor-length windows. Scores of green, white, and wine-colored candles encased in sterling, cast iron, and bronze holders are displayed in every room of the house. "Light, light, and more light," Colleen calls to the crew of decorators as she and my father survey the entry hallway, sitting rooms and dining room to approve each step of the house's transformation into a holiday vision. I smile and occasionally laugh at them. It seems they are acting out a play begun when they were children, singing a chant started by some long-ago aunt or mistress, or maybe my very young grandmother: light, light, and more light.

I am settling in at Moran and have grown to appreciate Colleen's routines. I am in no hurry to hit the floor in the morning and run like the Chicago Deidre did. I take Colleen's advice and reserve mornings for Macy or for doing whatever comes to mind. No visitors, no morning appointments to go to, and no phone calls to answer. Colleen nestles herself between me and the outside world by taking phone calls and writing down messages. I "work" my outside life for just a few hours in the afternoon, consult with Randall about legal matters and return Andres' phone calls from Chicago before transitioning to a more social world of late tea or walks outside.

This open space, created with Colleen's help, offers me time to contemplate the seriousness of the life changes that I face. I am not avoiding the decisions that face me; quite the contrary. By easing into Colleen's routine, I am afforded more rest and the opportunity to grieve the loss of the life I thought I had with Steven one small step at a time. As the shock over Steven being alive passes, and as I accept my life without him, I see my own life from a fresh perspective. I surely would not be healing if I had packed Macy up and returned to the hectic life of Chicago and the dance world.

County Cork, Ireland, 1981

The spring air and light have returned to Cork after an unusually dark and damp winter. The old part of Cork City pushes up ancient roots of plants that have been buried beneath it for centuries, and they grow half a foot each day in the warm, moist soil. Grasses turn green alongside the rivers, brick roads, and bridges. The sun is low in the surrounding hills and a multicolored sky announces the beginning of yet another spectacular sunset.

Cory and I make our way from his parked car to an old stone building that has housed several churches, a nurse training academy, a private girls' school, an elementary school, and now a performing arts center of the most rudimentary nature. Cory talked me into attending this evening's *Céili* performance of Irish dance by insisting that it is time for me to embrace all things Irish.

I am ambivalent at best and acutely conflicted at worst to interact with a part of my life that created so much joy because when I think of dance, I am also invaded by memories of Steven. If it had not been for my involvement with North River and my insistence on creating international dance themes for the company, I would not have been in London and crossed his path. But Cory reminded me he loves Irish traditional lyrics, instruments, and the athleticism of Irish step dancing much more than he loves stuffy Russian and American ballet. Teasing in his customary, over-the-top style, he insisted that I needed to see dance the way it was intended to be. I weakened.

Once inside, I look around the make-do staging area with its limited lighting and watch the crowd fill the main floor. People sit between the aisles and underneath the stage as the seating reaches capacity. There are no programs so I am unable to preview the music and dance selections or read short bios of the principal dancers and musicians, a habit with which I am accustomed.

Musicians set up a host of instruments: guitars of various sizes and shapes, an accordion, flutes, a harp, and two bagpipes. Stick microphones are also distributed on the stage. With no introduction, the musicians appear and the crowd breaks into a thunderous welcome. I listen to the music of my childhood and country as one Irish tune rolls into the next. It seems as if only a few minutes pass, but by the clock, it has been half an hour. Cold drinks are brought onto the stage for the musicians. A tall, dark haired woman in a long dress steps out from behind the backstage curtain and stands before one of the stick microphones to detail the second part of the program: the dance. She proudly informs the audience that the dancers are both young and not-so-young and are from the small villages and towns throughout the Cork area.

The musicians slide into a set of traditional reels and jigs. The youngest dancers appear on stage and dance in pairs to a polka dance, then break into circle dances, and then return to dancing in pairs. As one group of dancers finishes and exits, the next group, according to chronological age, appears and performs circle and paired dance. It is not until the dancers in their late teens and twenties appear on stage that the dance changes to solo step dancing. The musicians break into "The Gneeveguilla Reel" as individual dancers take the stage, one soloist interchanging for the next. The audience cheers and claps as the dancers and musicians perform. The last dancers are of a more mature age and have danced all of their lives. The musicians slow their selections to play "Danny Boy" and "I'll Take You Home Again Kathleen." The elder dancers partner and dance the waltz.

My head reels with the songs of my childhood as Cory and I walk the rustic Cork Bridge to the waiting car. I catch Cory's arm to stop him. At the center of the bridge, under the light of the spring moon, I wrap my arms around him and squeeze him tightly. I kiss him with all of the energy that is in my body. Cory stands motionlessly, soaking in every second. When I release him and step back, he flashes a wide smile and says "*Tá grá agam duit*"—I love you—to which I respond, "*Tá grá agam duit.*"

As we near the end of the bridge, Cory abruptly stops and turns to face me. "Is it time, Deidre?" My attention is somewhere else.

"It must be close to midnight," I respond rather absentmindedly.

"Deidre, come back from whatever planet you have landed upon. I asked you if it was time."

I look at Cory's confident and determined face and instantly recognize his meaning. "Yes, Cory. It is time."

"I have carried this in the lining of my pocket for some time now, Deidre. Once out, it cannot go back in. You understand, girl?" Cory asks quietly.

I smile and nod as Cory removes a small velvet box, opens it, and reveals a handmade gold ring with a Celtic cross engraved in its center. He lifts it from the box, reaches for my left hand, and places it on my ring finger.

"Not sure what kind of ring to call this, so if anyone asks, and until we figure it out, just say 'It's Cory's.' That should just about take care of the matter. And I have the mate at home, Deidre." We proceed toward Cory's parked car talking in soft voices, exchanging ideas about how we can merge two very different lives.

~ ~ ~ ~ ~

It is eight o'clock p.m. in Ireland and I want to prepare some notes before placing a long distance call to Andres. It is mid-afternoon in the States. If he still keeps the routine I witnessed for all the years we worked together, he will be winding down the major part of his day and retreating to his office.

I draw a T-chart on the paper in front of me. On one side, I write words and phrases I can use to support and agree with Andres' position or reactions to my proposal. On the other side of the T, I identify words that are meant to convey that I am firm in my decision. I know from past negotiations that a woman needs to repeat key words and phrases over and over again in a calm, pleasant tone in order for a man to accept the message. The more difficult a listener finds the message to accept, the more the need to repeat.

I put the call through, hear the phone ring, and sit back in my father's antique chair while I wait for Andres to pick up. "Deidre, good afternoon—or should I say good evening? I have to remind myself you are six hours later than we are in Chicago. I should know that from being over there with you, but you know how it is. Once you're back in your own world, you just think everybody else is right there with you."

I laugh and confess, "I had to sneak out of my bedroom and into the study so Colleen will not detect that I am plugging away at work in the evening. I don't have to remind you, Andres, of how Colleen still guards traditional roles for the women of the house. I am sure you noticed that trait in her when you stayed at Moran." I pause for a moment. "Andres, as you may have figured out, this call is not a social one. I am hoping you have an hour or so to devote to me."

"Yes, of course, Deidre. I recognize we are in a business mode when you send me an email marked 'urgent' two days in advance to set up a phone call so we can discuss dance."

"Guilty as charged. And with that open, I want to begin by noting that North River is successful largely due to your creative abilities. The basic business model and plans for the future are firmly in place, and it is just a matter of moving forward with that design."

Andres interrupts my entry before I can get to the meat of my message. "Deidre, don't tell me that you are thinking of moving back to part-time work again? I am not surprised, but I was really hoping..."

"Andres, let me finish. But I will expedite my conversation. I want to completely sell my partnership in North River as soon as possible."

I wait for Andres to respond, allowing silence to bring home my message.

"Deidre, I understand completely your need to settle down in one place and focus on your personal life after all the upheaval with Steven. I really do. But give up your interest in dance? I don't see that in you, Deidre."

"I appreciate your support, Andres, and I am glad that you recognize how much dance is in my blood. But I did not say anything about giving up dance. That is the second thing I need to talk with you about."

"Bringing North River to Ireland or creating a separate spin-off of North River?" Andres anticipates my next sentence. "Deidre, that tactic could be really complicated and financially risky. The entertainment demographics are enormously different in Ireland than they are in the US. I don't have to tell you of all people about that," Andres states.

"Exactly, Andres. I could not agree with you more. I want to start an entirely different kind of dance company in Ireland. But I can't do it without selling my interest in North River Dance, and I can't do it without you. When can you get on a plane and come over? I will have a full proposal and a small field trip put together whenever you can get here."

The telephone line becomes silent. I know that Andres is weighing how to respond to such a directive. Papers rustle on the other end of the phone line.

"I know better than to try and get you to change your mind once it is set, and from the sound of your voice, I would say you are committed to moving in another direction. Let me find my calendar, Deidre, and I will email you in a few hours. I'll clear my calendar and look at next week."

I have no more than hung up the phone when there is a soft knock on the study door. Colleen opens it and announces that Randal has arrived. She also informs me that she has put him in the breakfast room where she laid out some hot soup, bread, and brandy. She says that if I am going to work him at such uncivil times, the least Moran Manor can do is give the poor man something to eat and drink. I move from the study to find him eating the food put out for him.

"Randall, I commandeered my father's study for the bulk of the day and evening. He was at the Moran Hotel-Cork City this morning and is in Dublin overnight so I thought it would be a good time to focus on the changes I am making in my life. I have sorted things out in a way that I simply could not have done immediately after Steven's 'resurrection.'"

I hesitate then continue. "Randall, I do not feel it is in Macy's best interest to know about her father until she turns eighteen. Furthermore, I do not believe that Macy will be safe in Steven's custody no matter how short the visit. He has proven himself to be completely untrustworthy, and my first obligation is to protect my daughter. When Macy turns eighteen, and if Steven wants to make contact with her, I can't prevent it. But I can see no benefit in introducing Steven into Macy's life until then."

Randall asks a few more questions to aid in drafting the legal document. He assures me he can get a copy for me by tomorrow, and he will have it dispatched to London by legal courier by the end of the following day.

"Is there anything else I should know or do, Deidre?" Randall asks as he rises to exit the room. "I need to know everything related to you, Steven, and Macy so that I can advise you thoroughly. Has he tried to contact you or Macy?"

"No, not that I am aware of. I know this is difficult, but I do appreciate your help."

"I think you are wise to use legal tools to guide you as you make decisions where Macy is concerned. I see too many situations that become unnecessarily complex and end up creating unnecessary hurt and drama. For men, it is an automatic reflex to lean on a lawyer. Women too often allow themselves to be swayed by their emotions and either do nothing or take the advice of a man who has a vested interest in a particular outcome."

I nod to acknowledge his message.

"And by the way, Deidre—if I was in your situation, I would do exactly what you want done."

~ ~ ~ ~ ~

I slip into a vacant passenger drop-off and pick-up spot at Cork Airport. Andres slips inside the car. I ask him if he is up for one stop before we head to Moran. He responds, "Why not?" and I speed away.

I maneuver us from the busy airport and head for Cork City. We exchange small talk as I traverse the narrow streets and hills. We zip up a street that unexpectedly makes a circle and turn down an even narrower road. Andres rolls the window down and looks out as I make my way along the waterfront and through the village neighborhoods that locals have occupied for a century. I come to a sudden halt. Andres looks out at a three-story stone church that looks as if it has seen better days.

"I know better than to ask, Deidre, if there is a purpose in this stop. Just trying to figure out what it might be since neither of us are regulars at any church," Andres says with his eyebrows raised and a look of irony on his face. I lead us to a back door and we make our way to the basement. As we walk down the creaky wooden steps, the sounds of Irish folk music drift up to greet us. Andres looks at me with a knowing smile. "Ahhh, a dance rehearsal. I should have known."

We pull up folding chairs, sit down, and watch as a middle-aged man takes charge alongside a younger woman. The male instructor calls out to the dancers who are already warming up and to the others who are still entering the hall. The warm-up is unlike anything Andres has seen before. Unlike ballet or modern dance, where dancers warm up with a variety of stretches and poses, this rehearsal begins with slow tap patterns and leg lifts. After a few moments, the lead female instructor changes the CD and calls out the name of the dance they are to run through.

The school-age dancers perform in unison to a fast eight and then twelve-step pattern, which at times looks like tap but segues into a series of kicks and fast turns. Andres notes that the energy comes from the dancer's core and moves down to the feet, with backs and arms remaining straight and still. Halfway through the piece, the dancers drop back and a solo male dancer performs an increasingly athletic version of the dance, after which he steps back and a female solo dancer takes the stage. Confining her movements from the core to the floor, she performs a series of quick spins and turns with ballet-like grace, then returns to the small, quick steps and kicks. All dancers reunite and complete the dance in unison with increased speed and athleticism.

Andres looks at me and his eyes reveal his astonishment. We thank the dancers and instructors and climb the basement steps to the street.

"So, Deidre, cut to the chase. What do you have in mind here?"

"I think you know, Andres. But let's wait until tomorrow morning to talk more. I have two tickets for an Irish *Céili* dance tonight. Let's go to Moran so you can unpack and rest. We will have dinner at the house as Colleen will never forgive me if we do not show you the proper hospitality after your long flight from the US. Then, we can make our way back to Cork City for the dance. What do you think?" I ask.

"Sounds like you have done your homework, Ms. Deidre Moran. I am in your hands." Andres slides the car seat as far back into a reclining position as he can, pulls his dark glasses firmly over his face, and falls into a hard sleep while I speed along the narrow, foliage-lined roads to Moran Manor.

The morning finds me sipping on tea in the breakfast room and waiting for Andres to make an appearance. Last night's dance performance had impressed him, but he commented on the drive home that he could not see how one could build a dance business around Irish traditional dance. I refused the bait and chose instead to focus on rest and restoration and then resume our conversation today.

Once Andres finished breakfast and reviewed *The Irish Times*, I suggest that we get some fresh air and walk the 100 steps to the green grass and bay below. Once outside, I begin my pitch.

"Have you been to Hawaii, Andres?" I ask.

"Sure, Deidre. But what in the world does Hawaii have to do with building a dance company in Ireland?" Andres asks impatiently.

"Elvis Presley," I respond.

"You are kidding, right?" Andres responds with a sarcastic look on his face.

"When Elvis Presley did his televised Hawaii concert in 1973, few people had ever been to Hawaii and fewer yet had been exposed to Hawaiian culture or music. That program set the mold for every big music production since. Presley integrated live video of the people at strategically selected Hawaiian locations, and highlighted hula dance and original music from the Islands. Sure, the main deal was Elvis and his music, but that television show launched Hawaii tourism and introduced the world to Hawaii."

I take a breath and watch the expression on Andres face to see how effective my argument is. "That same idea can be used for Irish dance."

Andres turns and looks directly into my eyes. "I would say you have failed to calculate the biggest asset in that analogy, Deidre. Presley was the magnet that made that entire thing work. He was an established moneymaker, back from the service, in his 30s, and looking like the biggest stud on the planet with unlimited appeal to the young female market who, at that time, were the prime purchasers of record albums. Do you even remember how that guy came across on the cameras?"

"We can build that here."

"You don't have a star with a proven track record," interrupts Andres. "You have no experience in producing television events—or music events, for that matter. You would have to start from dirt level and grow everything from nothing."

"Are you saying developing an Irish dance company with television production is impossible?"

"No, it's possible. But here is the short list, Deidre. You would need to find and develop a male Irish dancer with the kind of talent and sex appeal that Presley had and center your company around him. That may not appeal to your female sensibilities, but that would be key to any kind of initial success because the dance market is 100 percent female driven. And, you would have to acquire significant funding to hire top-notch television producers here in Ireland. And that will cost you. Last, you would have to look at this project as a very long-term endeavor. It will take years to launch and even more years to turn a profit."

Andres sits on the lawn when we reach the bottom of the concrete steps. He perches his arms on his legs for support and leans over to gaze out at the blue-green water of Bantry Bay. I continue to watch him as he glues his eyes over the horizon to the mountains beyond.

"You are right, Andres. I have not given serious thought to the barriers you identify straight away. But here's the thing. I want to remain here and raise Macy in Ireland. I do not want to give up my love for dance, and I am committed to bringing the best of a modern Ireland to tourists and visitors. When you say 'Ireland' to most Americans, they think of elves and thatched cottages with no running water and a little Irish jig—the old Ireland. But the Ireland I know is changing."

"So tell me, Deidre, in one succinct statement, what is your goal here?"

I recognize the drill. "I want to revolutionize the Irish jig into a modern international professional dance form," I reply, staring at him in the face. "And, I want you to buy me out of my partnership in North River."

"And your bottom line on how you will determine if your project is viable?" Andres asks.

"I will give it a year. After one year of planning and conducting a few trial balloons, I will take it to a board of directors—headed up by you—for a thumbs up or down. Thumbs up, we continue the development. Thumbs down, we disband."

"Funding?" Andres asks. "It will take a lot of money to start-up. There won't be a lot of profit taken from your share of North River. We are still in the building stage, and we still depend upon nonprofit funding sources to keep us going."

"There is always this." I wave my hand toward Moran Manor. "It would be a hard sell, but I am thinking it is going to come my way eventually. Or at least, I can convince my father to use some of the estate as collateral for a bank loan to keep us afloat. I think he will be willing as long as Macy remaining here is part of the deal. We have done this before, Andres. But I can't do this without you. You are the brilliance behind forging the right creative team."

~ ~ ~ ~ ~

Within a month, Andres pulled together a "forecasting team" to arrive at Moran Manor. Its purpose is to predict the likelihood of success based on available information. Colleen is not happy that I commandeered the banquet table for the team but, in the end, she understands the need for a large table and space to accommodate ten people. An art historian from Trinity College arrives with a slide show of what he considers to be the most salient art pieces from the Book of Kells exhibition at Trinity College, a major tourist draw. Two *Céili* dance directors play tapes from shows and analyze components of the music and dance as they connect to Ireland's history. But, it is the representatives from the European and American production teams that choreographed the Elvis Presley Hawaii special that really captures

Andres's attention. What hits home to Andres is how the Presley show's influence imprinted a strategy for formulating future lucrative concert shows both in Europe and the US.

I leave Andres to his thoughts for the next couple of days. I use this down time to fulfill my promise to spend more time with Macy and her pony. We walk to the old stone riding stable and make our way to where the ponies have recently been separated from their mothers. With help from a stable hand, I hoist Macy onto a honey-colored quarter pony and grab onto a lead rope. I walk Macy and pony around the riding circle. She sits upright with a serious expression on her face as she tries to match the rhythm of the pony's body as it walks. Learning to post is something that comes naturally with enough time on a horse. I tell myself I need to put all the energies of my life aside and settle into this moment with Macy and the pony in order to keep my daughter safe and—equally important—to enjoy this special moment.

The sun begins its slow descent and casts a warm glow over the back patio, where I sit with lemonade while Macy peels off her riding clothes and boots. With my feet stretched in front of me on a footstool, I gaze down at the garden that has been so carefully laid out. It is late spring and the flowers are already in full bloom. Years ago, a Moran uncle had studied the gardens at the French and Italian royal palaces. He copied the designs and procured plants from all over the world to design the garden as it exists today. I often chastise myself for not taking more interest in studying the various plants that I trampled upon as a child and then walked alongside with a novel in hand as a teenager during my trips home from Chicago. Andres quietly slips into a chaise longue beside me while I am still in my garden reverie. I open my eyes and find him staring at me. He looks relaxed and refreshed.

"Trying to catch me off guard and in a weak moment?" I tease him while at the same time trying to read his impressions of the long planning sessions. He reaches over to the glass pitcher sitting on a table next to me, grabs a companion glass, and fills it with lemonade. He slides his chair closer to me to erase any sense of distance between us and prepares himself to deal with yet another one of my over-the-top plans.

"My wild Irish Deidre, what can I say? Yes, it is a fabulous idea. An idea that would not have been plausible ten years ago. Your sense of seeing the future of dance as a broad display of entertainment connected with Irish history is brilliant. And it has the potential to be extremely lucrative. But it will require a long development curve before there is any kind of pay-out. And Deidre, there is a limit to what I can do and to what Sissy can do without me. I can't see how I can be a major player in bringing this concept alive in Ireland and still keep the dance companies and student workshops going in Chicago and New York."

He pauses and I wait. I am certain of the direction he is going to head in, and I am ready.

"Listen, Deidre," he says. "Don't take this wrong way, but why don't you just sit back and enjoy the spot you are in? You are a financially secure woman living on this fabulous estate that your family has had for hundreds of years that is bound to be yours someday. You have a precious child and a man who has been patiently waiting to make you an honest woman for most of his life. Why keep pushing yourself?"

I put my beverage glass down with such force that the contents erupt all over the patio table. "The answer to all of that is in three words, Andres: Because I can. I can build an Irish dance company to put Ireland on an international stage. Yes, I have money—a great deal of it, left to me by a thoughtful mother. That money is growing by leaps and bounds in any number of investments. But, the money is tied up. I can use it for some essentials, but the majority of it is earmarked for asset development. I can buy and build hotels like my father has done, or I can develop apartment or business complexes. Or, I can build another dance company. This one in Ireland, for Ireland."

"Money from your mother?"

"Yes. During the years when we were building the dance company, Catherine told me that my mother left me money and that I should just go and ask my father for it. That is the main reason she financed North River. She knew I would eventually get my hands on the inheritance, even if the dance company failed."

I take another sip of my drink before continuing. "I won't go into all of the details, but my father felt the money was his to manage for me even beyond the years it became rightfully mine. He is willing to pull a large part of it out of the investments he made here as long as I invest the money in an Irish business, preferably, his. So yes, while it is true that I am a wealthy woman in my own right, there are restrictions on how I can use the money."

I reach for the lemonade and refill my glass. "I am well aware that men have long thought I was rich because of my father's holdings and because of Moran. I have watched men come and go in my life, but when they figured out they were not going to be able to tidily transport me into their lives as one of the supporting characters to build their own interests, I suddenly stopped being so attractive. Some hung in there, thinking that the money was reason enough and that they could get their hands on it. I was sure to make a man know early in any relationship that my money was tied down. And, Andres, it became pretty much of a game for me to guess how many days it would take before the would-be suitor would suddenly have a change of life or heart," I add.

"Deidre, you must think I am a real jerk," Andres says. "Sissy told me right after you and I met about your unique situation, including your bi-continental Ireland-US life. Your situation is so extraordinary that I tend to forget it, but that does not excuse me for playing the just-stay-home-and-be-a-good-little-woman song."

"Before I let you off the hook, let me say one more thing. You are building your case around the fact that I have inherited wealth. But for just a minute, let's consider the overwhelming majority of women who do not have wealth. They may not have any money whatsoever."

I describe the state of affairs in Ireland, even the relatively modern Ireland of our day. "The blokes around here would say that if a woman has money, then it becomes the husband's, and the woman should stay home where she belongs. She doesn't need to be working. And for a long time, that was Irish law. Married women's assets became their husbands'. Yet, these same men use the same excuse when it comes to the majority of women in Ireland who have no money of their own. Then they make the case that these women, married or not, should stay home and do what they can do to make a contribution because they can't make enough money to get by even if they were to try. But what men really mean, whether they are Irish or American or European, is that women should not be working for pay and taking opportunities away from men." I am nearly holding my breath as I speak.

Andres stands, stoops over me, and gives me a hug, which I quickly return. "Sadly," he says, "I have to agree with your analysis of women in the workplace, even if it does make men look like prehistoric dinosaurs with bodies far larger than their brains."

"We've been too good of friends and business partners to let hurt feelings get in the way of us," I say softly.

A maid makes an appearance and asks if she can bring some cocktails. We look at one another and laugh before giving our consent. While we wait for the drinks to appear, Andres turns to me and says, as if he is talking just to himself, "It is up to me entirely. Am I in or out? I am absolutely sure that your mind is cast in stone regarding the Irish dance concept."

I smile at him and nod.

"Damn it, Deidre. You know who you remind me of? Scarlett O'Hara!"

"Who is Scarlett O'Hara?" I ask with little interest while sipping my drink.

"You don't know who Scarlett O'Hara is? She's a famous American literary heroine—full-blooded Irish, and stubborn just like you. Maybe you are more so—stubborn, I mean. You had better find out who she is because if you intend to go ahead with this, I won't be the only one who is going to make that comparison. You will hear it the first time an Irish-American man finds himself hitting heads with you as you try to convince him to invest in your damn Irish *Céili* dance company!"

The drinks arrive. We sit back in our chairs and watch the sun slip down over Bantry Bay. As it makes its fast journey into darkness, it casts a fuchsia pink that the waters reflect back into the skies.

"So, Deidre, what are you going to call the company?" Andres asks rather nonchalantly, his eyes still glued to the sunset.

"Hadn't thought that far. Maybe Cork Dance, Dublin Dance, or North River Ireland after the Chicago company? Or Moran Steps Dance?"

~ ~ ~ ~ ~

I rise in the morning, pull the cord on the drapes of the floor-length window, and gaze at the water and hills out of habit. I make the sign of the cross, another habit, touching my forehead, chest, left shoulder, and right shoulder, thinking that my current run of good luck might abruptly end. The ritual reminds me of how superstitious the Irish are, using all of the old and new to ward away evildoers or extend bright days.

Andres returned to the States after signing a preliminary legal document naming me as President of Moran Steps Dance with him as creative director. Our understanding is that he will hire Irish and British producers, some used by the Presley group, while I will work with Irish dance companies to identify dancers. North River will buy out my partnership at a negotiated price still to be determined.

No sooner is Andres on his way to Cork Airport than the new company begins to take over Moran's second floor. The housekeeper instructs maids and butlers to push furniture from the unoccupied bedrooms and set up temporary workspaces. My father, while skeptical of the Irish dance project, is delighted that I am over my head in a project that requires Macy and me to remain at Moran and in Ireland. He cannot understand why I do not pick a simpler path, one that would use my business skills and abilities at the Moran Hotels. But he will not question any decision that his hard-headed daughter makes if it means I am at home with Macy after living abroad for years.

Colleen, to my surprise, enthusiastically jumps in once she learns of the new endeavor. She pushes the staff to get the second-story rooms readied and queries my father about redesigning a back door entrance so that it will be both functional and formal in appearance. She does not feel that business people should be forced to go in and out by way of the gardeners' and housemaids' entrance, yet she has reservations about them using the front door. No more has my father nodded his head to assure Colleen he will contemplate such a change than Colleen takes the nod to be an affirmative decision. A reconstructed back entrance and two functional hallways are carved into the old manor.

Colleen's knock pulls me away from my thoughts. I turn from the window to my door, which opens a sliver at a time. In a low voice, she tells me that my attorney is in the front reception room. She shares that Randall told her a gardener asked him whether he worked for the dance company or the house as the back door is now the expected entry and he would find hallway signs to direct him from there. He chuckled when telling Colleen he'd attempted to stump the gardener by saying he was looking for the nursery.

"It's not good news Deidre," Randall begins as I close the study door. "Steven is going to fight for full custody."

"Why in the world?" I query in disbelief.

"I think a lot of it centers on pride. He already has a grown son, so it isn't that he is giving away a chance at being a father. And he certainly isn't in it for the money as he has wealth of his own, from what I understand. I can't really put a clear picture together, Deidre, as Steven's life is shrouded."

"I have not changed my position, Randall. I think he believes I will back down and he will be able to maneuver his way back into all of our lives."

The attorney withholds any sign of agreement. "But it could get ugly and very public, Deidre. Steven may think that he has nothing to lose, and public opinion would favor him. Bad publicity for a woman in Ireland, and London still works in the old way. People are willing to believe that a woman is in the wrong before they will accept such from a man, even though everyone knows of personal examples where men have harbored mistresses for years, believing it is their right as long as they provide for family and hearth. It's the old notion that men are weaker in that respect but a woman is to be pure and diligent in the kind of life she lives."

"You paint Steven as a private person who controls every part of his life," I say. "I don't see him exposing himself to the media. That's a perfect formula for sacrificing that control."

Randall moves his head slightly to the right, signaling a different opinion. "Steven would build a picture of a rather unconventional American-Irish woman of wealth who jet sets between the US and Ireland. It could be costly to your image, to say nothing of the doors that would close to Macy. I would advise you to do nothing, and by all means, never contact Steven or his attorneys personally. With your approval, Deidre, I will hire the best private investigator that money can buy. We need to uncover who this man really is. In the meantime, do not agree to meet with him under any circumstances."

I assure Randall that I hear his warning and then watch as he walks out the front door and across the lawn. Perhaps I should have said a full rosary in my bedroom this morning.

~ ~ ~ ~ ~

As Deidre heads back to her bedroom, Patrick emerges from his second-floor bedroom and makes his way down the expansive staircase to the main floor. He is still in his cotton pajamas and is covered with a long robe. His worn leather slippers with rubber soles allow him to find his way to the study without making a sound. His age requires him to take a slower wake-up gait than he used to since blood must circulate to his nerves and cells before the arthritis pain subsides in his knees and feet. He knows that he should lose some weight and exercise regularly but, like many Irish men, his love for Jameson, Guinness, Irish cheese, and sandwiches get the best of him.

His doctor of many years has warned him that his heart shows signs of disease and weakness. Ignoring it will not make it go away. He hides the entirety of this from Colleen and his daughter. The last thing he wants is two women monitoring and directing him in the simple pleasures of his life, pleasures that he considers to be essential. He has no intention of giving up his favorite spirits and culinary delights by restricting his consumption.

He closes the heavy door and is relieved to see that Deidre has not commandeered the study. Now that she has working office areas upstairs, he finds he can return the study as a private sanctuary for his exclusive use. He had prompted Deidre when he asked her if she was finished using the study. She understood his meaning.

He muses to himself as he sits at the desk and gazes around the room at the paintings of Moran elders now in their graves. They would be pleased that the house is filled with the energy that was customary during their reign. In their day, the house was filled to the brim with the master's family, his wife's mother, and an assortment of extraneous family who preferred to be cared for by the estate rather than strike out on their own.

He smiles as he imagines how his sister Colleen, who has served in the role as mistress of Moran since his wife died, might have handled managing a house staff of thirty or more in Moran's heyday. She seems more than pleased that the house is fully occupied and being put to its proper use. "No sadder thing to see than a house that was meant to serve people sitting barren," she often mutters to Patrick when he raises his eyebrows at the newest house project or invasion of relatives, friends, and now Deidre's business endeavor.

Patrick adheres to the masculine principle that his house is his castle and serious work should be done at a place of business. He leans back in his chair, smiles slightly, and admits to himself that the argument over the proper use of the house is just another in the long list of arguments he has lost to Colleen and his increasingly assertive and confident daughter over the years. But times have indeed changed, and he reminds himself that he has been a willing participant in his daughter's modern upbringing by sending her to the States to be raised and educated while protecting her from the messages that Irish girls receive regarding their proper place.

He pushes his chair back, rises, and pulls the worn call cord to ring the kitchen. Within minutes, a kitchen maid appears with a tray of his favorite coffee, which is as strong as whiskey, and pieces of freshly made soda bread slathered with soft butter made from the milk of cows raised on the estate. Once again seated at his desk and in front of the wall-sized window, he watches as the sun climbs over the hills and mountains and burns off the heavy fog that sits over the bay.

He has to confess that the current scenario is not what he had in mind when he pushed for Deidre to remain in Ireland and raise his granddaughter at Moran. But watching the gradual transformation in Deidre, he has become her most ardent fan. He is also the strongest supporter of her endeavor to build a traditional Irish dance company even though he cannot see how it will be financially sustainable. Still, once he saw how Andres had piled on the project and how launching the company had fueled Deidre's renewed enthusiasm and energy, Patrick became a strong believer that Irish dance might be the very thing to heal his badly bruised daughter, profitable or not. The real jewel in the Irish dance haystack is that Macy's home is now in the very place where she is meant to be: Moran Manor. Patrick soaks in all of the four-year-old's laughter, which bounces off of the relic walls of every room in which she plays. He can only smile at each of the demands she makes as he hurries to make the child happy and secure.

Deidre has shared with him bits and pieces of the latest maneuvers concerning Steven, and he is aware that his attorney meets with Deidre often. He knows better than to ask Randall for an update, as the lawyer is old school and respects every client's rights, even when the client is another client's daughter. In time, Deidre will share the final arrangements concerning Macy and Steven. Until then, and for all time, Patrick will use any resource and influence that he can to make Macy happy.

Patrick finishes his breakfast and gazes at the grandfather clock across the room. At exactly eight o'clock a.m., he picks up the phone and begins to orchestrate his work day. When Brenda answers, he asks her to clear her morning schedule. He wants a couple of hours to go through some issues she brought to his attention that impact both the Cork and Dublin hotels. He also makes a mental note to call Colleen when he reaches the hotel to tell her he will not be home for dinner. He smiles in anticipation of his evening with Mrs. Dylan, his favorite female companion. He cannot imagine a life without the comforts of a woman who provides him access to a more intimate home than the rambling Moran house, yet he has no desire to marry a second time. Burying one wife is enough for him.

Patrick makes a few more calls that take a minute each, gathers up his briefcase, and slips out of the newly constructed back door exit, which, he has to admit, is the best new addition to the house. Why had it not occurred to him to construct such a convenient way to slip out of the house undetected by Colleen years ago?

~ ~ ~ ~ ~

Once introduced to the back door with its two corridors, Cory finds himself using it exclusively. Using the front door means having to confront Edwin or, if she gets there faster, Colleen. This seems like an unnecessary layer to Cory, who is used to things being simple and direct.

Taking the hallway that leads to the kitchen, he greets the cook and kitchen help, grabs a cup of coffee from the coffee maker, and asks if someone would be so kind as to let Deidre know he is in the kitchen. The cook gives him a disconcerting look and asks if he thinks she has nothing better to do than wait on a local man's social life when there is a house full of people who need three meals plus snacks and teas. Cory flashes a smile and a wink at the youngest kitchen assistant, and she quickly runs up to the first floor to catch Deidre.

Once out of the house with Cory carrying my small overnight bag, I tease him that I am on to his game. He avoids the front door so he can avoid Colleen, but he slips down to the kitchen so he will be noticed by the young girls who are certain to love his smiles and teases. He does not argue with my observation. Instead, he reminds me that is just one of the many reasons that I find him irresistible.

For the first time since Macy and I moved to Moran, Cory and I are slipping away for an entire weekend alone. He has set down the rules: no meeting up with other friends, no Macy, and no work business of any kind for either of us. I do not need convincing. I welcome escaping the Moran side of things in favor of spending time with Cory in the Cork countryside.

Cory rented a small cottage nestled in the hills of Skibbereen, a small village on the edge of the ocean. Like an ice cream eaten outside on a hot day, the afternoon hours melt away in what seems to be minutes. Cory has anchored his boat in a slip at a local marina, something easily accomplished as he has connections at every port around West Cork. Following an afternoon of sailing along the coast, drinking beer on board, and napping in the lower cabin, Cory sails back into port while the sun is still strong in the summer sky. Once off the boat, we head toward Skibbereen and go to a small, family restaurant hidden from the buses that clog the narrow roads and village towns in late August.

I know that Cory has more in mind that just smuggling the two of us away from Moran and all of its distractions. I am prepared to engage in a serious conversation about our future as a committed couple. Each time I think about how and where we could construct a private life of our own, I become bogged down in self-doubt. My father would be delighted if I moved Cory into Moran. It would be easy on my family and the best solution where Macy is concerned—at least, that would be my father's position, particularly since I have set up my business there as well.

But I do not see how Cory will fit into being the most recent player in the various Moran dramas. To be honest, I can't see myself there with a new husband, either. I married Steven at Moran and hoped to have some kind of life with him there when not in Chicago and London. Somehow, starting over with Cory at Moran has more negative associations than what I feel we could overcome. I want to find a nest all our own.

I follow Cory toward the back of the eatery as he makes small talk with the waitress, whom he obviously knows. My skin is hot and burned from the day's activities on the water. I neglected my usual sunscreen addiction as we were out of the elements and inside napping on the boat for a fair amount of time. My straight hair, disheveled by the wind and ocean air, has lost its center part and large strands cover my face.

"This place has great clams and the best stew I have ever had outside of my grandmother's kitchen," Cory says. "And I told the waitress I would slip some extra on her tip if she will keep these two back tables empty until we leave."

"If you feel that is really necessary," I reply to his concern for privacy.

"It is. You never know when one of those tour buses will unload fifty people in front of this place for an hour. God, I hate those buses. I know a lot of folks in these Cork villages depend on tourists to pay the bulk of their bills, but that doesn't mean I have to sit right in the middle of them. And clog the roads, don't they? You have to add one hour to any drive just in case you get caught up in the middle of a tourist caravan! And those same tourists complain about our cows blocking the roads!"

"Well, I am happy to hear that you at least acknowledge the importance of tourists to the island, Cory. You are among those who complain at the inconvenience of visitors, but I bet you aren't shy about taking the money that comes your way from their business."

Years ago, I established the habit of pushing back against Cory when his opinions differed from my own. By now, he expects it and enjoys the banter. It is one of the things he claims is attractive about me. So many of the girls he has known agree with anything he says just to smooth over the moment so they can get to the next date and then to the next month, hoping a wedding ring will be in the deal down the road.

Our meal arrives at the table and half a dozen pints of Guinness disappear. Once the waitress clears the dishes and leaves us alone, Cory leans across the table and clasps my hands in his own. I instantly become self-conscious and try to retract my hands so I can at least smooth down my hair or, better yet, escape to the women's bathroom where I can do a proper once-over. But Cory will not release me.

"I am awed by the natural beauty that is Deidre Moran. I see a woman with thick, straight red hair that frames azure eyes and high cheekbones. Her strength, both physical and intellectual, is my match and maybe more, and I am challenged by that in a good way. I admit that I do not know how I would have managed being pulled away from the country and land I loved as a child to be raised in a foreign country, no matter how well-heeled the situation was. But you have survived, and the traits that drew you to me as a childhood playmate have grown stronger and increasingly attractive to me."

He openly admits that most of his friends seek mild, traditionally oriented girls to marry; he has heard them say time and time again how that type of woman can be controlled. But he knows that controlled and boring is the last thing he will get with me, and it is not what he is looking for in a lover and partner.

Cory looks straight into my eyes. "Let's cut to the chase, girl. I have been running after you for a lifetime. Let's call it a damn tie. What do you have in mind in our living arrangement? Tell me what you want, don't want. I don't care. I just know this is bound to be a bit more complicated than dealing with an ordinary Irish lass who has lived at home in a small cottage with a large family all of her life and would trade away her best hat and rosary to move out of the house. I have just one condition. We don't move away from this table until we reach a mutually agreeable understanding."

"I am ready, Cory. And I love the force of your intent. I've been thinking that..."

The waitress turns her head from the table that she is serving to check on the handsome Cory in the back of the room. She sees the way he clasps the woman's hands in his. She also sees his head move into hers so that they are nearly touching. And most of all, she sees the look on his face as he listens intently to every word she says.

She turns away and heads toward the small service center near the kitchen, thinking that one of the best catches in Cork has just been reeled in.

~ ~ ~ ~ ~

Autumn weather in West Cork generally provides a mix of sun, rain, and fog. But this particular fall, the rain holds off until evenings. The fog lifts early in the morning and does not return until the middle of the night, leaving sunny and balmy days. I exit my car and climb the hill to where the construction crew is hard at work. The building began a month ago. The basement is already done, the rooms are framed up, and the roof is well underway.

For the first time in months if not years, I feel a sense of unrestrained exhilaration and joy. When I told my father and Colleen about our dream to build a one-story brick ranch house overlooking the sea on the outskirts of Schull, they were smart enough not to respond negatively. But privately, Colleen had commented to my father that at first appearance, the plan seemed like nothing but a distraction. Certainly, I was not going to actually live in such a small house and run back and forth between Moran and Schull. That would get old fast.

But I remained solid in my vision of raising Macy in a small home with Cory. I rather like the idea of all of us bumping into one another and not having multiple empty rooms to serve as isolating spaces, which is what happens at Moran more often than not. I seek to imitate the coziness of my Aunt Catherine and Sissy's homes in Evanston, but I also want my new family to be at Moran as much as possible. I crave intimacy in our living arrangement so I have said little more to my father and Colleen. The construction foreman has promised the house will be finished and ready to move into when spring returns to West Cork next year.

I wear the Celtic cross ring on my left hand, a promise to Cory that we will celebrate our new life in a commitment celebration. But

I have pushed him off of a formal wedding, at least for a few years, if indeed that. I have made it clear to Cory that while I love him with all of my heart, I cannot see my way clear to a traditional marriage. Indeed, why does it matter? We are committed to one another and financially independent, meaning he does not need my money and I do not need his. Still, I promised to reconsider a formal marriage if a new baby were to suddenly enter the picture—but I doubt very much there will be another baby given my age. Until that time, I am eager to begin my life with Cory at a celebration in our new home when spring turns the corner.

When friends question Cory about our marriage plans, he tells them that he is plumb worn out from chasing me all of these years. If I want to tie the knot officially, I would have to be the one to propose. And that seems to work well enough.

Donning high riding boots to protect my feet from the boards, nails, and debris that accompany construction sites, I walk through the center section that will comprise the home's large entryway and front room. As I walk in the direction of the sea, I enter into what is to be a huge kitchen. On either side of the center section, there will be wings housing bedrooms and baths. One wing is intended for Cory and me and with two extra bedrooms for what I hope will be infrequent guests. The other wing will house two bedrooms and a playroom, or what Cory calls "the young'un's quarters." As I continue my walk through the remainder of the house, what I see is on a much smaller scale than what I have been used to—but that is exactly the plan. I have no need to recreate Moran.

"Deidre girl," Cory calls in a sing-song fashion. I turn in his direction, but not before he catches me, lifts me off of my feet, and swings me around in two complete circles. With his arms still wrapped completely around me, he leads me into the soon-to-be kitchen. He nuzzles his head into my wind-mussed hair and pulls my cotton sweater over my head, mentioning that it is time we cook up something hot and sweet.

With my sweater removed, he peels off one bra strap and then the other before unhooking my bra from behind. Lifting my round, heavy breasts into his hands, he drags both of us to our knees. He circles his hands around the small of my back, pushing me into a slight backbend as he sucks hard on one nipple and then the other. I moan with delight. I slide my body underneath Cory and wiggle out of my jeans and bikini lingerie. Cory wastes no time pulling his shirt and jeans off and throwing them into the air. I pull Cory on top of me, and then roll over to mount him in a sitting position. I ride Cory softly, then hard. At times, I roll off to one side and the other. When I think he might come inside me, I lift my hips and pelvis entirely off of him and then push him back inside. At some point, Cory grabs me and demands that he be on top. He pushes me underneath his body and pushes himself inside of me in waves until we simultaneously experience the heat of orgasm. Cory lays on top of me until the lack of oxygen causes me to suddenly gasp. Exhausted, we fall asleep until the chill on the floor wakes us.

At first, I am disoriented, uncertain as to where I am. The room is dark. Cory's eyes partially open and he has a smile on his face. I turn my head to Cory and warn him that we need to stop meeting in out-of-the-way fields and construction sites—we really need to grow up. Cory turns his head and meets my eyes. With a full grin on his face, he assures me that he has no intention of taming either one of us.

~ ~ ~ ~ ~

Life at Moran Manor has settled into a predictably harried pace. Meals are prepared at regularly scheduled times, and it is assumed that the cook will serve a full dinner at six o'clock each evening, an hour earlier than what has traditionally been done at Moran, to accommodate our diverse work schedules: mine, my father's, and Cory's. We take for granted that Cory will be part of our evening dinner unless he notifies us that he has other plans. Additional phone lines with separate numbers are installed to provide service directly to the second floor thus securing the lines downstairs for use by family members only.

I coordinate my calendar with Colleen, providing schedules for Macy, the dance business, and private engagements. I suggest to Colleen during an unusually difficult planning session that perhaps it is time for me to hire a personal secretary to take over those events connected to the dance business, thus freeing Colleen to coordinate Macy and the family calendar. Colleen initially appears miffed at my suggestion, but she catches me on the main staircase terrace later in the day and admits that it is probably best to proceed with hiring yet another staff person who will use the backdoor path to the second floor.

Since Macy has begun a preschool program in the village, Colleen notes that it is more important for her to monitor Macy's day when I am working and to continue her responsibilities as unofficial mistress of Moran. Taking advantage of Colleen's unusual flexibility, I use the opportunity to suggest that she may want to hire a day housekeeper once again, reinstating the position that Colleen has absorbed for herself. Putting my arm around her shoulders, I remind Colleen that she is, after all, a member of the family, and her value as such is most judiciously used in direct contact with us. Colleen remains quiet and does not indicate her opinion of my suggestion one way or the other.

As men are prone to do, my father and Cory fall into highly predictable routines. Father rises several hours before any of us, defending his alone time in his study with coffee and breakfast served on a tray before heading out to begin his day. Since I have returned to

Ireland with Macy, he condenses his work day so it ends mid-afternoon, returning home to spend some private time with his granddaughter or have afternoon tea with family members that are home at the time. Colleen had raised her eyebrows the first time he cut his day short and returned home. He had dropped his briefcase on the entryway table and begun searching the house when he ran into Colleen. He asked for Macy but was told she had gone out for a walk with her nanny.

While my father did not ask that Macy be kept close to home mid-afternoons, Colleen knows her brother as well as the fingers on her hands. He would not change a long-established pattern without intending to replace it with another. On the third afternoon of arriving home early, he did not have to question the child's availability. Macy picked up on the new ritual and, as children will do, checks in with her grandfather at the end of every afternoon to make sure he will come home early the following afternoon to take her riding.

My father soaks in Macy's excitement as he lifts her into her child-size saddle and tightens down her stirrups. Each time he hears Macy laugh during their afternoons together, he silently congratulates himself for significantly expanding the numbers of hotel employees. He takes Brenda's advice, once she presents a detailed rationale, on just about everything regarding the running of the Moran hotels in Cork and Dublin. He has come to rely on her as his right-hand "man" and is fond of telling her so.

It is Cory's life that has taken the most dramatic turn. As a bachelor used to being on his own all of the time, he finds for the first time in his life that others depend upon his presence at designated times in the day. And he likes the feeling. He meets with me nearly every day in Schull at our construction site and looks forward to dinners with family each evening.

I suggested that he move into one of the available bedrooms at Moran, but he is not comfortable with the unintended signal that his presence may send to the house staff or, more to the point, to my father. He refused my offer with the excuse that he would not leave my bed to go to his own early in the morning just for the appearance of propriety. He prefers to stay in his bachelor cottage until March, when we will both leave our current living quarters for our new house by the sea. Until then, he assures me that he rather enjoys his gentle breaking-in as a captured stallion that has been put on a long lead.

I am closing out a long day in my newly appointed office on the second floor when the phone rings. "Hi Deidre, it's Sissy. Is it too late to talk about all the exciting things going on in Cork?"

"Sissy, it is so good to hear your voice. I can't tell you how many times you come to mind as I go through my day. All the phone calls around here have been from construction contractors lately. And I am sure Andres has given you all the latest on the Irish dance concept."

"Yes, he has. And I have to say, I think the idea is hot. It is the reason I am bothering you so late in your day, Deidre."

I sit back in my chair, readying myself for a long chat with my life-long friend and co-conspirator. I listen to Sissy and can hardly believe what she is sharing.

"Sissy, are you absolutely sure that this is what you want to do? Because you have to know that I am going to encourage you one-hundred percent. I could not be happier."

"I could not be surer about anything, other than how crazy I am about the two of you. I would love the opportunity to work with you to build the dance side of this idea—to work on the ground in Ireland and coordinate all of the dance-related activities. And yes, I am sure, Deidre. A ballet dancer's stage life is short, and I am nearly ready to expire.

Rather than do the customary exit from the stage to own and work at a dance studio here in Chicago, your idea is far more exciting," Sissy says.

"And Andres?" I ask. "How does he feel about you living over here and leaving him in Chicago?"

"He wasn't crazy about it at first, but he thinks no one is better qualified than me to do the work that is necessary on the ground in Ireland. Our days and evenings are spent apart as it is since he puts in extremely long work days, which often go into the late evenings, so our lifestyle resembles single people who are friends. And he knows that it will be for a finite period of time, just until the dance production gets to a level where my contribution will not be needed. In the meantime..." Sissy's voice drifts off.

I complete her sentence. "In the meantime, you can come to Cork, live at Moran, and spend your days building Moran Steps Dance and spend your evenings with me, Macy, and Cory—when we can pin him down. And I can't wait to show you the house..."

I detail all that is happening in my life—a life that, I confessed to Sissy many years ago, I had wondered if I was destined to live alone. I return the phone to its cradle and smile because things have taken such an unpredictable turn. Sissy will be at Moran working with me to boot up Moran Steps Dance. It seems too good to be true.

As is my life-long habit, I wonder what storm is just down the road to put a damper on my high spirits, and I know the answer to my self-imposed inquiry: Steven. My gut warns me that whatever my attorney and the private investigator bring to the surface, it will be dark. But I stop myself from hitting the emotional panic button. I already know that the real Steven is far from being the man he presented to me and to my family. When the real Steven is brought to light, I will accept it without being surprised.

Most importantly, I am learning to be kinder to myself. I have realized that trusting Steven when we first met does not reflect badly on me or my judgment. It is Steven who has engaged in deceit, not me. Whatever is uncovered about Steven's true nature, I will accept it without punishing myself. I will move on and keep my energy focused on Macy, Cory, and building this new life in Ireland.

~ ~ ~ ~ ~

Brenda looks at her wristwatch when she sees Patrick walk into the hotel entrance. She notices that he is at the hotel earlier and earlier and that there are fewer days when he works from home, as was his previous pattern.

Years have passed since Brenda was hired, and during that time, she has come to play a major role in how the Moran hotels operate. She doubled the number of hotel employees by adding housekeepers, kitchen help, front desk staff, and concierge to the mix, all of which transform the feel of the hotel into more than just a place to sleep.

Convincing Patrick to double the rates and aim at becoming the top-tier hotel chain in Cork and Dublin had been one of the most difficult challenges, along with hiring the best concierge staff. Brenda had brought in a hotel sales expert to make the pitch instead of trying to convince him herself. The expert persuaded Patrick that a top-notch concierge would not only book restaurant reservations and cabs for the guests but would also cater to high-end clients by securing last minute tickets to sold-out exhibits in Dublin or the Book of Kells tour at Trinity College.

But even as Patrick had been somewhat in doubt about the concierge idea, the biggest change was the number of women travelers who stayed at the hotel, both for business and vacation. In a glitzy slide presentation, the expert gave examples of women using concierge services at New York hotels and demonstrated how concierge excel at getting women to their destinations without having to wait for a husband—or, when traveling without a male companion, making them feel safe and secure in attending their desired events rather than being held captive in a five-star-hotel bedroom.

She reminds herself that any changes on the horizon will be miniature in comparison to the one Patrick had finally made: removing Michael from the hotels altogether. As the changes continued to ramp up at Moran Hotel-Dublin, he became increasingly more irritable and inappropriate. He blew up at any mention of new services and strategies aligned with increasing women clientele at the hotels. Brenda did not know what strategy Patrick had used to finally move him out, but she was thankful for his insight and action. He had telephoned her late one night from his Moran home office telling her to find a replacement for Michael. She had quickly done just that, acting before Patrick had a chance to change his mind.

Brenda enters Patrick's office. "Have a seat, Brenda." He points to the chair across from his desk. "It seems things are moving along well in both Cork and Dublin. And I have to hand it to you, Brenda. You were right with pushing me in this direction. I recently read an article in the *The Times* about how the hotels that do well are those that have catered to tourism, especially American tourism. I read specifically about the need for highly personalized services."

Seizing the opening, Brenda picks up the topic and carries it further. "Thank you, Patrick. But that is what you hired me for—to increase bookings and tap into a changing market. While we are on that topic, I would like to push a little bit further, if I may," she states more than asks.

Brenda pushes a thin leather notebook across the table and asks him to review the most recent report on hotel reservations. The report presents tables that show reservations by date and month, and it includes information about whether each guest was a business or leisure traveler. The report also includes gender information for the person who paid for the room and services.

"You can see two distinct trends in this data," Brenda says. "The first one is that the number of female business travelers is up significantly, and the duration of stay is increasing. The second most notable pattern is that the number of women making reservations for leisure travel is also up, even more so than the numbers for female business travelers. I met with our new concierge manager last week. He reviewed our customer requests and said that he had no difficulty making connections with the golf courses for golf reservations, even at the last minute if the client is flexible with the time."

She pauses, anticipating that Patrick may have one of his usual objections. Hearing none, she continues. "Requests have come up for finer cultural entertainment that includes writers, dancers, and concerts as opposed to pubs and drinking songs. Patrick, it comes up as a women's entertainment venue, but concierge says they also get requests for dance, massage, and exercise classes taught by women for women. As you already mentioned, the push is for finding those activities that appeal to the woman traveler over and above what we have arranged for in the past."

Patrick sits back in his chair. "You know, Brenda, don't get me wrong, but since you have come on board, the pace of work has tripled and expenses are way up—but so are the revenues. I think back to the days when I would come into the hotel at either Cork or Dublin, greet the one person at reception, and head for the office. Back then, things moved at a slow and predictable pace. I used to tell the staff when a customer asked for something out of the ordinary to say we don't provide that at this hotel, very sorry, and leave it at that. Now, every time a customer asks for something we don't deliver, it is logged in and every effort is made to meet the request, including routing the traveler to another hotel. That would have been unthinkable ten years ago as no hotel provided much more than a room with a bed, a hot bath, a full Irish breakfast in the dining room, and a taxi run to the pub."

Patrick puts the report back into the leather notebook and slides it across the desk to Brenda.

"I have a suggestion, Patrick, that may give us a kick start. The word is out that Deidre is working on putting together a dance company in Ireland. She no doubt has contacts in the dance community. Would she be willing to have one of her people work with our concierge director in identifying a list of events that we can advertise?" Brenda begins with the dance connection, thinking that Patrick will be more responsive to it than the other areas she has brought to his attention.

"Damn, Brenda, so you are thinking we are now going to get into the dance and entertainment businesses, too? I thought I was running a hotel business in Cork and Dublin, not a dance studio." He complains, all the while knowing he will follow through with her request. "Why can't we give visitors the Ireland we all know, the one that does not change!" He says this as a statement rather than as a question. He nevertheless adjusts his attitude and adds, "I guess it won't hurt if I talk with Deidre about your idea. But don't be surprised if she does not have time for this, given everything else she is focused on with getting that damn dance company up and going."

Brenda knows not to push the topic any further. She quickly stands, picks up the notebook, and nods to Patrick. She is on her way out of his office when he abruptly calls her back.

"Brenda, you will let me know right away if you decide to make any changes in your personal life, won't you?"

Brenda scrunches her eyebrows together, not following Patrick's new conversational drift.

"What I mean is, if you decide to get married, you will let me know immediately? While I stomp my feet about every new request you make, you have to know that I think you have really made all of the Moran hotels more financially successful. But Brenda, women don't work once they marry here in Ireland." He explains to make her understand his awkward request.

"No, I did not know that, Patrick," she smiles at him slyly. Of course, she knows that the archaic Irish tradition is being carved away a little bit at a time as the law that prohibited married women from working outside of the home was dropped. "I will let you know the minute I know if I am about to walk down the aisle. But Patrick, I am not Irish. I am not required to follow the outdated tradition that some men still expect Irish women to comply with, and I won't. Maybe in the next couple of years, more and more Irish women will throw that old custom along the side of the road where it belongs. That is another reason you were smart in hiring someone from America." Brenda smiles.

She understands what Patrick means by leaving the old Ireland alone. But she also knows that a big part of Ireland's economic troubles are just that: resistance to change. She has to give Patrick credit for pushing through his traditionally held beliefs and following his business instinct. And she laughs out loud when she thinks of his request to notify him immediately if she decides to marry as she will not be easily replaced. As if she would quit working just because she gets married!

~ ~ ~ ~ ~

There is a knock on the door of the second-floor bedroom that has been converted into my office. I call out for the visitor to come in. I am surprised to see my father as he has not been to the second floor's business wing to date and he is the last person I expect to see. He quickly surveys the room and notices that the ancient damask drapes are still on the window and an antique dresser is still tucked into the corner where it has always been. But I have moved a glass-top desk into the space where a large bed had been for years. A state-of-the-art-electric typewriter sits in the middle of the desk along with a detachable and movable phone. No cords for me; nothing to tie me down. A large calendar is tacked to a wall-size bulletin board, and flow charts and to-do lists completely fill the space.

My father explains his executive manager's request. I see he is a bit leery about running the dance and entertainment idea by me. I quickly assure him that it is a splendid idea and something that we do all the time in Chicago. Professional athletic teams have carried such a position for years; the dance and cultural world had simply stolen the move from their playbook.

I also tell my father that Sissy will be coming to Cork to play a major role in launching the dance company. I know that my father has developed an unusually cordial relationship with her, and he seems delighted that someone from my Chicago inner circle will be transplanted to Moran.

"Look, Dad. Just as soon as Sissy arrives, I will send her over to the hotel to talk with Brenda about the promotional strategies we use in Chicago that you can adopt here. Sound good?"

My father smiles. "Sure." He heads down the two flights of stairs to find Macy. He is beginning to see me in another light, one that he continually fights against. I am obviously a successful businesswoman in addition to being the mother of his sole grandchild. Yet, he still cannot free the lock on his heart to tell me so.

Chicago, 1981

The view of Lake Michigan from the high-rise condominium is one of the things Sissy will miss most. She and Andres moved into what had been Deidre and Steven's place when Deidre moved to her house in Evanston. From Sissy's perch in front of the living room window, she watches red, yellow, and white sails dart over the water as sailors enjoy the last of the late autumn days. She returns to her bedroom and examines the contents of her suitcase, which lies on the bed. Deidre—who is in town to help with Sissy's transition to Ireland—has encouraged her to pack light. Once Sissy adjusts to Ireland's cool and rainy fall weather, she is sure to trade most of her Chicago wardrobe for one that includes the woolens and modern weaves common in Ireland.

Sissy anticipated that Andres would have a change of heart and decide that he needed her to remain in Chicago. But he has not. True, their lives center completely around North River and dance—to the exclusion of just about everything else, including having a family of their own. Neither one of them had pushed the other to slow down, nor had they ever had a serious conversation about having a baby. Each had thought the other would bring up the subject when it became a burning desire. But neither she nor Andres ever did. And, at the age of forty-four, she holds no regrets about her childless state.

Sissy gives up packing and stretches out on the bed. When Andres first began talking about the possibility of growing yet another dance company in Ireland, Sissy's first thought had been that she would like to play an active part in the work. As she stares at the ceiling, she thought about her long career in ballet and the dance world. As a young twenty-year-old fresh from college, she never expected to be as successful as she proved to be, particularly when she joined Andres's company. She rose to a solo dancer and starred in all of the roles she had watched other dancers do in complete envy and admiration. She had collaborated with the New York City Ballet and the American Ballet Theatre and performed all of her favorites, including *Giselle.*

She thought she would be prepared to release her prima dance career to younger dancers. But she found that moving away from center stage to conducting rehearsals was not the easy move as she had told herself it would be. She had watched other ballet dancers go through the "retirement" transition, so she expected to be no different. But it was different. It was painful and continues to be. When the opportunity arose to leave Chicago and the US dance scene to work in Ireland with her very best friend, she knew she had to take the leap.

Sissy and Deidre had worked side by side from the time they were eighteen years old at Northwestern. Sissy admits that her pain is as much about missing Deidre as it is about leaving her role as a major dancer. They have shared all of the highs together and have been there for each other through major life-altering events. Sissy grimaces into her pillow with the reminder that she and Deidre are midlife friends and not young women anymore. Making a fast dance-like transition, Sissy leaps off of the bed she shares with Andres and closes the suitcase without giving packing another thought. Deidre is right. She will buy clothes in Cork and let the shop women costume her for her new role.

The buzzer to the apartment sounds and Deidre, who had spent the morning at North River with Andres tying up loose ends, asks if Sissy needs help with her luggage. In no time, the suitcases are loaded into the cab and the women huddle together in the back seat.

"Sissy," Deidre says, "as I have been moving my life back to Ireland, one thought keeps resurfacing and haunting me at the most unpredictable times. I know this is not on our itinerary, but I am hoping you will accompany me on this one stop."

~ ~ ~ ~ ~

The driver announces that we have arrived at the police precinct. Sissy and I head inside. What we find seems like chaos. Ringing phones go unanswered and a hundred conversations go on at once. Uniformed police accompany adults, teenagers, and children as they pass through the corridors. Business-suited women sit with individuals in varying states of emotional distress. Parents showing varying degrees of distress wait in chairs, and others are calm and patient, as if they are waiting in a line that they have found themselves in many times before.

I look past the zoo of humans, walk to the main reception desk, and ask to speak with a female officer. When asked what it is in regard to, I reply that it is an unsolved crime.

Once inside the small conference room with Sissy and a woman officer, I detail the night years ago when I was brutally attacked and raped. I describe it in such a way that it seems like the attack has just happened. The sounds from the streets, the intruder's smell, and the pounding of my heart are present in the confined space that Sissy, the policewoman, and I now occupy. As I talk, the officer records every detail and alternates her gaze from a notebook to Sissy to looking me directly in the eyes. I end my story with an apology for not reporting the crime when it occurred. I know it could have helped other girls, as I have come to understand over the years that a violent stranger rapist is likely to rape one victim after another until he is stopped. Sissy holds her head down, emotionally overcome by my confession. It seems to her that I feel as guilty as any criminal held in a precinct jail.

The officer asks if she can bring a female assault counselor into the room to talk with us. I refuse, adding that I have been in therapy with a woman therapist on and off for years. I do ask the policewoman whether a man with such a profile has been convicted. We leave the precinct with a promise that the officer will contact me if she has something to share.

We walk from the precinct to the cab in silence. Both of us are numb and re-living those awful days in the basement apartment all over again. We complete our carefully compiled errand list and are seated for lunch at our favorite café, which is not far from North River, when the manager notifies me that she has a call from the dance studio.

After lunch, we jump back in the cab to head to O'Hare International, but I ask the driver to make an unexpected stop first. He does, and he waits while we walk into the precinct for the second time that day. Once we are checked in at the main reception desk, we are led into a private conference room and greeted by the waiting policewoman.

"I never expected to get a call back quite this fast."

The officer smiles and acknowledges that she knows we are trying to catch an international flight. "This won't take long, Ms. Moran."

"It is common that survivors of a rape can remember the details of the crime no matter how much time has gone by. You are no different, Ms. Moran. When I sent an email out to detectives at the precinct who worked on assault and rape crimes twenty years ago, your description of what the perpetrator did after he attacked you caught the attention of a senior detective who worked the Michigan Avenue neighborhood back then."

Sissy and I wait to hear which part of my story ignited a memory trace in the detective. "He showed you pictures of his wife and kids," the officer explains. "That is unforgettable and stands out among the rape reports we get in."

The officer watch for a response but, seeing none, goes on. "He was caught, convicted of multiple attacks, and sent to a state prison in Illinois. The evidence provided by one of the victims is what got him to a lineup and eventually locked up. Just as you described in your assault, the perpetrator got out his wallet to show her his wife and kids. She took a really good look and flipped the photos around to see if she could get a glimpse of his driver's license. The assailant grabbed the wallet back, sensing what she was doing."

"That girl had courage in excess. All I could think of was to go along so he would not hurt me anymore and would just leave," I respond.

"Anyway, with that lead to go on, officers went back and interviewed a number of assault victims as to whether the attacker had shared anything with them that was out of the ordinary. They found two more girls who, when presented with that general question, provided the same account as the 'courageous girl' did—and as you did just this morning." The detective pauses. "Can I ask you a personal question, Ms. Moran? And before I do, the reason I am asking is that your answer can help us when we are working with other victims of rape and assault."

"You want to know why it took me so long to come in. Why didn't I report it right away? For all of the usual reasons. I was shocked, numbed, overcome, in disbelief. And after a few weeks and even months went by, I was embarrassed that I had been so careless, fearful of being judged by my friends and the dancers that I worked with. I felt like somehow I must have deserved to be attacked or it would not have happened," I explain. "And when I finally did see a therapist, I was focused on healing and moving forward. I could not bear the thought of re-living the attack by reporting it or testifying."

"And now?" the officer questions.

"And now I want it out of my unconscious, where it ended up living only to come alive and remind me at the most unexpected times. And now, I am strong enough to report it. I very much regret that it took me years to come forward and that I could have helped stop that horrific man from hurting other women, and maybe even young girls."

I stand, signaling to Sissy that I want to escape to the waiting cab as quickly as I can. I hesitate. I know I should thank the officer for everything she does to help girls and women like me. I look at her and offer an expression that is half smile, half grimace. It is the best I can do.

County Cork, Ireland

Colleen sips a strong cup of black tea at the antique oak table in the kitchen. She finds herself rising early in the morning, matching Patrick's habit. Before Deidre and Macy moved home, she and her brother had fallen into the habit of getting up around nine o'clock. Patrick had also worked at home a day or two each week. But their daily routines have altered to work around those of Deidre, Macy, Sissy, and the people who come to work at the house for the dance company. With a raised eyebrow, Colleen remembers that Patrick had told her in the past how much he wished Deidre and Macy would return to Moran. He can now count that blessing as having been dished out to him, but neither of them could have predicted the upheaval in their routines.

Sissy has created the most change and energy. Colleen takes a long sip of her tea and reflects on exactly why that is so. Certainly, having a four-year-old in the house again, while delightful, has challenged them all. Cory's presence at dinner every evening brings with it an aura of the townspeople's concerns as his days are spent interacting with them rather than being isolated at Moran. But Sissy brings something familiar.

Like Sissy, Deidre's mother had been an American woman—but unlike Sissy, Suzanne had spent a good deal of time in London and had acquired some of the British habits and manner. And, she was from an older generation of women. Sissy, on the other hand, is modern and 100 percent American. No matter that she has taken to wearing exclusively Irish and British dress: long woolen skirts with ankle boots and a collection of hats. It is the way Sissy takes over the room, but not in a brash or unappealing way, that reminds Colleen of Deidre's mother. When she arrived, she leaped to where Macy was sitting and picked up the child while exclaiming how she missed her very favorite Moran. On another occasion, Sissy had approached Colleen, who was relaxing with a book, and begged her to help choose proper riding and day clothes that would flatter her blond hair and slim figure. Without giving Colleen a chance to reply, she said that she absolutely trusted Colleen to make sure that she was dressed attractively without trying to imitate Irish dress completely. "After all," she had pleaded to Colleen, "I am an American woman and don't want that to be lost with my appearance." Colleen smiles, thinking that there is not a chance Sissy's sense of American style and audaciousness will ever be lost.

Colleen has to admit that she likes Sissy. She is pleasant and generous with words of appreciation for anything Colleen or the house staff does for her. She brings a badly needed exuberance to the house. Colleen does have to admit that she finds Sissy's life as a performer to be more than what she is accustomed to since, once married, Irish women do not work or hold any type of public position. And it is unheard of in Ireland for a married woman to be congenially separated from her husband with his apparent blessing, even if it's only temporary. It bothers Colleen as she does not want to support a lifestyle she feels is immoral, yet immoral it is not. She hears similar rumblings from the maids, as Sissy no doubt provides a source of gossip and entertainment for them. In the end, Colleen tells herself that Sissy is Deidre's dear friend, and while the woman may be guilty of turning the house decorum upside down, she is welcomed by Deidre and Patrick, so that is all that matters. Quickly finishing her tea, Colleen decides that she will begin to drop positive comments to the staff concerning Sissy's energy and sense of light, which they all should welcome and imitate.

Colleen is hardly on her feet when Sissy sweeps into the kitchen and sings her usual "Good morning, Colleen" in a loud, cheery voice. Sissy spends more time in the kitchen than any other family member. It had annoyed Colleen initially, but she has grown accustomed to Sissy's morning greetings and now looks forward to them.

"Colleen, I have asked Brenda to go riding later this morning. I am wondering if it would be too much of an imposition for us to have lunch on the outdoor back patio facing the magnificent French garden."

"No, of course it will be no trouble, Sissy. I will relay your request to the cook."

Sissy adds, "I know you would not ask, Colleen, but I want you to know that Deidre has asked me to meet Brenda and follow-up on an idea involving Irish dance and other Irish cultural events."

Colleen raises both eyebrows and widens her eyes to express interest, but she shows no sign of approval or disapproval. While Deidre has not made the specifics entirely clear to Colleen, she knows Sissy's entry into their lives is connected to the Irish dance project. But involving Moran Hotels is an unprecedented path.

Sissy reads Colleen's raised eyebrows and quickly adds, "Patrick has directed Brenda to get ideas from Deidre and me on how North River Dance uses our cultural director, as he wants to create a similar position for the Moran Hotels." Colleen nods to indicate that she understands, but she does not engage in any further conversation on the matter. She cannot help but wonder what kind of storms will be stirred up with the further involvement of women in the Moran Hotel business, which Patrick considers to be the domain of men.

Colleen collects scrambled eggs, hot Irish oats, milk, and two slices of fresh brown bread on a plate, climbs the steps to the first-floor breakfast room, and sits down in her usual place. She gazes out at the bay and far beyond to the sea. She observes that the wind has kicked up the tides and has put on full whitecaps. *Not much different out there from what is going on inside this house,* she muses as she enjoys a solitary breakfast and a quiet moment to herself.

~ ~ ~ ~ ~

In the earliest hours after midnight, the spirits of Moran Manor sense the rise of energy in the house. Moran has lain dormant for years, markedly so after the death of Mistress Suzanne. The energy from the sheer number of people living in and visiting the estate has now called the spirits out to roam. It is like times gone by when the house was full. As the sun begins to rise, and with Patrick's early appearance, the spirits recede back into the walls or to unused rooms where the light is low.

When Patrick takes his solo journey from his bedroom to his study, he sometimes feels as though he is being followed, and on more than one occasion, he has turned to check over his shoulder.

~ ~ ~ ~ ~

Once Andres arrives at Moran, he loses no time pushing the project forward. The long, winding driveway leading to Moran is now occupied by personal cars and delivery trucks. Taxis arrive and deposit guests that are somehow connected to the dance company project. The cast and crew include production professionals from London and

Chicago, Irish dance studio owners from Cork and Dublin, history and art professors from Cork and Trinity colleges, and music recording specialists from Dublin, London, and Chicago. Edwin stands at the front door to ensure that arrivals are properly instructed to use the back door and follow the sign that will lead them to the second-floor business wing. He insists on being given an updated list of expected visitors to the house each morning so that he knows who is to be welcomed through the front door, such as guests who are staying at the house for an extended stay, and those who are scheduled to meet with Deidre to be directed to the back entry.

The newly hired head housekeeper has convinced Colleen of the need for a handful of experienced and older live-in maids, one to take care of all housekeeping needs on the second-floor business wing and another to see to the personal bedrooms on the other side of the second floor. With Sissy and Andres living at Moran full time, she thinks it is essential that one maid spend a few hours each day tending to their rooms as well as to their clothes and errands, rather than hiring a ladies maid for Sissy—not that Sissy would tolerate one. She told one of the maids that she could clean her own room as well as Andres's so the maids do not have to bother with their rooms at all. But Colleen will not settle for such an outrageous suggestion.

When Colleen runs the additional staffing needs past Patrick, she also adds two full-time first-floor maids who will also work in the kitchen if needed. Patrick sighs aloud as he listens to his sister's rationale for adding to the house budget, and he anticipates that there will be more. The second-floor live-in maids will somehow need day staff, and no doubt Edwin, not to be left out, will see his way to adding staff as well.

As the maids, cooks, and butler hustle around the house learning their new roles and responsibilities, they also observe something unique to both Moran Manor and to any Irish estate house. In the business wing on the second floor, Deidre and Andres are deep into day-long planning meetings. One room is completely cleared of furniture, and a large table with folding chairs is set up to accommodate the planning team. As maids deliver drinks, coffee, tea, and sandwiches during the extended meetings, which do not break for lunch, they observe Deidre and Andres taking charge, one and then the other, as they explain the process they will use in bringing the dance show to the stage.

Deidre and Andres use the same process that worked for them hundreds of times during North River's productions. They each know their role and responsibility and allow the other to have the floor and authority when it comes to describing their part of the staging process.

The local women have never seen a woman in a leadership position, seemingly with the same influence and power as a man. They squabble over turns to make the second-floor "refreshment run," as they call it, so they can have a chance to see firsthand. In the kitchen, the staff chats about the Irish dance company's progress, particularly the fact the Deidre Moran leads along with Andres. The maid assigned to Sissy's bedroom has asked the cordial American woman if it is her husband or Deidre that is in charge. Sissy smiles at the girl and replies that they are equally in charge. Deidre heads up operations and finance and Andres oversees everything that involves dance production. She adds that she has known Deidre for almost her entire life and no one is ever going to be in charge of Deidre Moran except Deidre Moran. The young maid retreats from the room to report the startling news to the kitchen staff: an Irish woman in charge of a business!

One day runs into another until a month slips by. At the culmination of each day, Sissy, Deidre, and Andres hold a debriefing meeting just before the family cocktail hour. On this day, the maid finds the threesome out on the French garden patio. She brings a large tray holding cold glasses of tea, biscuits, and a selection of Irish cheeses while still another maid steers an antique serving cart piled high with buckets of ice and a selection of liquor and beer.

"I still can't believe that the housekeeper has Sissy and I assigned to separate bedrooms," Andres comments to Deidre, eyeing the refreshment cart. "I told her that it is just a waste of time and energy since I am in Sissy's room most of the time anyway."

"Some things are not going to change around here, Andres, and that is one of them. It is just a long-held custom for ladies to have rooms separate from their husbands. I guess Virginia Woolf would refer to it as a room of her own?" I surprise myself at how quickly that analogy resurfaces. Not wanting memories of Steven during our early years in London to show on my face, I quickly move the conversation in another direction.

"You know, Andres, I think that many women and men would love to have that kind of privacy. And I have to believe that one's sex life may be a bit hotter when some things are reserved for the personal and not shared with one's spouse?" Andres thinks about that for a minute. A smile comes to his face as he contemplates the advantages he had not considered.

Next, I call his attention back to the dance production agenda. "I have one day set aside next week for signing the contracts, given that our attorney in Chicago has reviewed them and sees no issues. We will have dance practice locations in Dublin, most of them in local church basements as that is the best I could find on a short notice."

Andres shrugs and puts his hands in the air. "Not surprised, Deidre. What is different for me in this case is that I will not be involved directly with the dance training or rehearsals. We both agreed that it made sense to hire Irish dance teachers for that as they have the Irish dance history and the step dancing repertoire down, and I would just have to have them teach me anyway. Sissy will take on the role of coordinating the timeline of events on this end."

I nod, hearing what I expected him to say.

"But I am working on finding a male Irish step dancer in Chicago, and I think I have a lead," Andres reports.

"What? This is news to me. I thought we would find a male lead here," I say.

"We have seen the talent here. It's still the traditional step dancing. There is modern talent to be found on the south side of Chicago. I checked out a few Irish dance studios—I didn't know they existed. They're small and located in the Irish neighborhoods. But the style I am seeing is, like I said, modern. The Chicago dancer that I scouted has honed the athleticism of the male solo in ballet and applied it to Irish step dance. And I reluctantly have to admit, he is a real looker. I would like to fly him over here for you and Sissy to meet. Put him with a select few of the local dancers and see what he does with them."

My first instinct is to push for developing a male lead who is already in Ireland. But I have seen the best of the dancers, and Andres is right in that their style is dated. My pitch all along has been to modernize Irish dance and merge components of international dance within a new dance form.

"I haven't given up on the possibility of finding a male lead here, but hearing your argument, you're right. Tell me more about this Chicago dancer?"

"From what I hear, he is second-generation Irish. His parents moved to Chicago just a few weeks before he was born. He was raised in the Irish neighborhood on the south side and has hung around Irish dance neighborhood studios for a while. He also does boxing and judo. Just your average Irish Chicago kid," Andres smiles at me as he explains.

"Right, average kid," Sissy says. She smiles at me as well. "Come on, Deidre. Let's get him on a plane as soon as we can. Let's see what this hot stuff from Chicago can do."

"I would like to make one more recommendation, though," Andres says. "I think we need to move up the trial show date from May to mid-March, in time for St. Patrick's Day. I am thinking you and Sissy can schedule a show date in one of the bigger theaters in Dublin. Advertise the hell out of it. You know, the usual."

I look at Andres with eyes wide open. "Of course, but do you think we will be ready by then?"

"Only one way to find out. Get a date and produce as good as we can by then," answers Andres. "We agreed to a year's timeline to see if this thing is viable or not. We need a trial balloon."

"Just so you know," I add, "the time around St. Patrick's day is going to be over the top for me. The house is to be done in March and Cory has his heart set on moving in as soon as it is complete."

"That's not the only thing Cory has his heart set on doing in March, Deidre Moran," Cory says as he turns the corner on the sidewalk that circles the manor to join the group for the after-work meltdown session. "Did you tell the extended Moran family and workgroup that you are getting committed in March?" he says to Deidre. Then, turning to Sissy and Andres, he teases, "I won't use the word 'marriage' in fear of scaring off the lady."

Sissy jumps out of her seat with glee and nearly climbs into my lap as she wraps her arms around me. "Deidre Moran, how could you have kept this a secret from me?" Andres stands and extends his hand to Cory in congratulations.

"I am not sure whether I should congratulate you or issue you a warning, Cory. You will have your hands full with that lady," he says.

Cory laughs in the easy way he always does when confronted with teasing or a challenge. "I hope so. I like a challenge, Andres. We both know that Deidre is that."

Cory joins the group as Andres moves to serve him a room-temperature Guinness from the refreshment cart. "You take care of the dance business," Cory says. "I've got the house and Deidre." We laugh and enjoy the celebratory moment until Edwin appears to direct us to the dining room. "And, just for the record," Cory says while pointing to Edwin, who has just left the patio, "that is one interruption we won't have when you come for a Guinness at our little house on the sea. No butlers or maids!" With Cory getting the last laugh, as usual, we head in for dinner.

Colleen brings Macy to the table and seats her next to me—no dinner with the nanny in a separate room for my daughter. Catherine had pretty much destroyed that practice years ago during her visit to Moran.

My father gazes around the table at me, Cory, Sissy, Andres, Macy, and Colleen. He holds his glass high to signal a toast. "To a new beginning. To my new family. *Sláinte chuig na fir, agus go mairfidh na mná go deo.*"

"Whatever does that mean?" asks Sissy.

"Health to the men, and may the women live forever!" answers Cory, flashing a big smile.

~ ~ ~ ~ ~

My ritual of drifting down the halls, into the study, and through the large reception rooms begins hours before my father's early morning rise. I remember how I rooted in closets and hung from second-floor windows as a young, lost girl after my mother's death. I can still recall my imaginary friend, Susan, who somehow had magically appeared after my mother went away. She came to me in dreams, flying out of the clouds, and would scoop me up to safety when I had one of my many nightmares. I had hung on to Susan during the first few years in Evanston, but her visits waned as I became focused on my new life in the States.

Being in therapy helped me to understand those behaviors, and I now accept them for what they were: trauma and grief pouring out of a very young girl. But lately, since the most recent news about Steven, I wake at two o'clock in the morning with incoherent thoughts running through my head. It is as if my body and psyche are alerting me and triggering latent memories of Susan, casting me into a hypervigilant state so I can deal with whatever develops or accept whatever already is.

During this particular middle-of-the-night meandering, I creep down the stairs and slowly walk through one room after another. I stand before wall-size windows and study the quiet bay waters, which are between low and high tides. The bay looks as if it is resting, waiting, and preparing to deal with the energy that the waves will produce like clockwork the following day.

I find myself sitting in the breakfast room, gazing at Moran's grounds and the sea below. I rise from my seat and turn to go back to my bedroom when a photo on the wall catches my eye. It is a large framed picture of my mother, Suzanne Moran. It has never been there before. After my mother's death, my father removed all the pictures and the one oil portrait he had commissioned of her. When had this picture been returned to the wall?

I step closer to the photo to compare it to the memory I carry in my head. She sits in front of the French Garden, legs casually crossed with her bare feet on the patio. She looks directly at the observer with her emerald green eyes, which seem to glow with happiness. A full, thick head of chestnut-brown hair falls to her shoulders in thick waves. Her complexion is smooth and transparent, illuminated by a low-setting sun in the background. She wears a cornflower-blue, knee-length sundress that reveals long, lean legs and a slim figure.

I stand transfixed for several minutes, locked in a stare with my mother. At times, it appears that she tips her head to one side, then tucks her chin down slightly and raises her eyes to me. After shaking myself a bit to remind me that it is an inanimate picture, I do recall that my mother looked at me in just that way when I was a little girl. She used that look when I did something that captured her attention and pleased her.

On the quiet shuffle back to my bedroom, I remind myself of my therapist's suggestion for dealing with grief and troubling memories. "Go back," she had encouraged, "but do not get stuck there. Set a limit and remind yourself that grief and loss are now part of your strength and resilience." And I do feel stronger every time I go "back."

I turn the corner on the second-floor terrace and, like I did as a young child, whisper to the ghosts of the house, asking them to walk alongside me and keep me safe. How I love the old, rambling house with its severely dated décor. But I believe that behind the old damask drapes and cracked walls covered with heavy wallpaper and fabric, the spirits still know me, welcome me, and protect me. They, better than anyone else, know how I suffered within these walls. And yet these walls kept me safe at a time when my adult family members were drowning in their own sadness. I gently open the door to my bedroom and close it behind me.

Much further down the hallway, another door opens as quietly
as the one I closed. My father, in his usual cotton pajamas and robe,
shuffles along the hallway in his leather slippers. His usual path is the
most direct route to his study. But this morning, he makes his way to
the breakfast room, pulls up one of the chairs at the table, and swings
it around to face the framed picture of my mother. He settles back into
the chair and whispers to the picture in low tones.

"My dear, the house is alive again, but you would never guess how
things are changing since your remarkable daughter has returned with
your granddaughter. Her name is Macy. She has your spirit, and she
would have captured your heart the very first time you laid eyes on her.
Like you captured mine."

~ ~ ~ ~ ~

"Colleen, may I talk to you privately, please?" I direct my inquiry
to Colleen while we are in the kitchen, before she has a chance to stroll
to the breakfast room for one of the day's few leisurely moments. We
walk to a small room outside of the kitchen. Its purpose has changed
over the years from a butler's serving pantry to a dish cabinet and, most
recently, into a small telephone room.

"I don't want to raise the alarm, but I have noticed something odd
in my bedroom. Things are out of place—out of order is the only way
I can describe it. A vase that I keep in the center of the dresser was
moved to the end of the dresser, or a blouse turns up in the portion of
my closet where all my long pants and full dresses are hung. A pair of
shoes that I have not worn for ages shows up under a chair. Nothing
is missing, just moved. I did mention it to Mary, who takes care of my
room. She noticed it right away but figured I had worn the shoes or had

a preference for the vase to be at the end of the dresser. She had not noticed the blouse out of order."

"Well, I am not surprised at all. I have been telling your father that with all of the traffic going up and down the second-floor staircase and terrace and through the hallway, we have left ourselves open to people being out of place, either by accident or on purpose. Maybe someone has decided to snoop around or maybe that someone is taking a long look to see what they might want to take when they come back another time. Either way, Deidre, I can't remember a time when so many people have had the freedom to enter the second floor, where private bedrooms have been ever since this house was built. Proper butlers and head housekeepers would not have tolerated it! But what is a butler or housekeeper to say when it is the grown daughter that insists on turning over long-held rules of the house?"

I listen intently to Colleen's sound reasoning and criticism. "I didn't want to mention this to Father or anyone else before talking to you. And I think you are right, Colleen. I didn't intend for the second floor to become so available when I grabbed some of the rooms to use as an office and planning rooms for the dance business. It just got out of hand," I admit to my aunt. I say, "Please, Colleen, don't concern Father with this. If you will arrange to have locks installed on all of the private bedrooms, I will begin to look for office space in another building on the grounds to house the dance business. That will stop all outside traffic to the second floor, and most of the recent traffic to the house as well. I am so sorry for not having had the foresight to see that our family security could be so easily breached."

In an effort to calm me and ease my mind, Colleen assures me that no harm has been done other than a few personal things moved around. She assures me she will see to it that locks are installed on all of the bedrooms by the end of the day and will offer no explanation for the order.

But Colleen lives by her instincts and a keenly developed sense of order. The bedroom situation that I have described is more than enough to warrant action. She hurries to Macy's bedroom. She knows the room and its possessions better than anyone else. If something is out of order or disturbed from its usual place, she will detect it in a flash. Seeing nothing of concern, she makes her way downstairs and pushes open the study door. She finds my father still at his desk, taking a slower morning than usual before going to Cork City for the day. Within half an hour, Colleen leaves the study having fully informed him of not only the need for tighter house security but her unease regarding my sense that an intruder has made his or her way into my bedroom.

~ ~ ~ ~ ~

Patrick sits in front of his attorney. He called Randall right after his talk with Colleen to set up a meeting in Cork for an update on the Steven Whitney investigation. Patrick acknowledges that Deidre is Randall's private client. However, he makes the case that if someone has entered his house and his daughter's bedroom, it is his responsibility to take action. Ireland still hangs on to its old traditions and modern laws can be laid aside when a strong case is made and a large legal fee is paid in a timely fashion.

Randall says the private investigator came up empty in finding personal information on Steven. His lifestyle leaves no hint that can be traced. He has no permanent address and there are no marriage or divorce records, and no birth records indicating Steven as the father of any child. He did work for the British MI6, but the nature of his work is vague, and the investigator failed to get any details when he interviewed the MI6 director. Steven pays no taxes and does not license a vehicle in his name. He simply does not leave a trail.

Patrick eases into a waiting taxi, and within two hours he is on the ground at Heathrow Airport and in yet another taxi, this one headed for St. Ermin's Hotel and the MI6 office. It is late afternoon by the time the cab weaves through London traffic, but he is not going to leave without talking to the director. He has a deep feeling in his gut that there is much more to Steven's story, most of it hidden by the MI6. He will require the secretary to call the director back to the office if need be—Patrick knows he is available, as his attorney has called the MI6 office to give a heads-up that Patrick is on his way.

When he arrives at the office, the same buttoned-down secretary has strong tea, sandwiches, and whiskey waiting for Patrick. She indicates that the director has turned his car around to return to the office. Patrick has had two shots of whiskey and is halfway through a sandwich when the director walks through the reception door, tosses his long trench coat on the empty chair, and signals for Patrick to follow him. He closes the door, buzzes his secretary, and instructs her to lock his phone and close up the office for the day. The director wastes no time by offering an apology.

"It has become necessary to debrief you in full, Mr. Moran, regarding the status of Steven Whitney. Moran Manor has been under the agency's surveillance since the time your daughter, Ms. Moran, moved back to your estate. The stakeout includes MI6 men on the grounds, long-distance cameras, and close scrutiny of the various people in and off of the estate. The agency security team has run profiles on everyone who is living at or employed by the Manor, including kitchen help and groundskeepers. Nobody was omitted, including a Mrs. and Mr. Andres Soto, and you."

Patrick is stunned. The director swirls his chair around to the credenza behind his desk. He lifts a carafe of liquor with one hand and a glass with the other. He pours a drink and hands it to Patrick, who quietly accepts the signal that anesthesia in addition to the drinks he consumed in the reception room is necessary.

The director continues. "Your investigator cannot find anything on Steven Whitney because his life has been purged by the Intelligence Agency. For public purposes, Steven Whitney does not exist. He was not in medical support. He worked in intelligence for the British M16. He is a trained executioner, assassin, eradicator. He is one of the top in the world."

The director warns Patrick not to underestimate Steven's profile. "He is extremely intelligent. He can memorize a classified file in less than an hour. He is charismatic, charming, and socially outgoing. He speaks five languages fluently. He always appears to be telling the truth because his truth is all that he knows, and that truth centers around the task or the job at the moment or the obstacle that needs to be destroyed. He covers his tracks flawlessly, and he can detect immediately when he is being followed."

Patrick leans back into his chair and takes a long swig of straight whiskey. The picture painted by the director is that of a consummate professional killer at the top of his game. Blood rushes from his face, and even the whiskey cannot mask the tinge of yellow that begins to spread from his neck to his forehead. His heart races and his pulse runs fast.

The director transitions again. "After your last visit here, I made it clear to Steven that he had to clean up the situation with Ms. Moran. End it. Walk away. But one thing about men who have a profile that makes them super effective spies and killers is that they are egocentric and narcissistic. They believe they have power beyond any ordinary man, and certainly beyond their employer. They are loners who work for themselves and get paid millions of pounds for their results. They don't take orders well when it comes to their private lives. They feel they have earned the right to live a life with no rules, or at least only those that they determine."

"So, you don't have any kind of influence or power over him?"

"No. He isn't one of us; a part of this agency. And, he no longer has any kind of relationship with us."

The director pauses, and then says, "The agency does not want to see a long, protracted child custody trial involving a prominent British-Irish family that would be spread to every tabloid and television station in London. Every third-rate news reporter would soon find out, much like you did, that the man at the center has no public record. That kind of publicity could unveil activities about the agency that would damage its reputation and, worse, expose its activities. Trying to contain Steven under such circumstances is too risky. And frankly, it is something that Steven would never permit. He is in control of outcomes. That is what he gets paid to do, and frankly, that is what we relied on him to do."

Patrick, still stunned, manages to ask, "What can I do to protect my daughter?"

The director's response sends a chill down Patrick's back. He curtly replies, "I am not altogether certain. But I can tell you this. From my experience working with men like Steven, I do not think it is your daughter that he is after. He wants his child."

"His child," Patrick repeats struggling to follow the deputy's train of thought.

"He wants his child. Why the child? Because he knows the child is his bloodline. It belongs to him. His rules. Deidre is in the way, true. That makes her life at risk."

~ ~ ~ ~ ~

Patrick takes the red-eye back to Cork City and is on Moran grounds by early morning. He approaches the manor house front door and does a visual survey, attempting to spot the surveillance team in action. He detects nothing. Once inside, he instructs Colleen to call Deidre downstairs to his study immediately.

Still in her nightclothes, she stands in front of her father and listens to his directive. "I need you to move the dance operation out of the house as soon as possible. I know this explanation may seem shallow but I can no longer tolerate the disruption to my private life. I know you might find a different location on the grounds, but the new location has to be a significant distance from Moran. Look at Cork City or Dublin. I own a townhouse in Dublin that could be converted to meet the needs of your dance business."

"Your need to have more privacy in your own home and affairs does not surprise me, Father, as I am aware of how quickly Moran has gone from being an extremely private residence to looking more like a bustling business." What catches Deidre's attention is the look of stress on his face. "Is something more to your request than what you are telling me now, Father?"

"No, not all, Deidre. It's just that I am getting old and simply don't have the stamina for all of this upheaval. Of course, I am only referring to the dance operation moving—not you, your friends, or certainly Macy. It's just everything connected in one way or another with the dance production."

"The timing is good, Deidre," Andres says during a phone conversation to Chicago as he listens to Deidre outline the need for the Irish dance company to find a permanent location. "I am returning to Ireland at the end of the week, and by then we can sign a lease in Dublin to house the dance company. Cork City is too small and not centrally located for our purposes. Sissy and I will find an apartment in Dublin or wherever the company lands."

"No, Sissy and you will not find an apartment in Dublin. You are more than just part of the dance company. You are my closest friends in the world. Father did not say a word about either of you moving out of Moran. I need you both here. And Macy would be heartbroken," Deidre pleads.

By the end of the day, the dance company equipment is loaded on a moving truck and is in transit to Dublin for storage. Patrick asks Cory if he can borrow part of the crew that is building the house. Within days, the builders have walled off the back hallway up to the second story and installed armor-gauge, bullet-resistant doors made from five-inch steel. The house has also been equipped with a security system at the back and front entries. Patrick, Colleen, Deidre, and Edwin possess the combination to open the door, but no others—including Cory. Doors are to remain closed and locked at all times. Patrick instructs Colleen to refrain from answering the front door and allow Edwin to do his job. Colleen raises her eyes upon hearing this order. "There is no partial way to address the security issues you raised to me, Colleen. Securing the front door is a basic step."

Patrick spends the next three days locked in his study. He unwinds the dusty, tightly rolled Moran blueprints of the original structure on his desk along with the blueprints for each of the two additions. For hours, aided by a series of desktop magnifying glasses of varying sizes, he pours over the details of the plans and scribbles a list of notations in a small notebook. Stuffing the notebook in his pocket, he then walks deliberately through the house with a newly informed set of eyes. The notebook guides his investigation and analysis of each room, hallway, nook, and cranny along with every possible entry point into the house. He also surveys each storage closet and unfinished rafter on the third-floor. As he does, he realizes that he has not been on the manor's third floor since he was a boy using it as his hideaway. It has either housed servants or served as storage for all of the time he has lived at Moran.

Next, he exits a third floor door, climbs onto the roof, and moves along the various roof platforms to examine the turrets and battlements. At each side of the roof, he halts, stares over the grounds below, and then looks over the hills that are far beyond the estate. When he finishes with one section of the roof, he carefully walks to another until he completes the same exercise on all three sections. This activity does not go unnoticed by Colleen. While she is spared from seeing her brother standing on top of the roof, she is certain that he has never conducted such a critical analysis of the house.

~ ~ ~ ~ ~

Late autumn of 1981 settles into Bantry Bay and sends the usual signals. The leaves drop from the oak trees that line the narrow countryside roads surrounding Moran Manor. The French garden in front of the west patio loses its roses and most of the perennial flowers, leaving only the hardiest marigolds and purple coneflowers for the slow-moving bees and butterflies that gather whatever pollen remains. The mists off of the ocean last longer in the morning and move in earlier in the afternoon to coat the lawn with a thin blanket of slick moisture. The air is pungent with the smells of crop residue and decay as plants are well past their summer peak. The cool air and tangy ocean scent are far more noticeable in early November as the perfumed aromas of the summer and early fall have all but disappeared.

Once admitted through locked doors, Cory saunters into the house, arriving earlier than usual to catch Patrick before the cocktail hour. At Colleen's direction, he follows the hallway to Patrick's study but finds the room empty. He skirts Colleen and takes the hallway down to the kitchen to see if the any of the kitchen help may have a clue as to Patrick Moran's newly acquired habits. A stable hand, taking an early supper in the kitchen, tells Cory to try the stable as Mr. Moran has been spending more and more time around the horses with his granddaughter. Cory raises his eyebrows and heads outside.

He walks through the stone arches that lead to the collection of stable buildings. One building is designated to store the hay bundles needed to get the estate's livestock through the rainy and sunless winter months when the weather prevents them from grazing. Next to the hay, the farm hands have piled barrels of oats and large bins of corn cobs and apples to supplement the livestock diet.

The buildings on either side of the feed barns house wagons and a collection of wheels, tools, antique scythes, sickles, and hay mowers. Several buildings are dedicated to an enormous collection of horse tack. Rather than discard a piece of equipment when a newer variety appears on the market, it is the custom of the Moran livery to keep every piece that has ever been used. Huge nails and hooks hold reins, bridles, stirrups, headgear, breastplates, and mouth bits of every size and thickness. On the other side of the tack building, deep boxed shelving starts at ground level and reaches ten feet off of the ground. The shelves hold an assortment of English saddles. They are organized according to rider size, be it a child, growing adolescent, or adult. The boxes highest off of the ground contain saddles constructed from the finest of leathers and ornamentation.

Cory enjoys examining this part of the Moran estate. He notes with some curiosity that the number of stable hires has not been weeded down from the last expansion upon Deidre's return. Cory walks into the horse barn and finds Patrick talking with one of the newer hires. When he sees Cory, Patrick cuts off his conversation with the stable hand and walks towards him. Patrick leads Cory to a small office between the two bays. It is equipped with a rudimentary wooden desk and several unsteady, makeshift chairs.

"I apologize for interrupting your private time," Cory says, "but I need to know what the rush is to clear out Moran and to seal up the back entry. My workers on loan to you heard some gossip while building the wall and installing the security doors. They said this all appears to be a push-out by you." Cory confronts Patrick in an understated tone.

"I admit, Cory, the drive to clear the dance company out of Moran and seal off the back entryway is out of the ordinary, but Ireland is in the middle of extraordinary times. Money is tight all around. With the increase in tourism and the well-heeled coming to the Island, both for investment's sake and for vacation, shady people follow. Crime follows the money. Deidre has keenly observed that the house may have already been breached by unsavory characters connected with the dance business or the various delivery people coming and going." Patrick avoids making eye contact with Cory.

"Are you sure that is all it is then?" asks Cory, eyeing his soon-to-be father-in-law seriously.

Patrick hesitates before responding, remembering how the director of the MI6 had cautioned him. "Absolutely," Patrick replies, nodding and looking over Cory's head.

"All right, then. Guess I will take you at your word. I will see you up at the house for dinner?" Cory does not expect an answer.

Patrick turns his back to Cory as he contemplates his next task. Cory strolls through the cement arches that partition the stables from the grounds, and he turns toward the house. His head is down and he watches each foot as he takes deliberate steps forward. He could not help but notice that Patrick did not look him directly in the eye when explaining his reasons for the relocation of the dance operation. He remains unconvinced.

~ ~ ~ ~ ~

Patrick walks the cobbled courtyard from the house to the stables. His black riding pants pull taut across his stomach and provide another reminder of the weight he has gained. Swinging his helmet in his hand, he looks up at the second-story stable roof and gazes at the cupola, as has been his automatic daily routine over the last month. He appreciates the stables in a way he previously had not. When he studied the stable maps, blueprints, and history, he acquired a keen appreciation of the architectural design's dual purpose: to house horses and to function as a defensive lookout.

Built by an Earl in 1845, the walls are stone and reinforced at each corner with red brick. At the top of the center wall sits a stunning copper-domed cupola with multiple columns, designed in the Tuscan Corinthian style. He remembers that he thought it looked like an upside down teacup when he was a child. Patrick recalls how his early ancestors had viewed cupolas, temples, and castles on their way through the "tour of the continent," as it was then commonly known. His descendants were among many who duplicated a variety of Greek structures on their own land and, when finished, wondered what function they would serve.

Glancing at the cupola above the second story of the roofed stables, he is now acutely aware that constructing a stable in such a fashion, complete with roofs and battlements, is as much about defense from intruders as it is about ornamentation.

He has a date with Macy. He promised to take her for her first real horse ride around the estate; she will be seated in front of him on his horse. Her nanny agreed to escort her to the stables once she finishes her lunch. Patrick gazes up at the azure blue skies and at the sun low on the horizon. They have been enjoying a run of sunny, rain-free days that are unusual for the middle of November. Patrick knows that darker, wetter days are ahead as West Cork winter weather is less about snow and much more about days of dark, oceanic rain.

He can see Macy skipping down the courtyard. He leads his horse out of its bay and mumbles a few words at the stable hand, who has equipped the horse for the ride. Once the nanny deposits the small child in the stable yard, she makes her way along the cobblestone path and back to the house while Patrick chats with his excited granddaughter, who cannot stand still. Patrick turns to face the child and directs her his way. He tells her he will walk her around the courtyard on his horse so she can get used to being in a taller seat. Holding the child in his arms, he approaches the horse while the stable hand holds on to the horse by its reins. Patrick hoists Macy into the saddle.

Unnoticed by the preoccupied Patrick, a tall man dressed in English riding breeches, high boots, mask-like aviator glasses and a helmet walks out of the horse bay.

"Mr. Moran," he says. "And Macy," he bows slightly to the child. "I have been instructed by your mother to give you the riding lesson. You are wanted up at the house, sir—an urgent matter."

In one fluid movement, Patrick removes the child from her seat on his horse and deposits her on the ground, tucking her into his chest. He stoops over the child so his head meets the back of hers and whispers into her ear. In an instant, the child bolts down the courtyard and out of view faster than a horse startled by lightning.

"Very clever, Patrick. What did you say to the child?"

"Two words," answers Patrick. "Macy, bolt."

"So, you practiced with her. You knew I was coming. Very astute."

"What do you want, Steven?" Patrick's tone is flat.

"I already have what I want. I have someone waiting around the corner as backup, and he has Macy by now."

"I think you are bluffing, Steven. About the man waiting around the corner. This place has been under surveillance for months," Patrick says, looking straight into Steven's eyes.

"I expected it to be."

Patrick pulls a handgun from beneath his vest and points it at Steven. Steven takes one step toward Patrick. "Put the gun down. Let's talk things out."

Before Patrick can utter one word, Steven hits the ground face down and lands near Patrick's boots. Stunned, Patrick squints at a small bullet hole in the back of Steven's head. Blood trickles down his neck and onto either side of his ears. When Patrick looks up, he sees a stable hand with a pistol. The shooter tucks the gun inside his coat and another stable hand appears within seconds. They pull Steven's body inside the bay.

"The child is okay," says yet another man who steps up to Patrick and is also disguised as a stable hand. "By now she is back up at the house and has heard nothing."

"Was there a silencer on the gun?" Patrick questions the killer, still stunned by the events and not able to believe what he has just witnessed.

"We will take care of everything and will be gone before you get back up to the house." He ignores Patrick's question about a silencer.

"What do I say about Steven?" asks Patrick.

"Nothing. There is nothing to say. It has been handled. Go up to the house." The stable hand-turned-agent is stern as he directs Patrick. Patrick hurries up to the house on trembling legs and, once inside, is greeted by an exuberant Macy.

"I bolted, Grandpa! I bolted really fast, just like we practiced in our game. I bolted just like a stallion afraid of lightning," Macy exclaims with delight.

Patrick picks the child up and holds her tightly against his chest attempting to mask the tears that well up in his eyes. "You bolted as fast as the wind, Macy. Just like my stallion. You passed the bolting lesson perfectly. We can go out for the rest of that ride just as soon as your mother gives us the go- ahead."

~ ~ ~ ~ ~

The December rains move in and fog hangs thick, blocking the morning light and my view of any movement outdoors. Two men dressed in long, black trench coats pull up in front of Moran in a Mercedes van. I hear the doorbell ring. A few minutes later, the butler appears and tells me that two men are at the door asking to see a Mrs. Deidre Whitney.

When I appear at the front door, one of the men notifies me that he has an official letter for a Deidre Moran Whitney.

I walk to my father's study, hand him the letter, and ask him to read it out loud. It contains only two sentences.

"Dear Mrs. Whitney." Patrick reads slowly. "The purpose of this notice is to update you on Steven Whitney's status. On the behalf of

Britain, we extend our condolences on Mr. Whitney's untimely death in the line of duty with the MI6."

Patrick observes his daughter and tries to gauge her reaction. In his most cautious and calm voice, he advises, "Let the letter be the last of Steven, Deidre. After all, it is an event we have already mourned."

I am stunned. I look at my father closely, trying to decipher if he has more knowledge about this latest episode of Steven's life than what he has just revealed.

"It seems too expedient, too fast," I say. "Until this moment, I have been in the middle of a messy if not costly child custody battle, and suddenly Steven is gone? Again? Will he reappear tomorrow, next month, or in a year? And, what's with the Mrs. Whitney if I am not legally married?"

"Time will tell, Deidre. For right now? Get through this day. See what tomorrow brings. Embrace the Irish saying: may the best day of your past be the worst day of your future."

My stomach muscles contract and I am overtaken by light headedness. I cave into the closest chair I can find.

"Always an Irish proverb to show the way, Dad? I wonder what Mother would have said about all of this. How would she have advised me?"

"Well, that I don't know. But I do know this. She wants you to be happy. Wherever you need to go on your journey to find happiness that is the right direction." Then he quickly adds, "As long as it is in Ireland."

I can't help but smile at his predictability. But I have learned one thing about him as an adult that I was ignorant of for the many years abroad. He is miserable at being the instrument of pain. Since I have returned home, I have come to know him as an adult woman rather than a hurt child. My father is best at building and protecting, and he is heavy-handed at most everything else but particularly so when it comes to his family. And for that, I am grateful.

He holds his arms out toward me. I nod my head, indicating acceptance. Today I will trust in my dad's wisdom and release what remains of Steven's clandestine life. I simply have exhausted any energy that may be required to deal with the Steven saga today. I surrender into the comfort and safety of my father's arms, and in this moment, I find peace.

County Cork, Ireland, 1996

I leave open the bedroom drapes to maximize my morning view of the grounds in late May. Formerly father's study, this room is now our bedroom. Still in bed, I roll to my right side and stretch my body to its full vertical capacity, then roll to the left and repeat the same movement before gently pushing to my feet. I look back at the bed to see if Cory is awake but see that he is sound asleep.

I turn my attention to my dresser and pick up my favorite boar bristle hairbrush. With fifty strokes, I draw the moisture from my scalp throughout my shoulder length blunt cut hair. Now forty-nine years old, my physical appearance takes on certain characteristics of the bay I love. My auburn hair, while still thick, is now streaked with hints of white, like the foam on a night sea. I try to remind myself to carry my frame straight, like the dancer I had been.

There are noticeable changes in my physical appearance. I share with my grown daughter that I view the sea as a living entity that is ever-changing, just like a woman. A part of it dies each day and then births again.

Pulling the bedroom door quietly behind me, I stroll across the two first floor drawing rooms, the front foyer, and the room that still serves as both the breakfast and luncheon room. We have spent our life split between the Cottage on the Sea, officially christened by Cory, and Moran Manor while my father and Aunt Colleen still lived here.

I enter the breakfast room and my eyes are drawn to the bouquet of blue spring gentians arranged in a pink marble vase. "It seems like yesterday when I ran down those same hills where the gentians still flourish in abundance," I whisper to myself. "I can still feel the warm ground under my bare feet. I still remember promising myself I will never stop running, never."

No sooner have I finished the last whispered word than Sissy saunters into the breakfast room and heads over to the coffee service on the buffet. "Whatever has you talking to yourself on this fabulous spring morning, Deidre?" she teases me.

"Oh, you know, talking to the ghosts," I answer softly.

"Do they talk back?" Sissy asks as she walks over to me and wraps her arms around me.

"Yes, sometimes I think they do."

"I think I saw a few of my own in the upstairs bedroom I have been camped in."

"Really?" I am caught a bit off guard as Sissy has never paid much attention to the Moran ghost stories that I have shared with her over the years.

"Except mine aren't nearly as intriguing as yours are," Sissy confesses. "My ghost is a young Andres running back and forth between my bedroom and his," Sissy teases.

"Speaking of Andres, he is one wonderful man. He is such a good sport about you putting boots on Moran Grounds to help me navigate through these changes."

I smile and gaze at Sissy. She has not lost one ounce of her stunning Chicagoan looks. She has swept bangs and layered ash blond hair that falls to her shoulders, and she still throws her head from side to side to emphasize a point. Toned and pencil thin, Sissy never talks about weight or body issues; rather, she commits herself to daily strength-building classes along with balance routines. If a woman complains to Sissy about the ravages of growing older, she curtly cuts the woman off and asks her what she is doing to take care of herself.

"Is Cory not joining us?" Sissy asks.

"He is sound asleep. His plan is to slip out undetected by the women of the house, grab some coffee and pastry in Bantry, and then pick me up to go home before we make our way to London," I explain.

When we finish our breakfast, Sissy turns to me. "Let's look at where we are with this. I have filled in the names that we talked about for each of the rooms, along with the designated purpose. Macy can always change her mind, but the sooner we lock in this plan, the sooner the designers can be contracted,—well, you get the point, Deidre. Macy isn't opening up a new Moran Hotel here. We want to hang on to as much of the old manor charm—which I happen to love—yet redesign unpretentiously so the rooms and outdoor venues fit this historic manor house."

"What do you think of calling this room 'Colleen's Sunroom'?" Sissy asks while looking around at what seems to be everyone's favorite room of the expansive estate.

I smile, remembering how much Colleen loved her "small breakfast room," as she had referred to it. "Perfect," I say. "I can still see her sitting in front of the window, gazing out at the bay and relishing her morning tea and breakfast. No one dared interrupt or rush the one ritual she held faithfully. I still miss her, Sissy," I say. "She was a second mother to me, not that I don't love and appreciate all that my Aunt Catherine did. But Catherine was more like an older sister who pushed me to take charge of my own life. Colleen—she stepped into my mother's place, and that could not have been an easy thing for her to do."

"She seemed to lose her spunk after your father died, don't you think, Deidre?" Sissy is commenting, not asking for my opinion.

"Very true. Except for the one year that she went to Chicago with Aunt Catherine, her whole life was taking care of my dad and Moran. After Dad died, she talked of moving to Dublin or Cork, but she never did."

"Can't really blame her, Deidre. After all, where would she be able to have the kind of views that she had here? And, Moran was as much her home as your dad's even though he had a hard time saying that out loud," Sissy adds.

"And, Sissy. I want my bedroom upstairs to be called Deidre. And don't look at me with your eyebrows raised. I know I have a bedroom down here. But, I am still very attached to my childhood bedroom. And someday, Cory and I won't be here at all anymore; at least staying overnight. So I do want my name on that upstairs bedroom!"

"And so it will be, Lady Deidre," Sissy affirms with a smile.

Sissy musters the courage to turn the conversation in another direction. "We are so different, Deidre. I came to the dance stage with a college degree, a pair of dance slippers, and change in my pockets. No family to go home to for an extra twenty-dollar bill. Once I left my parents' house, I was on my own. And you with Catherine's bank account that you could tap into when you needed money and an ocean between you, your father, and Colleen—we were so very different. But the differences never got in the way. And look at us now. Especially Andres and me! We lived from paycheck to paycheck for years because he came to the dance business in the same financial shape as I did. Who could have ever predicted the success of North River Dance in Chicago?"

"And you and I have been so very lucky, Sissy," I say. "Can you believe how far we have come since our early Chicago days of dance lessons and my horrible experience in that dreadful basement apartment? Turns out my dad was right about that. He told me two young women had no business living in a basement apartment off the main drag."

The women sit in silence, reflecting on those memories. Sissy lifts her head from her coffee and says, "Deidre have you ever thought you made a mistake in selling off Moran Steps Dance just as it was getting its roots into the ground?"

"Take a long look at me, Sissy, and tell me who you see sitting across from you. I admit that my head and heart wanted to hang on to the company, but my body provided the voice of reason. Andres and I knew after the first year that the concept would eventually take wings. But the wings we counted on emerging in three years were years down the road and required much more money."

Sissy pushes a bit further. "I realize that, but doesn't it seem unfair that a television producer from Dublin was the one that capitalized on your company big time and not you?"

"I understand completely where you are coming from. That's the thing about business, Sissy. You make your best guess and take a risk. I thought it would take another eight years or so to bring the Irish dance company to an international audience. Moya Doherty was in the right place with connections to television production and, equally important, she was in her thirties with plenty of drive and energy while my fifth decade was staring me straight in the face. I still am pleased that a local woman from Ireland, raised by two school teachers, was the one that bought me out. I am also pleased that she continues with the original concept that Andres and I had envisioned when we began."

"Yes, but Deidre, Moya Doherty is the richest woman in Ireland due to the mammoth success of the company you started. And all she did was rename the company," Sissy goads me.

I laugh out loud. "Oh, I think she did a little more than that. Yes, I have to hand it to her. She took it to more than the next level. And continues to do so. But, Sissy, I ran out of energy after the Steven drama, then the deaths of my father and Colleen not long after. Never thought that my boundless energy supply would dwindle and refuse to rekindle at the same level, but that is what happened. And, truthfully, I got the price for the dance company that I thought was fair at the time. My mother's inheritance came my way but the real surprise was my dad leaving Moran and the estate to Macy and by-passing me. He never once gave me an inkling of his intention."

"Any ideas on what his motivation was for that?"

"None. It came as a complete surprise."

"And speaking of this estate," Sissy says, lifting her arms over her head in the direction of the expansive interior rooms. "How are you adjusting to transitioning the home that so many of the Morans grew up in, including you and Macy, from a private residence to one that will be open to the public?"

"To be honest, I am doing my best to not dwell on the loss side of the change. You are right in that this house has been my emotional anchor. In the days and years when I did not know who I was or where I belonged, putting my feet down on any floor of this house, whether the floor was covered with worn carpet, painted boards, or old kitchen tiles, centered me—for the time being, at least. And during the challenges of the Chicago years, just knowing Moran was here comforted me."

The two women sit in silence engulfed in their own private thoughts.

"Macy is faced with inheritance taxes on all of this, taxes that will go up every year," Deidre breaks their silence as she waves her arms over her head pointing to the walls and ceilings of Moran.

"Now I get why Macy has been determined to establish Moran Manor as an event site. It preserves the best of the old world. By setting aside rooms for you and your guests, she can still designate the greater part of Moran into a business." Deidre smiles at Sissy acknowledging the closure she so expertly put to the Moran Manor story.

"Thanks, Sissy, for being the manager in residence until Cory and I return from our visit with Macy in London. Are you sure you can handle...? But of course you can. Probably better than I can. I should have reconsidered and hired a butler after the last one left, just to hold the place down during the transition."

Deidre continues. "I am uneasy about the trip to London. In her last telephone call a few days ago, Macy said another option for Moran has come to light; one she believes has enormous merit. She was not willing to share any details preferring to go over it in person when Cory and I arrive in London. And, Cory reminded me that Macy does not need my approval for whatever decisions she makes about Moran including tearing the whole place down."

"Oh, well. You will get through it. Our reminiscing this morning made me think of one other thing. Is it okay if I ask you a very personal question?"

"Sissy, after all of these years, nothing is out of bounds."

"It's about Steven. Something that Macy has said over the years about being in the riding stables with her grandfather, your dad, and running away from a tall man. Are you sure that Steven is really dead, Deidre?"

I rustle my hair with both hands, as has been my habit since childhood when I am asked a difficult question that has no easy answer. "As my father was fond of saying, he was sent into the Irish mist. I 'buried' Steven in London," putting quotation marks into the air with my hands. "And after a period of time, I let him go emotionally right here at Moran." I move my eyes to the ceiling and beyond.

Sissy observes me for any signs of wavering. Seeing none, she nods in acceptance and accompanies me to the front door. She hugs me and turns to go back inside.

I watch my friend as she closes the massive oak door, which has been darkened by time with all of its divots, scratches, and scrapes. It has kept unfriendly forces away from my family for three centuries. For the time being, Sissy will play the role that a Moran butler and my Aunt Colleen had diligently preserved.

A black Jeep speeds up the paved driveway and leaves a path of dust in its wake. A man bounds from the vehicle and stands beside me. Streaks of silver thread through the still-thick, black hair on Cory McInnis's head. Slim in a long grey pair of knit running pants and matching long-sleeve fitted shirt, he still turns the heads of most women that he passes, no matter their age.

"What, my lady? No luggage?" he teases. Cory knows that when I do a quick overnight at Moran, I take my purse as my overnight bag.

I look at the man that is the glue that holds me to County Cork. I then gaze up at the second-floor window at what was once my bedroom. The winds swirl the long tapestry drapes in the open windows. As I hold my gaze, I picture a small girl standing behind the drapes and peering over the estate.

"See a ghost up there?" Cory asks following my eyes to the second story window.

I turn and smile at him. "Not exactly. I was just thinking that when I was a very small girl, I used to pretend that I could fly from that very window that had no storms or screens. I had this imaginary friend who did fly," I recall. "I shudder at what could have happened, Cory. It was years later when I learned that it is not uncommon for traumatized children to have dreams and visions of flight, to sleepwalk, and to acquire imaginary friends, all of which I did."

Cory looks at the woman he has known for as long as he can remember. "Naw, never would have happened," he says in a confident, matter-of-fact fashion. He smiles, grabs my hand, and leads me to the Jeep. "Let's go home to our cottage on the sea. Moran Manor has been here for more than three hundred years. It will be here for another day."

I abruptly turn to face him with an irritated look on my face. "Cory McInnis, are you really going to dismiss me and this memory that has haunted me all the years of my life?"

Cory turns me around and looks me head-on. "You forget one thing. I was the scrappy little boy lying on your bedroom floor and holding your feet to the ground, my sweet, Irish Deidre. I was not going to let you go anywhere without having my say about it first."

I turn back to look out the rear window to catch a departing glimpse and smile at the little girl who is still there, still waving.

Cory maneuvers the jeep down the drive lined with centuries-old oaks. An Audi Sportback with tinted windows passes us and heads towards Moran.

"There is something that unsettles me when I see one of those turbos with blackened-out windows," Cory confesses to me. "I'm thinking that if putting shades on your face isn't disguise enough, what is accomplished by camouflaging your vehicle except for no good?"

In a reflex reaction, I wrench by body to take another look out the back window just in time to see the Sportback pull up to the oversized front door of Moran.

Author's Note

I drew the inspiration for *Wild Dreams* in part from my own life. Like Deidre, I was haunted by childhood memories of my enormous family home perched on a hill overlooking a small rural town in Wisconsin. After the untimely death of my 35 year old mother when I was six, I was relocated to suburban Milwaukee at age nine to live with a maternal aunt along with my two brothers, ages five and ten and one sister, age eight. I never returned to the "big white house on the hill" and while I was in college, it was torn down.

Within a year or so of my "removal", my father was no longer allowed to visit us as it was thought to be too disruptive to our settling into our new suburban life...especially for me; or so I was told. In less than a year, my youngest brother—then age five—was sent away to live with a relative in another state. While in high school my oldest brother was forced into the service near the end of his junior year of high school. Such cutting away limb by limb of a nuclear family is not allowed today. I can bear testimony to the life-long pain and lasting effects on my brothers, sister and me that destruction of a family causes. And, at age 18 when the State considered us no longer children needing support and protection, where did we belong? And how does one navigate back to a father who had endured years of pain from family trauma? While my novel does not answer these questions, it does address the themes of trauma, identity, connectedness and security.

A gift came to me near the final revision of *Wild Dreams*. Had I called upon ghosts of the past or was it that I was relentlessly searching through historical photo sites in northern Wisconsin, or both? I found a picture of my family home high on a hill surrounded by the small town I was born in and where both of my parents and their families were raised.

While completing the first draft of the novel, I stumbled across a photo and information on the Bantry House Estate in Cork, Ireland. I visited Bantry House the following summer and it became the inspiration for Moran Manor. The characters and Moran Manor are entirely fictional and no connection between them and the former or current owners of the Bantry House Estate exists.

Moya Doherty is the cofounder of Riverdance, the Irish dance and music performance company. It began as a performance act in 1994. With Doherty's tenacity, Riverdance grew into a stand-alone international phenomenon. I use dramatic license to link Moran Steps Dance to Moya and Riverdance, entirely a fictional connection.

Acknowledgments

To the hardworking professionals at Orange Hat Publishing, thank you for your expertise and support: Shannon Ishizaki, Kaeley Dunteman, Lauren Lisak and Carolyn Washburne. A special thanks to Signe Jorgenson, copy editor extraordinaire, who worked with me closely to enhance the readability, conciseness and style of my writing during the final revision. I extend my appreciation to Kendra Burdick, professional photographer, for her magic in creating a perfect profile photo of me—even though it took 88 shots for her to get what she was after! You are amazing.

For your beautiful photo of Bantry House, thank you to Nicholas O'Donnel freelance photographer based in Bray, County Wicklow for providing me the rights to the photo of Bantry House to use as the book cover of *Wild Dreams.*

I extend my sincere gratitude to Sandra Schofield, published novelist and instructor at the Summer Iowa Writers' Workshop. I appreciate your willingness to work with me beyond the summer workshop. Your instruction on the essentials of novel structure and your critical feedback on an early draft helped me enormously.

To my beta reader team of Jennifer Cook, Kay Daro, Dianne Leudert, Arlene Radtke and CeCelia Zorn, you are a courageous group who provided me with honest feedback. I appreciate your time and effort in completing such a task.

To my many friends and supporters on Facebook, thank you for your comments and support as I navigated the road to novel writing.

To my granddaughter Lauren, you kept asking for six years how the novel was progressing and pointed to the framed photos of my nonfiction books and said there will be a third one on that wall soon. Thank you for your faith. Finally, to Hannah, Jack, Leo and Bill—just a little push from their grandmother Maureen to follow your wildest dream.

CPSIA information can be obtained
at www.ICGtesting.com
Printed in the USA
FFHW011046141019
55524818-61348FF